THE TREASURE OF PARAGON BOOK 5

# THE DRAGON OF CECIL COURT

*USA TODAY* BESTSELLING AUTHOR
# GENEVIEVE JACK

**The Dragon of Cecil Court: The Treasure of Paragon, Book 5**

Copyright © Genevieve Jack 2020

Published by Carpe Luna Ltd, PO Box 5932, Bloomington, IL 61702

First Edition: August 2020

eISBN: 978-1-940675-56-5

Paperback: 978-1-940675-52-7

V 2.1

# ABOUT THIS BOOK

**Old flames still burn hot.**

*He's only ever had one weakness.*

Nathaniel Clarke has a secret. Before he became the owner of an occult bookshop on Bookseller's Row, he was a prince of the kingdom of Paragon. Now the dragon shifter is the high priest of the Order of the Dragon, a society of the most powerful supernatural beings in London. He's only ever had one weakness, and he hasn't seen her in a decade.

*She's only ever been good at one thing.*

American pop singer Clarissa Black survived by singing on street corners before Nathaniel came into her life and unlocked the latent magic inside her. Despite their passionate affair, she refused Nathaniel's proposal in order to pursue her music career. Her multiplatinum albums have made her a star but one with few people she can trust.

*It only takes one spark to change two lives forever.*

When Clarissa's voice fails her during a show in London, it's an excuse to reconnect with the man who remains her deepest regret. Nathaniel is reluctant to open old wounds but can't refuse Clarissa's plea for help or the passion her nearness awakens in him. But as he closes in on breaking the curse, Nathaniel learns the cause of what ails her is tangled with the deadly past he left behind.

# AUTHOR'S NOTE

**Dear Reader,**

Love is the truest magic and the most fulfilling fantasy. Thank you for coming along on this journey as I share the tale of the Treasure of Paragon, nine exiled royal dragon shifters destined to find love and their way home.

There are three things you can expect from a Genevieve Jack novel: magic will play a key role, unexpected twists are the norm, and love will conquer all.

## *The Treasure of Paragon Reading Order*

The Dragon of New Orleans, Book 1
Windy City Dragon, Book 2,
Manhattan Dragon, Book 3
The Dragon of Sedona, Book 4
The Dragon of Cecil Court, Book 5
Highland Dragon, Book 6
Hidden Dragon, Book 7
The Dragons of Paragon, Book 8
The Last Dragon, Book 9

Keep in touch to stay in the know about new releases, sales, and giveaways.

Join my VIP reader group
Sign up for my newsletter

Now, let's spread our wings (or at least our pages) and escape together!

*Genevieve Jack*

## *Paragon*

Aborella woke in her chambers, feeling like she'd been torn apart and pieced back together, and of course she had. That damned dragon, Alexander, had bitten her in two and left her to die. Only by siphoning the life force of the plants around her had she managed to magically repair herself. But then that witch Raven had further drained her power, almost to the point of death.

She curled onto her side and closed her eyes. At least she'd had the last laugh. Raven, Gabriel, and Tobias were now imprisoned in the dungeons of Paragon. They'd be punished for their insurrection. She would not be surprised if Eleanor, Empress of Paragon, ordered their beheading this very day. She'd avenge Aborella. Oh, how she'd enjoy watching the witch die. The brothers too, but the witch most of all.

She opened her silver eyes and smiled against the sheets. The usually dark purple skin of her hand was a gray shade of lavender. Still not fully healed then. What she needed now was rest and time in the forest to rejuvenate. After the sacrifices she'd made for the kingdom, she'd likely be lauded a hero and given all the time away she needed.

The heavy iron door to her bedroom swung open without the benefit of a knock. Eleanor strode in, her black gown swooshing with her steps. "Aborella, thank the Mountain you're awake."

"Good morn, Your Highness," the fairy said softly, pushing herself higher on the pillows and bowing her head in lieu of a curtsy. All of her muscles ached, and fatigue gripped her at the slightest effort. "I trust you've had a moment to speak with the Guard about the security of our new prisoners?"

"Yes, about that..."

Aborella waited patiently for the praise due her. She'd almost died bringing Raven, Gabriel, and Tobias back to Paragon, quite a feat considering the power the witch, Raven, wielded. She expected Eleanor would want to reward her in some way, and certainly her hungry belly felt overdue for a banquet in her honor.

But the empress's mouth bent into a scowl. "You left the egg behind."

An uncomfortable prickle ran along the underside of her skin at the sight of Eleanor's tightly drawn lips.

"It couldn't be avoided," Aborella said. "Raven's powers are immeasurable. Had I waited to return until I had the egg, she would have killed me."

"Then perhaps you should have died." Eleanor narrowed her eyes.

Aborella frowned and reached for the silver robe that hung on her bedpost. "If I had died, none of the heirs would be in your dungeon, least of all the eldest and the witch."

Eleanor let out a huff. "Yes, well, be that as it may, I am

2

pleased that you've returned in one piece. There is much more work to do."

The silver robe dragged on the floor as Aborella painfully hobbled to the bar cart the servants had left in her chambers and poured herself a glass of water from the pitcher. It was flavored with bullhorn root. The refreshing, spicy beverage tingled in her throat and temporarily revived her. The effect was not unlike human coffee, although even more temporary for a fairy.

"What are your plans for the prisoners?" Aborella asked. "Will you use them as bait to draw out the others?"

"Yes, most certainly, but I have greater plans for Gabriel. Ransom has captured the leader of the resistance. He resides in the dungeon even now."

"Who? Who is it?"

Eleanor coupled her hands in front of her hips. "I cannot tell you. For now his identity is secret, for good reason. Suffice it to say, we have our work cut out for us to squelch the rumblings he's started among our citizens."

"What sort of rumblings?" Aborella's eyes narrowed. She'd not seen this in her visions.

"Some of the people do not believe that Brynhoff's actions against my children were justified. They refuse to see the evidence of their traitorous intent or accept that Marius's rule would have driven Paragon to ruin. The rebels say that Brynhoff and I have no claim to the throne and that the longer we're here, the more severe the goddess's wrath. Can you believe such nonsense?"

Of course Aborella could believe it. Both of them knew that Eleanor had eliminated her children for precisely the goal of securing the throne for herself. But that didn't mean it wasn't the right thing to do. Eleanor and Brynhoff understood what Paragon needed, that a common and supreme ruler was necessary to keep control over the five kingdoms. At the moment, the kingdoms were only loosely united by a mutually-agreed-upon pact that had been in place for centuries. As a result of that pact, Paragon held a precarious position as the leader of the five cooperative but independent kingdoms. But if Eleanor had her way, she would become the supreme ruler of all, conquer the other kingdoms, and make them her subjects. The unification of their world would improve life for every Paragonian and most of the other kingdoms as well... if they cooperated.

Aborella longed to see that day. All those fairies in the kingdom of Everfield who had taunted her and tortured her for being different would fall to their knees when Eleanor succeeded. And when that happened, it would be Aborella by her side. She'd rain hellfire down on anyone who'd ever been against her.

"They are jealous of your leadership, Empress. If you have a list of names, the right potion might change their minds, or ruin them if necessary," Aborella said of the gossipers.

"No. The true identities of the rebels have been well hidden. What I wish to do is control Gabriel. If my eldest son comes to my defense, admits his wrongdoing, and agrees to rule at my side, it will put all the rumblings to rest."

"Hmmm." Aborella rubbed her chin. "Controlling Gabriel won't be easy."

"You sound unsure of your abilities." A muscle in Eleanor's angular jaw tensed.

"My influence does not work on dragons, Empress, as you well know. There are complex spells I can try, but their ongoing effectiveness can't be guaranteed. Your kind are powerful magical creatures after all."

"What if the two of us combine forces and work together on a spell?"

"Maybe. I need time to recover and research the possibilities."

"How long?"

"For a spell as complicated as dragon compulsion? At least a week."

Eleanor grunted in disappointment and paced the room, her hands curling into fists.

"And then there is the matter of Raven," Aborella said.

"What about her?"

"She is an extremely powerful witch. She has likely already covered Gabriel in protective enchantments. I will never be confident he is truly under our compulsion as long as she's alive."

The empress tilted her chin up. "It would be foolish to execute her. We might need her. If you truly can't compel Gabriel magically, we will have to use her to force his compliance. Not to mention she may prove useful when it comes to the others. Her power is inconvenient though. Every moment she remains in the dungeon, I worry she schemes to kill us all. Power like that can never be trusted."

A vision ignited inside Aborella's head, like a ray of light shining directly into her eyes. At first it almost knocked her off her feet. But once she interpreted it, the thought spread her mouth into an eager grin. "You're absolutely right," she said slowly. "We don't need to magically compel Gabriel's cooperation, Empress. All we need to do is incentivize him."

Eleanor folded her arms. "And how do you suppose we do that?"

"By threatening his mate."

Eleanor scoffed. "She's had his tooth and in your own words is a witch of immeasurable power. How exactly do you plan to do that? If we kill her, all we will inspire is his wrath."

Aborella poured another glass of water and took a sip. "When I was living with the humans, her father told me she was once an ordinary girl, one who was dying of cancer until she swallowed Gabriel's tooth. What can be done can be undone."

"Don't waste my time, Aborella. A dragon's tooth cannot be removed from its host. It would kill her." Eleanor drummed her fingers in obvious annoyance.

The fairy gave her wings a good stretch and rolled her neck. "I must use my crystals to know for sure, but I've sensed there is another way. The secret is to undo what made her a witch before the tooth enhanced her power. If we can do that, if we can neutralize Raven, then I predict Gabriel will be far more motivated to preserve his vulnerable mate."

Slowly, Eleanor's lips spread into an angular and wicked grin. "I know that twinkle in your eye, Aborella. You sense this is the answer. You've seen it, haven't you?"

Aborella raised her chin and gave a confident nod.

The empress's lips pulled back from her teeth in a tight smile. "Then take your time. We must get this right. The kingdom depends on it."

# CHAPTER ONE

*Paragon*

The good thing about being locked in a dungeon in Paragon without visitors or explanation was that Raven had plenty of time to think. That was the end of her list of good things. The bad things were far more numerous. Many hours had passed since Aborella had captured them and brought them to Paragon, although just how many she couldn't be sure. There were no windows in the dungeon, and no reliable way to tell the time. Long enough for her to sleep and wake up hungry.

They'd been offered nothing in that time—not food, not water, not clothing. She was still dressed in the same outfit she'd been wearing in Sedona. Unfortunately, Gabriel and his brother Tobias were completely naked because they'd shifted from their dragon forms moments before being captured. Not that she minded so much about Gabriel, but Tobias's state of undress was awkward, especially considering the floor and walls were made of reflective, polished obsidian.

"How are you feeling?" Tobias asked her.

Last time Raven was in Paragon, she'd become ill to the point of death. At the time, their best theory was that she'd absorbed the realm's magic and overwhelmed her human body. But the true cause of her illness had been ultimately unknown, and so far, she was in complete control of her magical resources.

"So far, so good," she said through cracked lips.

"Excellent! It would be a shame if you were ill for our beheading."

"Tobias!" Gabriel barked.

"Brother, your mate knows what we are in for. She's not an idiot. If Mother and Brynhoff meant to keep us alive, we'd have water."

He was right. Raven did know. And she was already searching her magical arsenal for how to get them out of this. "I'd like to conjure food and water but the way my spell works, I have to know precisely where what I'm after is and what it looks like. I don't know anything about Paragon. I'd be casting a net into the void. The only beverage I've tried here is Tribiscal wine, and the Silver Sunset must be too far away because I can't seem to sense the drink when I cast in order to draw it to me. Already tried."

Damn, it was hot. At least the brothers were more tolerant of the heat than she was. The dungeon had to be at least ninety degrees. Sweat dripped down her temple.

"Don't bother," Gabriel said. "The obsidian in the walls is enchanted against all forms of magic. Otherwise Tobias and I could melt the door with our dragon fire. Believe me, your magic won't work here."

Raven raised an eyebrow at the challenge. "The walls are enchanted? What about..."

She tipped her head back and murmured an incantation

under her breath. To her relief, it started to snow. "Oh, thank the Mountain," she said. "There's moisture in the air." She caught a snowflake on her tongue and relished the cool feel against her skin.

"Shhh. Do you hear that?" Tobias said.

Raven quieted. Footsteps on stone reached her ears. Snapping her fingers, she stopped the snow above her and shoved her brain into gear, sorting through the spells she'd absorbed, practiced, and kept at the ready. Was Aborella finally coming to finish them off?

The fairy appeared on the other side of the cell door, and Raven had to smile. She looked drained, almost white, and the symbols on her skin had faded to dull scars.

"You look peaked, Aborella," Raven said through her teeth. "Maybe you should go lie down." *And die*, she added in her head.

The fairy showed her sharp yellow teeth. "I feel well enough for this."

"For what exactly?" Tobias asked, a muscle in his jaw twitching.

An intimidatingly tall woman dressed in a purple silk gown stepped into view. Raven would never forget her face or the long dark hair that reminded her of her own. Although she appeared thinner now than before, her features sharp, merciless. Empress Eleanor.

"Hello, Mother," Gabriel said.

"My sons, it is so good to see you again." She sent them each a smile through the bars of the cell door, her thin lips stretching in a way that made her nose look exceptionally pointed. Then she turned a scowl on her. "Raven," she added by way of greeting. "I'm afraid our family reunion will have to wait until we've mitigated an unfortunate unpredictability."

Gabriel frowned. "What unpredictability is that exactly?"

"I'll need a strand of her hair," Aborella said, pointing at Raven.

"You will have no such thing," Gabriel snarled.

But the dragon queen swept her hand through the air, her citrine ring glowing gold on her finger.

Raven felt a tug on the side of her head. "Ow!"

Before any of them could react, a strand of her hair, root intact, floated through the door and into Aborella's hands.

"What are you doing?" Raven ran for the door but was greeted with a repelling force like she'd run into the side of a rubber ball. Not only could she not reach through the bars, she couldn't even touch them. She hurled every spell in her arsenal toward Aborella, but they all bounced harmlessly back at her.

Raven watched in horror as Aborella retrieved a second black hair from her pocket and a third, lighter one from an envelope she'd had tucked under her arm. Mumbling something, she began braiding the three together.

Backing away from the door, Raven clung to Gabriel's side and whispered in his ear, "Can you understand what she's saying?"

"Yes, she's speaking Paragonian."

"Tell me."

"Three sisters at last are found, three hairs are braided round, three witches power bound, I tie thee, one, two, three."

Aborella bent the braid into a knot.

"Stop her!" Raven said frantically. She wasn't sure exactly what Aborella was doing, but she could feel it, like a needle passing under her skin.

Gabriel rushed the door but bounced back, presumably

off the same force that had impeded her. He ended up back at her side, shaking his head. Tobias stood on her right, his eyes betraying his worry. The corners of his mouth sank grimly.

Aborella paused. "Now your blood, Empress."

Eleanor made a tsking sound but pricked her finger with the sharp tip of her thumbnail. "If I must."

"There is no other way than dragon magic, Empress." Aborella pressed the braided knot into the ruby bead that bubbled on Eleanor's finger, and Raven watched as the blood permeated the strands until each was made red from end to tip. Her blood felt hot in her veins.

Aborella began to untie the knot. "I break your link, one from another; I break your past, mother from child; I break your power, witch from witch." With the knot completely untied, she began to unbraid the three strands of hair. "Together no more. Power no more. Three sisters no more."

Raven gasped. It felt like she'd been stabbed through the heart with a giant needle, and a thread was being tugged through her flesh. She collapsed to her knees. The three hairs, now unbraided, dropped to the obsidian floor and burned into ash.

Gabriel rushed to her and gathered her into his arms. "What have you done to her?"

It was as if Aborella had extracted part of her soul. Raven felt hollowed out, completely empty. She clung to Gabriel, suppressing a sob. She wouldn't give the bitch the satisfaction.

The door clicked and Aborella and the empress strolled into the cell. A threatening growl rumbled in Gabriel's chest.

Aborella snorted. "Relax, dragon. I've simply neutralized your mate's power at its source."

The empress stared down her nose at Raven. "Now you will join me for dinner," she said in a low, cool tone. "And if you try anything, Gabriel, or you, Tobias"—she leveled a stare at each of them—"I will kill her. Without her magic, it will take no more than a flick of my wrist and her neck will snap. Do you understand?"

Raven thought her mate's jaw might crack from how tightly he ground his teeth, but he gave her a definitive nod. Tobias did as well.

At a snap of the empress's fingers, two prison guards jogged into the room, one with arms laden with clothing, the other with a washbowl and a basket of bathroom sundries. Both were placed on the floor before them.

"Dress," Eleanor said. "Clean up. Then we celebrate. Welcome home, my sons. The kingdom of Paragon has missed you."

# CHAPTER TWO

## *London*

Nathaniel Clarke lingered outside Relics and Runes occult bookstore, his pipe nestled in his palm. Not so long ago, he'd have fired the Turkish tobacco, loosely tamped within its bent rosewood bowl, in the comfort of his office, but smoking indoors was illegal these days in London. Bad for humans. He supposed when your lifespan was a mere hundred years or less, cutting it short by a decade or more for the sake of a smoke was reckless.

As an immortal dragon, Nathaniel couldn't get cancer or any other human disease, and considering he could breathe fire, a little smoke was completely harmless to his composition. Humans, however, were important to Nathaniel, making up the majority of the occult book market. Plus he enjoyed the company of a few of them. He'd prefer to keep them alive.

No matter—it was early and Cecil Court had yet to suffer the tread of visitors' footsteps, which gave him an opportunity to both enjoy his favorite smoke and make use of the enchanting properties of this particular tobacco blend. Specially developed by a friend—a wizard and master tobacconist—the heady smoke served a number of purposes. For one, it alerted him of imminent danger. This morning though, his use for it was far more mundane, to render his storefront irresistible to shoppers.

He flipped the top of his butane lighter and circled the flame over the tobacco, then let it burn out. A good false light. Ah yes, the scent was heavenly. He lit it again and took a ceremonious puff. The thick smoke curled along his tongue before he blew it out in a perfect, cloudlike ring that floated toward the summer sky.

"Honestly, Clarke, are you still flushing good money away on that dreadful habit?" Mr. Greene, owner of the neighboring bookshop, appeared beside him, broom in hand, and raised his bushy gray eyebrows. He stared point-edly at Nathaniel's pipe. "You're going to blow an artery if you keep that up."

"Not everyone can be the picture of health as you are, Greene." Nathaniel pointed a knuckle at the man and winked. "I'm of the mind to enjoy what years I have with a good smoke."

"Because you're a young chap. Wait until you're old like me and regret comes to roost." He straightened his sweater vest over his overlarge paunch.

"I daresay, I predict you'll outlive us all."

The elderly man chuckled. "From your lips to God's ears." He gave his doorstep a few half-hearted sweeps. "Speaking of regrets of the past and all that, have you heard the news this morning?"

"I haven't had the pleasure." Nathaniel puffed his pipe and blew a smoke ring over Greene's head. Actually, he took no pleasure in current events. The world was in a constant state of wearying political angst. After three hundred years, he'd seen empires rise and fall. It didn't matter to him which blowhard was in office or who was seen hobnobbing with whom. Nathaniel existed above it all. And if he didn't like something, all he had to do was wait. Everything ended eventually, aside from him.

Greene wagged his finger. "Oh dear. I would have thought you'd be the first to know."

"Hmm? What's that?" He sent a tiny smoke ring through the center of a bigger one. The enchantment was taking hold. Already the brass around his door appeared shinier and the red paint that coated its wood gleamed as if he'd painted it yesterday.

"That fling of yours from a few years ago, the songbird from the States. You know, the pretty one."

Nathaniel released his smoke in an uncontrolled and unattractive exhale. "You don't mean..."

"The fish that got away, Clarke. You know the one. The woman. Ahh, I've lost my head." Greene tapped the heel of his palm against his temple. "Can't think of it. Something... Clarissa! That's it."

"Clarissa is in London?" An uninvited tingle radiated from the back of Nathaniel's neck, down his arms, and made his hands go numb. For the love of the Mountain, he did not need to hear Clarissa was in town today.

"She is! But that's not why everyone's talking about her. It seems she was performing for a corporate audience, the people who make those home gadgets. Tanaka Corp. Anyhow, her voice gave out completely in the middle of her performance. She had to be escorted from the stage. The Tanaka people were royally cheesed off over it. And, well, there are all sorts of rumors now going round about why.

Drugs or whatnot. People are suggesting she might have to cancel her concert at the O2 later this month."

"Hmm." Nathaniel ground his teeth. Clarissa was a witch, a powerful one, and if her voice had given out, there was a dark reason for it. He stared down into his pipe. Today might be a good day to close up shop and take a holiday. Bora-Bora sounded like a nice diversion.

"So you hadn't heard. You two don't keep in touch then?"

Nathaniel sighed. "No. It was a fleeting affair. She has her career, and I have..." He gestured vaguely in the direction of Relics and Runes.

"Righto! Dodged a bullet, I'd say. Bad luck to have a woman that beautiful, if you don't mind my saying so. My Minerva, rest her soul, wasn't a looker, but she was a dab hand in the kitchen. That's the type of woman you can rely on. Good cook. Loyal soul."

"If only there were more Minervas out there." Nathaniel pictured the heavyset woman with wild gray hair who'd passed away a few years ago and carefully kept his expression reverential.

"God broke the mold when he made her." Greene wiped a tear from his eye and glanced at his watch. "Is that the time? Oh dear. We'll be opening soon. I'd better ready the shop. Good day, Clarke."

"Good day." Returning the man's little wave, Nathaniel watched him disappear inside his shop, then leaned against the doorframe and closed his eyes. So Clarissa was in town. It didn't mean anything. And her voice giving out could have a number of causes, perhaps a virus of the throat or a nodule on the vocal cords. She was probably visiting a doctor even now. With any luck, she'd be on a plane back to America in no time.

He opened his eyes. Bringing his pipe to his lips, he allowed the thick smoke to linger on his tongue before slowly and deliberately blowing a perfect ring... that morphed into a crimson heart as it floated toward the clear blue sky.

"Fuck."

He whirled and fumbled with the door, setting his pipe on the counter and mumbling incoherently as he passed the books on witchcraft, Jungian theory, the tarot cards, the crystals, the grimoires and the yoga magazines, to the small greenhouse of magical herbs at the back. He plucked two potted rosemary plants from the sill and hurried to place them on either side of the front door before ducking back inside again.

"With any luck...," he mumbled. Where were his cards? He needed to read his cards.

The bell above the door rang.

"Jesus, Nathaniel, rosemary? It only protects you against those who would do you harm. When have I ever wanted to hurt you?"

Clarissa stepped across his threshold as if she'd been summoned by his earlier use of her name, like the devil or a demon. A real possibility now that he thought of it. Her blond hair was covered in a rose-colored scarf, and large dark glasses hid her blue eyes. But there was no mistaking her lithe figure and catlike grace. Or her scent. The floral and earthy notes of lilies and moss hit his nose.

She reached up and removed her glasses. "I think I'm being followed."

"Then you'd better be on your way. Where's your security?"

"Everyone wants to know what happened last night." Her gaze roved over his face. His suit. "You look exactly the same. I mean, I knew you didn't age, but my God. Is that the pocket square I bought you?"

"I hear footsteps in the alley. You should go before the paparazzi arrive."

She shuffled closer to him. "Hide me. Please!"

The door opened. Cursing his own stupidity, he curled her into his arms and cloaked both of them in invisibility. He pressed a finger to his lips, although she of all people knew to remain silent.

Two men entered the store, one tall and suave, the other looking like he'd slept on the floor of a pub the night before. Both had cameras ready. They swept through the rooms, searched behind the counter.

"I know she came in here. I saw her," the taller one said. He eyed the still-smoking pipe. "Hello?" he called. "Anyone here?"

The slovenly one squinted his eyes. "There's a lower level." The two jogged down the stairs to where Nathaniel shelved the books on fairies and druids among other things.

Nathaniel lowered his finger from his mouth, but not the invisibility that cloaked them both.

"You've got a lot of nerve coming back here after all this time," he whispered to her.

"I need your help." Her lips were red. He had a strong desire to smear her lipstick.

"No."

"Believe me, if I had any other choice, I would have made it. You're the only one who can help me."

"No." It was out of the question really. Not after how they'd left things.

The two men jogged back up the stairs, visibly baffled. "Gone. Just gone," the tall man said. "Into thin air."

"Are you sure it was her?"

Tall Man rubbed his chin. "Could've been a decoy, I suppose. It was odd she had no security."

"There's a back door," the short man said, pointing with his chin.

They rushed into the courtyard. Nathaniel waited until he could no longer hear their footsteps or their voices before he dropped the invisibility.

"Next time I'll let them find you." He dusted off his hands as if holding her had filthied them.

"That hurts, Nate. It really does. After all we've meant to each other."

"Ancient history."

"But a pleasant one. As pasts go, I'm happy with ours."

"Speak for yourself." He smoothed the sleeve of his jacket and moved behind the counter. Better. He'd prefer a lead wall between them, but the counter would have to do. "Enjoy the pleasant weather." He gestured toward the door.

"There's something wrong with my voice."

"See a doctor."

"It's not that type of problem," she whispered.

The bell above the door dinged and the first customer of the day strolled in. Nathaniel greeted the man, who beelined straight to the section on witchcraft.

He shrugged. "I don't know anything about vocal performance. But best of luck to you." He gestured toward the door again.

She took a deep breath and blew it out slowly, then approached the counter. "Please... Nathaniel... If you ever cared for me... If what we had ever meant anything to you... I need your help."

He narrowed his eyes on her. "You can do it yourself."

Slowly she shook her head. "No. I. Can't."

Realization dawned and he leaned forward to sniff her

throat. As usual, she smelled of lilies and moss, but the magical tang that always accompanied her scent was missing. Clarissa's magical Bunsen burner was on the fritz. Interesting. Not interesting enough for him to feed his heart into a meat grinder by allowing her back into his life, but interesting.

Still, it was impossible not to remember the good times what with her standing right in front of him. He met her gaze and held it.

"Nathaniel?" she pleaded.

"No," he said again. And he meant it.

# CHAPTER THREE

The most tangled ball of emotions twisted in Clarissa's chest. Without a shadow of doubt, she believed Nathaniel was the only person in the world who could save her career. Her former lover and mentor was a powerful dragon. Everything she'd ever learned about magic started with him.

That was the problem. She'd treated him terribly. Rejected him at the moment he was most vulnerable and left without explanation. Of course there was an explanation, but not one he wanted to hear. Not one he was willing to understand at the time. She was so young then, barely twenty. And he was ancient. Although he looked to be in his early thirties, he'd lived in London for three centuries and in his native land for even longer.

They'd barely spoken over the past decade. With her tour schedule and the chip on his shoulder, the hiatus wasn't surprising. But she'd never thought it would come to this. Some part of her had thought that what they'd shared was sacred and that if she ever needed him—really needed him, like now—he'd be there for her.

She pressed her hips against the counter and leaned toward him. "Nate..."

He frowned.

"Nathaniel..." She made her voice soft and inviting. "I'm begging you. I will pay you anything."

"Don't insult me."

"I will *do* anything." She loaded her expression with promise and held his dark stare. By God, he looked good in a suit, but then the supernatural creatures that acted as his servants excelled in the domestic arts. Few others would understand the bespoke three-piece was handmade, its classic style owing to the fact it might have been created eighty years or more ago. She parted her lips and whispered, "You know I'm not lying."

His eyes narrowed. Those fathomless pits sparked with amethyst fire as he registered her offer, making her wonder what lecherous thoughts had crossed his mind in the moment. Nathaniel danced with the dark arts. If she leaned closer, she might catch a whiff of sulfur clinging to his perfectly tailored suit. At best, the predatory gleam in his eyes was sexual. More likely though, he was thinking of spells that used witch's blood or worse, her ground bones.

"Careful, Clarissa, you have no idea the things I've dreamt of doing to you over the years."

She forced herself to hold her ground although the heat coming off him quickly became uncomfortable, not to mention the squirm-worthy weight of his stare. Her phone vibrated in her pocket—no doubt Tom, her manager, calling again. There would be repercussions for what happened last night at Tanaka. The press would hound her. Her manager would expect a doctor's explanation for what happened. But no human doctor could fix what ailed her.

Her voice hadn't given out. Her magic had. And what

was left of her witchy common sense told her she'd been targeted with black magic.

The lone customer approached and tossed a handbook about Wiccan altars onto the counter. "Has anyone ever told you you look a lot like that American pop star Clarissa?"

She cleared her throat and replied in her best cockney accent. "Ya think so, eh? I do wish I 'ad 'er bank account." She added a few nasal laughs for good measure.

The man withdrew a phone from his pocket and snapped a selfie with her in the background. "You don't mind, do you?" the man asked, although it was clear he didn't care what her answer was. "Too good a story to pass up."

Clarissa frowned but held her tongue. If she told him she did mind, it would only be confessing to her true identity.

A curl of dark smoke rose from Nathaniel's pipe. He mumbled the price to the patron, tugged the man's credit card from his hand in a way that bordered on aggression, and ran it through the reader. Nathaniel dropped the book into a bag and handed it to the customer but did not let go. Instead, he took another puff from the pipe and blew a mouthful of dark smoke in the customer's face.

Shadowy tendrils clouded around the stranger's head, then twisted and slid inside his ears. His eyelashes fluttered. All the light bled from his expression until it was utterly blank. Clarissa might as well have been staring at a giant walking carrot for how much control the man had over his own mind.

"You came in, bought this book, and then you left," Nathaniel said to the man, never breaking eye contact. He yanked the phone from the man's hand and deleted the picture. "You never saw this woman and you will never mention her to anyone."

"I never saw the woman," the man parroted absently.

"Now leave. Enjoy your book."

The man scurried off and out the door.

She was saved. He *did* care, at least enough to protect her from idle gossip. Maybe there was hope if she pulled the right strings. "Thank you, Nate. Now please, can we talk about this? There's so much I need to say to you. I want to apologize—"

"Only so I will help you." He rolled his eyes.

"I want to explain."

"You want to give me an excuse."

"Stop! Can't you find it in your heart to listen?" She watched him slowly raise his pipe to his lips. Without her magic, if he blew a spell into her face, she'd act just as his last customer had, mind blank as she shuffled out the door, straight into certain ruin. She covered her nose and mouth with her hands and held her breath.

Lifting an eyebrow, he blew the smoke over his shoulder in a ring that quickly bent into a heart before it dissipated. That heart told her everything she needed to know. It was a sign of the magical entanglement he'd offered her and she'd refused. She hadn't expected any of it to remain with him.

"Still?" she asked.

"I told you it was forever." His voice was ominously soft, and her skin tingled at the memory of that tone under sweeter circumstances.

"But if you feel a connection to me even now, why aren't you helping me? You must know how desperate I am."

"And you must know that you left what was between us in ashes." His lips bent into a scowl, and his pupils became black holes of rage. "I have asked you nicely, Clarissa, but now I am losing my patience. Do not make me use magic or physical force to remove you from this store. You will not enjoy either."

She planted her palms on the counter between them, her fingers spread as if her hands could anchor her there. She'd pleaded. She'd begged. He was going to leave her with no other choice but to say the word she knew he could not refuse, not because of what he'd once shared with her but because the rule of magic would demand his cooperation.

He drew in smoke from his pipe.

"Sanctuary," she blurted.

The smoke left his mouth in a deep purple rush. "What did you say?"

"I call on my fellow members of the secret Order of the Dragon to shelter me from my enemies. Sanctuary."

"How dare you?" His voice hissed between his teeth. "You haven't participated in the order in a decade." On the countertop, a set of talons sprouted from his first knuckles and pressed their razor-sharp tips into the glass.

"But I am a member by blood oath, and I require sanctuary." She lifted her chin, her spine ramrod straight. "Unless the code of the order has changed—"

"It hasn't changed."

Oh, how she wanted to run from his deadly visage. She'd cornered the beast, and if she wasn't careful, he'd tear her apart liberating himself. Despite her internal fear, she forced her outward appearance to remain calm.

Rolling his neck, Nathaniel brushed the arms of his suit jacket as if they weren't already meticulously cleaned and pressed, then leveled an indifferent stare at her. "Very well, Clarissa. You may go to Mistwood."

She gulped. Mistwood, his Oxfordshire manor, was remote and protected by magic. It was the type of place where no one would find her, but also no one could hear her scream. She would be safe there, yes, but entirely at his mercy. She nodded.

"I offer you sanctuary in the name of the order," he said through a wicked smile. "And I take in return what you have offered."

"And that is?" She couldn't keep the tremble from her voice.

He was around the counter in the blink of an eye, pressed against her back. He brought one talon to the side of her throat. Her heart pounded, and not completely out of fear. She'd never stopped wanting Nathaniel.

His hot breath brushed her cheek as he articulated his next word. "An-y-thing."

Panting, she felt his nose brush her ear and his stubble graze the delicate skin of her cheek. Her knees almost gave out, but she forced herself to nod. What choice did she have?

He shoved her toward the exit. She snatched her sunglasses off the counter and backed out the door, a breath of relief rushing from her lungs as soon as it was closed between them.

Swallowing, she fished her phone from her purse and tapped Tom's number while she jogged toward her car.

"Finally! Clarissa, you'd better have a good explanation for why you snuck past your security this morning. Everyone has been out of their minds looking for you. I came within an inch of getting the police involved. The Tanaka guys are livid. The press is going bananas over this. You need to come back to the hotel this instant."

"Can't." She turned the corner and walked faster

toward the place where her hired driver, dressed in a plain sweatshirt and cap, waited in an understated brown coupe. No one would guess she'd choose a car like this or a driver who looked like he delivered pizzas in his off time. Hopefully it would keep the paparazzi off her trail.

"What do you mean you can't?" Tom's tone was irate.

"I've just come from the specialist." She forced a cough and made her voice sound raspy. "Rare condition of the vocal cords. He can fix it, but I have to go to a treatment facility immediately. Total secrecy, and the treatment will take several days. He said it was imperative that I completely rest my voice after the procedure. No phone or visitors."

"Who? Which doctor? Not Kline? Please tell me my future isn't in the hands of that butcher."

"Not Kline. I've got to go, Tom. I'll be in touch when I'm cleared to speak again."

"Bu—"

She hung up on him and turned off her phone. No one else would call. One of the consequences of being both an orphan and a celebrity was that there were few people personally obliged to check up on her. She had friends, but they were the kind who expected her to call *them*. After all, she was frequently busy. They wouldn't want to interrupt. If she could call anyone a best friend, she'd suppose it would have to be Tom. He was certainly the one she spoke to the most. But he was her manager. Could someone who was paid to keep you happy technically be called a friend?

She climbed in the passenger side and turned to the driver. "Oxfordshire."

He opened his mouth to protest the distance and likely the time commitment. Mistwood was an hour and a half from Cecil Court. She reached into her wallet and handed him a hundred quid. "If that's not enough, I'll pay you whatever you want."

With a nod of his head, he turned his eyes to the road. Clarissa leaned back in her seat and prepared herself for whatever Nathaniel had in store for her.

## CHAPTER FOUR

"Here. Stop. Please!" Clarissa shook the driver by the shoulder and the car jerked as he hit the brakes.

"What are ya playin' at? Ain't nothin' round here as far as the eye can see."

"I know. I'm... meeting someone."

"All the way out here?" The spotty-faced man wrinkled his nose. "Wouldn't ya rather I keep on to someplace..." He surveyed the wall-to-wall green surrounding them. "Well, someplace else?"

She popped open the door and grabbed her rolling bag from the trunk, then walked around to his window and handed him another wad of bills. "Thank you for your help. I have my phone fully charged should I need any additional assistance. Don't you worry." She held the device up as evidence and then backed away from the car.

He gave her a curt nod and slowly drove away.

Among the rolling, bucolic hills near Waterleys Copse in Bicester, Clarissa stood at a crossroads facing north. How apropos that this was where she'd end up. Four directions. Four choices. And none of them led to her destination. Just as in life, she'd reached a point where no paved road would take her where she needed to go, no list of pros and cons would lead her to a decision that could solve this problem with her voice, a problem that would ruin her, would ruin all she had in the world if Nate couldn't fix it.

With a firm grip on her bag, she moved to the center of the crossroads, closed her eyes, and spun thrice around to her right and once to her left. Once she stopped, she said in a loud, clear voice, "By the blood of the dragon, open."

The rumbling clank of a portcullis rising vibrated against her skin, and she opened her eyes to find the crossroads gone. She stood at the base of a cobblestone drive leading to the house she hoped would be her salvation.

Mistwood Manor had been erected in 1699 by an architect named Nicholas Hawksmoor who was a member of the first Order of the Dragon. To Clarissa, it would always remind her of Downton Abbey, although Mistwood, with its magical upkeep, had better weathered the ravages of time. Despite the castle-like sound the magical gate had made when it opened, this was not a medieval fortress but a grand estate, a marvel of seventeenth-century architecture that always gave her a sense of airy lightness. She was safe here to be sure, and not because anyone would be shooting arrows from the roof but because the magic that saturated every inch of this property was the strongest she'd ever encountered as a witch. Not to mention it was usually guarded by the fiercest, most unforgiving dragon.

She swallowed the lump in her throat as memories of her old life at Mistwood came flooding back. The first time Nathaniel had brought her here, she couldn't keep her mouth from gaping. By that time he'd revealed what he was to her, although she could scarcely believe it. He'd swept her off her feet. The idea of going home with him had seemed so romantic, far better than another night in the cheapest hostel she could find. So she'd said yes and proceeded to be blown away by the history, the magic, the excitement she'd found behind the doors of the house on the hill. If only those things had been enough.

Hoofbeats pounded on the drive behind her, and the carriage that always brought guests to the manor arrived. Pulled by one of Nate's prized sleek black Percherons, the carriage had no driver. The door opened for her of its own accord, and she climbed inside. The moment she was seated, the vehicle lurched forward and headed for the estate.

By the scene out the window, things at Mistwood hadn't changed much since she'd left. The same brook traversed the property, bubbling over rocks worn smooth from its current. Off to her right, she could see the orchard, as green and lush as when she'd left. The walnut, apple, and fig trees bore their fruit year-round thanks to Nate's magic, and she remembered the scent of the blossoms like the first time she'd walked its rows. She wondered if *everything* was the same in the orchard, but that was a question for another time. She could drive herself crazy thinking about it now.

The carriage passed a strip of packed dirt that carved through the rolling green, and she wondered if Nate still rode the trails every morning before breakfast. What was his horse's name? Diablo. Was the stallion still alive? She supposed yes. How long did horses live?

They rounded the circular garden in front of the estate, and the carriage came to an abrupt halt. The door opened. When no help appeared, she grunted and wrestled her luggage out herself. She stumbled down the step and had to use her bag to steady herself. The scent of eucalyptus filled her nose.

"Tempest, I don't expect you to help me, but you could say hello. It's not as if we've never met before." The oread was here. He was the source of the scent. But the mountain nymphs who cared for Nate and this estate, Tempest and Laurel, were notoriously shy and secretive. She'd lived here just over a year, and it had taken months for them to trust her enough to reveal themselves to her then.

"I'd prefer it this way, madam. You won't be long in our care, and a professional distance seems appropriate." The oread's deep tenor had a tinny quality, and she pictured his polished marble skin, blond curls, and gossamer wings despite his invisibility. The cold shoulder didn't surprise her. Oreads bonded to magical creatures like Nathanial with unparalleled loyalty.

She snorted. "For what it's worth, it's nice to, um, hear you. I've missed this place."

A puff of air grazed her cheek and the heavy wooden door with its iron lion's-head knocker swung open for her.

When Tempest's voice came again, it was curt. "Your room is prepared. I assume you remember where it is."

"Of course I do." She stepped into the marble foyer, and the door closed behind her. Another draft fluttered her hair and he was gone, his herbal scent fading like a dying rose. He did not offer to carry her bag. "Okay then, I'll just find my own way," she called in his wake.

She popped the telescoping handle of her bag and strode toward the curving staircase, the rattle of the caster wheels echoing through the wide, empty foyer. The place looked like a museum, all cream marble and white and gold trim with a red runner that she followed like the yellow brick road up the majestic staircase.

Hoisting her bag, she climbed to the second floor, cursing her blasted stilettos the entire time, and rolled her way to the room where she'd stayed all those years ago. But when she opened the door, she wasn't prepared for the emotions that flooded her heart.

Nothing had changed.

"Holy crap," she whispered. It was exactly the same. Exactly. Down to the Rihanna pin she'd wedged into the side of her mirror. The place was like a shrine.

It was the first and only place that ever felt like home to her. She had no idea who her real parents were, but her adoptive parents were killed in a freak accident when she was five. She barely remembered them, but she'd been told a sinkhole had opened up and swallowed half her Florida home, taking her parents with it. Although her memory of that day consisted only of blurry, timeworn images, the social worker told her she'd been recovered while dangling her legs over the side of the hole.

After that she'd become a ward of the state and gone from foster home to foster home, and the accidents had followed. Every time a family sent her to her room, the pipes would burst and flood the rest of the house. One time, when she was ten, a guardian had tried to paddle her for smoking his cigarettes. The curtains caught fire and soon the entire house was engulfed in flame. When she was sixteen, a wealthy host family had served her escargot. The snails had animated and climbed off her plate, sending Barb, her foster mom, into hysterics. She actually liked that family, although they seemed indifferent when she moved out a year and a half later.

College wasn't in her future, but she'd always had a talent for music, so she'd earned enough money singing on street corners and in the subway terminal to get by until the summer of her twentieth year when she'd saved enough to come to London. She'd longed to visit Liverpool, the home of the Beatles, and follow their musical journey. Young and foolish, she'd run out of cash in days and was singing for her supper in the tubes of London when Nathaniel found her.

She remembered it like it was yesterday. The song by Norah Jones that was her go-to when she was desperate for tips. Clarissa's version of "Come Away with Me" always held a certain power, but that day the sound had become a palpable thing in the underground. The crowd exiting the trains stopped to listen. That's when he strolled up to her. She noticed him right away. Everyone noticed him. All that dark energy moving toward her, framed by white subway tiles. She was never the same.

"He refuses to let me change anything." A silvery voice rang behind her. She whirled to find the delicate, pale features of Laurel, Tempest's mate and the other oread who cared for the house. Her gossamer wings swayed gently behind her. "The master hasn't been the same since you left."

"Laurel, it's so good to see you!" She opened her arms to hug the nymph but embraced only cool air. The oread had disappeared. Clarissa sighed. Truly she had no allies here.

"You must excuse me." Laurel's voice came as if from a distance. "The room may be the same, but nothing else is. You're a ghost here now. We've grieved you, you understand. And I'm told your visit won't be a long one."

"He told you that?" She frowned. Although it was true she didn't plan to stay any longer than it took for him to fix her, it was a bad sign that Nathaniel was counting the days until her departure. She had two weeks at most. If her voice hadn't recovered by then, she might as well return to America and look into business school because her career as a pop star would effectively be over.

"Can you answer me one thing?" Laurel asked from the shadows. "Did you ever love him, or was it all just...?"

She didn't finish the question, but Clarissa knew what she meant. Nathaniel had been her muse. Still, she froze at the word *love*, the faces of foster families rushing through her mind. She couldn't even remember most of their names. And then Nate. Darkly handsome Nate. How tempting it had been to curl up with the devil in his magical estate back then, when he had become her everything. But their time together had always had an expiration date. How long could it last? Until the ceiling caved in on her, or he returned to the place he'd come from and said goodbye? Did anyone stay in love with the person they loved when they were twenty?

She cleared her throat. "Laurel, I learned many things living here. Magic is real. Dragons are real. Nymphs like you are real. I learned that I am a witch and during a full moon, I can feel the night itself like warm velvet against my skin. But there is one thing I know down to my soul, and it's something I learned long before I ever came here."

"What's that, miss?"

"Love isn't real." She lowered her eyes, slipped into her room with her bag trailing behind her, and closed the door.

# CHAPTER FIVE

Avery Tanglewood wanted her sister, Raven, back, and the best way she knew to make that happen was the professor she was about to meet in a place called the Latner Room, Saint Peter's College, Oxford University. Beside her, Rowan hugged a book to her chest. Avery still had trouble coming to terms with the fact the woman could transform into a dragon and that her seven brothers were exiled princes of a realm called Paragon, but two of those brothers had been captured with Raven. No one wanted to get them back more than Rowan.

They'd come under the guise of showing the professor a book Rowan's gallery had procured, a rare seventeenth-century text on dragons.

"I still don't understand why you wanted me to pose as your assistant," Avery said. "Nick is stronger and probably knows more about your business."

"Nick wants to touch base with his contacts in the London Police Department. Besides, I have it on good authority that this particular professor has an eye for young women. No offense to Nick, but I think you are the better honey to catch this fly."

Avery straightened the neck of her blouse, not exactly comfortable with being visual bait. Still, she couldn't deny she was the only practical choice. Maiara was so new to the modern world she still couldn't stop herself from playing with every light switch she came across. The Native American healer was Alexander's mate and only recently returned to her human form after centuries of soul-inhabiting her hawk familiar. Tobias's mate, Sabrina, was undoubtedly beautiful, but as a hybrid vampire she preferred to sleep during the day. Besides, she hadn't reached London yet. At least Avery knew Raven's egg was safe under the watchful eye of Alexander back at the apartment. The egg, or Li'l Puff as she'd started to call it, was her first priority in her sister's absence.

"I don't know anything about history. Just pray he doesn't put me on the spot," Avery warned.

"Don't worry about it. I'll do the talking."

"What's this guy's name again?"

"Dr. Peter Wallace, professor of medieval history with a specialization in mythology and folklore. He has an interest in dragons. Wrote several papers on the cultural role the wyvern myth played during the European witch trials." Rowan stopped in front of a lovely old building and caught the door as a man in a suit hurried out.

Avery followed her inside and to the room where a wiry and ancient-looking man sat at a ridiculously large conference table.

"Professor Wallace?" Rowan extended her hand when the man gave her a nod of greeting.

"A pleasure to meet you, Ms. Valor. I must say, when I spoke to you on the phone about the piece you found, I wasn't expecting such a lovely young woman to be behind the call."

Rowan offered him a smile worthy of a car salesman. "Well, I'm older than I look and old enough to know a valuable manuscript when I see one."

They laughed together for exactly three beats, and Avery folded her hands like an awkward teenager.

"Oh, Professor, this is my assistant, Avery."

The moment Professor Wallace's gaze fell on Avery, his demeanor changed drastically. His easy smile sagged and his eyes narrowed. Avery got the immediate sense that he hated her. An instant and inexplicable loathing flowed her way. It couldn't have anything to do with her personally— they'd only just met— but it hurt just the same.

"Avery, you say?"

"Avery Tanglewood," she filled in, adding her last name in the hopes that her full introduction would chase the cobwebs of abhorrence in his eyes from whatever memory her presence was drawing up. "I'm Rowan's assistant."

He pursed his lips and nodded slowly. "Well, two lovely young women... My year is made." He turned away from her. "You'll excuse me for not offering you a drink, but I don't believe it would be prudent until I've assessed the authenticity of what you've brought me." He gave a low rumbling laugh.

"I own a gallery in New York, Professor. I can spot a fake from across Manhattan. I promise you, you won't be disappointed." Rowan placed the bundle she was carrying on the table and pulled on a pair of white archival gloves. The leather-bound volume was swaddled in soft white cloth, and she unwrapped it to reveal the rich mahogany of the ancient volume.

"My, the binding does look authentic," the professor

mumbled. He drew his own pair of soft white gloves from an inner pocket of his jacket and gestured for Rowan to move out of the way. Carefully, as if he were handling a bomb, he lifted the cover and opened the book to the first page. "My word, is this...?"

"Ancient Greek and Latin," Rowan said. "The date in the corner suggests it was transcribed in 1699."

Filled with curiosity, Avery leaned forward to get a better look. She'd never seen a book like this or anything written in ancient Greek other than possibly at a museum. The symbols on the page meant nothing to her, but when Wallace turned the page, the illustrations made her inhale sharply. Dragons.

"Alas, I can read the Latin, but my Greek is a bit rusty. I'd like to consult with a colleague..." Professor Wallace rubbed his silver beard.

Rowan smiled. "I believe we're all a little rusty when it comes to ancient languages, but I know enough to tell you what this says if you'd care for the translation of a nonacademic."

He lowered his head and stared at her expectantly over the top of his glasses.

"I believe it's a health manual written by a group that believed in dragons. There are recipes that include dragon scales, dragon blood, and even dancing with dragons."

"Mmm. Yes." He flipped the page. "Recipes for vitality, or perhaps potions. Belief in dragons was often tied to the early practice of magic and religion."

"Were there actually dragons here?" Avery blurted. "You wouldn't put all this effort into a cookbook with recipes calling for ingredients that don't exist, right? I mean, according to legend, were they thought to be real at the time?"

Professor Wallace cleared his throat and gave her an odd look like she was completely daft. "Of course not. Dragons never actually existed, my dear. They were invented for political reasons, to inspire fear among the people and subsequent relief and praise when a monarch slew the nonexistent creature."

Her shoulders slumped. "You're telling me you don't believe in any dragon-like creature at all? Not an overlarge alligator or a prehistoric sturgeon being confused for the Loch Ness Monster?"

He shook his head. "It's poppycock. No more real than the griffins or fairies of yore. Human beings, my dear, have extremely active imaginations. You must never underestimate man's ability to lie."

Rowan placed a hand on Avery's arm. "This conversation is fascinating. Perhaps you can slake my associate's thirst for knowledge with some resources on dragon legends in the area?"

He mumbled something and nodded his head, engrossed in the pages in front of him. "This belongs in the Bodleian collection. Are you willing to part with it?"

"For the right price," Rowan said softly, and Avery could have sworn the color of her suit became redder as she raised her chin and smiled confidently at the man. All at once, her own navy suit seemed frumpy and ill-tailored.

The professor removed his glasses and stared down his nose at Rowan. "I will have to consult with the department. Do you mind if I borrow this for a few days for further analysis? I can assure you it will be handled with utmost care."

Rowan withdrew a card from her pocket and handed it to him. "I'm staying in London proper for a few weeks, buying for my gallery. My number is on the back. I have a car, so I can be here within the hour when you're ready to talk business."

He nodded and carefully closed the book, rewrapping it in the white fabric.

Avery cleared her throat. "I'm interested in local dragon lore, especially areas where the locals believed dragons were real. Can you recommend any places to visit or books to read?"

He gave her a demeaning look and gathered the book into his arms. "I'm afraid the resources at the Bodleian are only available to fellows. Are you an academic?" The way he asked it, Avery was quite certain he knew she wasn't.

"No."

Professor Wallace gave her a patronizing smile. "Then I'd suggest you begin with a Google search. It sounds rudimentary, but it will be the most effective use of your time in the short period you are here." He tucked his chin into his chest. "Now, if you will both excuse me, I must get back to my work. Allow me to show you out."

Rowan extended her hand for a firm shake and an exchange of pleasantries. Before Avery knew it, she and Rowan had been ushered to the parklike setting outside the building with a hasty and rather clipped goodbye.

"What an asshole! Did you see how he looked at me? It was like he hated me from the moment I walked into the room." Avery took a deep breath and blew it out in an exasperated huff.

Rowan twisted a piece of her hair around her finger. "No... He didn't hate *you*. It was almost like he thought he recognized you and whoever it was you reminded him of, they were not someone he admired."

Avery sighed. "Now what do we do? He couldn't have been less helpful if he'd tried."

"Yes. That was odd, wasn't it? We still have an in with him since he took the book, but he almost seemed reluctant to give us any information in return. Did you notice?"

Avery thought back. "I did. You had to tell him what the book was about. It was rather strange."

"Very strange. Have you ever in your life heard of a professor who didn't love to talk about his area of expertise?"

Avery shrugged. She'd never had the chance to go to college. She was older than Raven by a year, but when Raven became ill, all her family's resources had been devoted to making her better and giving her the chance at an education because no one knew how long she had to live. Avery, it was assumed, had plenty of time, was perfectly healthy, and was happy enough to work at the Three Sisters. She knew nothing about professors. Aside from a few dates with young members of the profession who seemed more interested in the physical aspects of their relationship than sharing their intellectual opinions with her, she had no experience at all.

"Where did you get that book anyway?" Avery asked.

Rowan did a double take and laughed. "Don't tell my brothers or Nick, but my claim that my gallery procured it *recently* wasn't exactly true by human standards. In fact, I obtained it when it was relatively new. A Scottish gentleman I once... spent considerable time with gave it to me as a gift in the late seventeen hundreds."

Avery flashed her a wry smile. "Ooooh. A Scottish lover? Do tell."

Rowan bobbed her eyebrows. "Let's just say that if you ever wanted to know what it would feel like to hold thunder itself between your thighs, you should make love to a Scot."

"Considering that's the word of a dragon, I'm going to take that literally."

They both laughed.

"Seriously, Rowan, where do we go from here?"

Rowan paused and looked up at the sky. "There are other places to do research besides the Bodleian."

# CHAPTER SIX

"Take a deep breath, Albert. I have full confidence you can handle the store without me this afternoon." Nathaniel pressed the phone to his ear and leaned against the leather backseat of his car. His eyes closed in frustration as his driver Emory hastened home to Mistwood. He must be patient. After all, the boy was relatively new. Although Albert had been working for him for several months, this was the first time he'd requested the boy close Relics and Runes on his own. He supposed it was a big responsibility for the young man.

"What 'bout the till?" Albert asked in a tone that rose with his excitement into a high squeak.

"Leave it for the morning. I trust you." Truthfully, Nathaniel didn't need trust. If the boy stole a penny from him, it would be well and obvious the next time he saw Albert. The spell he'd cast would render him or any other thief bald as a cue ball until the sum was returned. Steal a book and the filcher would find themselves with a strange new mole on the hand that lifted it from the shelf.

"Mr. Clarke, I won't let you down."

Nathaniel could picture the poor chap's knees wobbling with his words. "I know you won't. Thank you for doing this. If all is well in the morning, there will be a bonus in it for you."

"Thank you, sir."

He hated to heap this kind of responsibility on the boy without the proper training, but he had no choice. This Clarissa situation must be dealt with as expediently as possible. He took an absent puff from his pipe. The smoke that left his mouth morphed into a dark pink heart. *Fuck.*

Frantically, he thumbed through his phone contacts and dialed Warwick.

"To what do I owe the pleasure?" The wizard's smooth voice crooned into his ear.

"How do I break a blood oath to the Order of the Dragon?"

"Why on earth would you want to do that?"

Nathaniel took another calming puff on his pipe, and thankfully his exhale was dark with his anger this time. The smoke ring squeezed in the center in a way that made it look like a skull. His driver Emory's eyes met his in the rearview mirror and then flicked back to the road.

"Clarissa is back, and she's claimed sanctuary."

"Bollocks!" Warwick released a string of curses. "Where did you put her?"

"Mistwood for now, until I find a more suitable arrangement. This whole situation is more than a little odd. She lost her magic rather abruptly. Wants me to help her get it back."

The wizard huffed. "Lost her magic? How?"

"I have no idea."

"Well, you'd better find out for the sake of the order! If it's catching, we're all in danger!"

Catching. Nathaniel hadn't thought of that. A very strong curse could spread, another reason he needed to get her out of here as soon as possible.

"Tell me how to cut her loose and I'll send her packing straight away. The coven will be safe when she's back in America."

He scoffed. "There's no way except to kill you, Nathaniel. She swore on your blood. Your magic fuels the Order of the Dragon. As long as you are alive, there is a binding magical contract for you to offer her basic protection."

"Bloody hell."

"If it is some sort of a curse, it's safer for everyone having her there until you know exactly what she's dealing with. No one in the order has better defenses against malicious magic than you."

Nathaniel closed his eyes and ground his teeth. "Very well. She will stay here until I have it sorted."

Silence stretched on the other end of the line. When Warwick spoke again, his voice was as firm as a schoolmaster's. "You don't have to speak to her. You don't have to like her. All you have to do is give her just enough to survive. If you want her to leave, I wouldn't make things... comfortable for her beyond what's absolutely necessary under the circumstances."

He grunted.

"You have plenty of my tobacco, I assume."

"Should be enough."

"Good. That should help you manage your feelings for her."

"Should it? So far it's done little but blow puffy red hearts every time I think of her." Nathaniel rubbed his eyes with his thumb and forefinger.

"Oh dear. I'll send over a different blend to, uh, calm your nerves. I'll need more of your blood. My reserves are running low." It was an unfortunate reality that Nathaniel's blood was a necessary ingredient in binding Warwick's magic to the tobacco.

"I'd appreciate that. I'll get you what you need." Nate rubbed a muscle in his jaw that had started to ache.

"But please, Nathaniel, while you have her there, don't just cure her, find out what happened to her power. Perhaps we have an enemy. There are those who would love to see the elimination of the order. That coven from Edinburgh comes to mind. We need to know for sure she's not a Trojan horse."

He took another puff from his pipe and was happy the smoke blew in a traditional ring at his command. "I'll take care of it."

"Good luck, my dear friend."

His driver met his eyes again in the mirror as they turned off the road, passed through the protective wards around Mistwood, and traveled up the drive.

"What do you have to say, Emory? If it weren't for the mirror, I'd turn to stone under that stare of yours."

"I was just wondering, sir... Not to be presumptuous, but might this be an opportunity for Clarissa to heal old wounds?"

The growl that rumbled up Nathaniel's throat had the driver's knuckles turning white on the steering wheel.

"Watch yourself. There will be no healing. There is nothing left to heal. Clarissa is a devil, and there is only room for one in this hell of mine. I plan to deal with this thing that plagues her as soon as possible and send her on her way. The faster, the better."

Emory nodded. "Of course. You're right, sir. Glad to know your head is on straight."

Emory came to a stop in front of Mistwood and popped out to open the door for him.

Nathaniel grabbed his attaché case and strode toward the manor. "Take the rest of the day off. I won't be leaving again until tomorrow morning."

"Yes, sir. Thank you, sir." The man climbed behind the wheel and made haste back down the drive.

"She's been in her old chambers since noon," Tempest said, appearing in the suddenly open door, arms crossed and looking as rumpled as an oread could look. "If you like, I could forget to remove my gloves after mucking Diablo's stall and feel my way around her room."

Nathaniel groaned. "If I thought a bit of manure would solve this problem, I'd take you up on that offer. Unfortunately, Warwick has advised me that until I fix what ails Clarissa, she is our permanent guest. Let's try to make the best of it."

With a bow of his head, Tempest disappeared, sending a disgruntled puff of wind in his direction. Well, he couldn't agree more with the sentiment. He took a long, fortifying drag on his pipe. The smoke blew from his lips a cautionary orange. He tamped out the tobacco and plugged the bowl with a wind cap before sliding it into his pocket.

"You're a dragon, Nathaniel. Be a dragon," he whispered to himself. He took the stairs three at a time. If she thought she could simply come back here and he'd treat her like nothing had changed between them, she was sadly mistaken. This visit would be on his terms and, with any luck, mercifully short.

He barged into her room without knocking.

She rose from the chair where she'd been reading in one

quick movement. "You might knock before entering some-one's room, Nathaniel. What if I'd been dressing?"

His dragon twisted hot and rough in his chest, and his tongue burned with the need to lash out. "May I remind you, Clarissa, that this is not your room. It's mine, as is the rest of this house and the grounds. I've agreed to give you sanctuary, not privacy. As for your potential nakedness, I doubt there's anything I haven't seen before, unless you've added a secret tattoo since our last joining? No? As such, your state of dress is of no concern to me."

"You can be such a fucking brute." She narrowed her eyes and shook her head.

"As you know, and still you came to me for help." He sneered in her direction.

"If I had any other choice, believe me, I'd take it." She folded her arms over her filmy floral dress in a way that threatened to drive him to distraction. Her skin would feel soft if he touched her, like the petal of a rose.

He stared down his nose at her. "Since you've made your choice, Ms. Black, let's not prolong your purpose. Tell me exactly how this happened, everything you remember."

# CHAPTER SEVEN

## *Tanaka Auditorium*
## *Before*

Tanaka Auditorium was standing room only, which was saying something considering the size of the theater. As private events went, it was huge. Tom had relayed that the tech giant had hired Clarissa as a perk for the employees who'd worked to develop some sort of new gadget that would give the iPhone a run for its money. They'd certainly gone all out.

At the moment, Blue Radio was opening for her. She waited backstage, using her last moments before the show to center herself. Out of nowhere, a sophisticated-looking woman in a light gray business suit appeared beside her. Before Clarissa could say a word, the stranger reached out and plucked a hair from her head.

"Wow! What the fuck?" Clarissa snapped. The redheaded woman started to walk away, but Clarissa grabbed her arm. "Who the hell are you?"

"Hair and makeup," the woman said, her voice gritty and low like she might have a cold. "Cleaning up a stray."

"Next time ask permission before you touch me." She released the woman's elbow and searched for Tom. He was going to get an earful over this. It wasn't about the hair. Everyone knew she counted on these last moments of meditation to do her best work. Time alone to center herself was part of her creative process. Allowing a stranger backstage this close to the performance completely threw her off.

When she couldn't find Tom, she turned back to explain the rules to the woman herself, only she'd disappeared. Probably knew she was in trouble. She'd talk to Tom about it after the show. Whatever company she worked for, they needed to know they couldn't bring in new blood at zero hour.

For the rest of the opening act, she pushed the incident from her mind, instead choosing to focus on the show ahead of her. By the time Blue Radio left the stage and Tom appeared again, she'd forgotten all about it. She watched him exchange hand signals with the soundman while tech readied the stage. The lights dimmed. At once, the roar of the crowd became deafening.

White and red pyrotechnics blazed to life with the opening beats and her dancers flooded the stage. Their black leotards were designed to give the impression of scales, and they weaved like snakes, dancing their way into the hearts of the audience. Her people were the best in the business. Some looked positively boneless.

Her latest album, *The Serpent's Strike*, was all about being bitten by love, how the poison got into your blood and changed you forever. How fitting that she should be performing in London. The only man she'd ever thought she could love lived here, and she'd never succeeded in curing herself from his romantic venom.

When the stage manager waved a finger, she strode onto the stage in a black snakeskin bustier, a skirt that desperately wanted to be a belt, and a train that weighed hundreds of pounds and had to be carried and positioned by a second set of dancers.

*Bring the night!* She sang and the crowd went wild. She broke into her dance, singing the series of notes that led into the first verse. Her voice ignited the air around her, syncing the dancers with her body and making the room twinkle with living energy.

Clarissa was a witch and her voice was her wand. Tonight, as she did every night, she would take her audience on a magical journey they would never forget.

*Your night, it crawls to meet*
*the darkness inside me.*
*Don't you know that your energy*
*is the thing making me me?*

The train she was wearing detached and rose behind her as if carried by a breeze. As she sang, it folded itself into an origami beast, a dark sparkling dragon with huge wings that flapped above her and the dancers. The crowd went crazy. Lights flashed as they tried their best to capture a picture that would do it justice. When she sang again, they sang along with her.

*I was once a dying thing.*
*You helped me to find my wings.*
*Though you were my everything,*
*I broke away and felt the sting.*
*Free from you, free from us.*
*Free to rule the skies above.*
*Bring on the night.*

*I will be its queen.*
*Bring on the night.*
*I will rule the wind.*
*Bring on the night.*
*I welcome it. I'm ready. I'm ready.*

Something was wrong. During this part of the performance, the origami dragon was supposed to fly over her head, circle the crowd, and then return to the stage where she would pretend to slay it with her dance moves. It wasn't happening. She kept moving, performing the dance steps as always, but her magic drained from the room like the rush of water from an unplugged bathtub. Her throat caught, constricted. It felt like she'd swallowed a bee.

In abject horror, she cast a frantic, desperate look toward Tom backstage and patted her throat. All he could do was spread his hands and yell into his headset.

Fabric rustled above her. She tipped her head back just in time to watch hundreds of pounds of black twinkling cloth give up its dragon form and drop, flattening her to the stage.

# CHAPTER EIGHT

The story was not what Nathaniel had expected. If someone had been able to use a hair plucked from Clarissa's head to sabotage her performance so quickly, the perpetrator must be a truly powerful magical being. The attack was targeted and malicious. Someone wanted not only to hurt her but to embarrass her too.

"They took me to the hospital after the show. I was physically fine, but my magic was gone."

"I see. You said you didn't recognize the redheaded woman?"

She shook her head.

"Is there anyone who would want to hurt you?"

"No one has threatened me explicitly. If this is personal, I don't know why."

He scoffed. "Of course not. It couldn't possibly be personal. What have you ever done that was your fault?"

Her eyes narrowed at his sarcastic tone. "I'm sorry, Nathaniel. I'm sorry about what happened between us."

"Don't waste your breath on false words. I'll get to work this afternoon on a spell to reveal the source of this curse."

"And until then, I should wait here for you to burst into the room at your next whim?"

He scowled at her. "Yes. This is my home after all, despite your using the Order of the Dragon against me. Besides, you did offer me... anything... to help you."

"I see. So is that what this is all about? My offer?"

She stood and strode toward him, stepping out of her stilettos on the way. She stopped less than six inches in front of him, close enough she knew he could catch her scent. His lips pulled back from his teeth as the natural lily fragrance of her skin filled his nose and his inner dragon woke from its slumber.

He wanted her. He'd always wanted her. And she was using it against him.

In a few quick moves, she pulled her dress over her head. Underneath, the lacy pale pink bra and panty set she wore teased him mercilessly. His gaze flicked down to the edge of the lace where it cut across her breasts, her nipples hidden under a panel of silk. Immediately his body responded and his instant erection twitched with need. She noticed. She always noticed.

Her fists landed on her hips. "Well? I offered you everything. Are you going to take it? I won't say no. I'm too desperate."

His mouth was as dry as a stone. It would serve her right if he called her bluff. He could have her on that bed before she could blink, body spread out under him like his own personal buffet. But that's what she wanted. Sex with her would give her control. It would awaken all the feelings he'd fought so hard to repress over the years, the offered bond that she'd rejected. Oh no, he wouldn't give her the satisfaction.

He ground his teeth and stared down his nose at her.

Two could play at this game, and her buttons were just as easy to push. "What makes you think I'd give *you* pleasure in exchange for my magic? Hardly seems like a fair trade." He moved in closer, his voice all grit as his dragon raised the temperature in the room and his stare burned into hers. "No, if I take from you it will be for *my* pleasure and mine alone. Be careful, Clarissa—you don't want to give me any ideas."

He turned on his heel and strode toward the door. "Meet me in the ritual room in an hour. I recommend skipping lunch. The tests I will run on you to discover your malady tend to empty the stomach."

One last glance out of the corner of his eye showed her to be visibly shaken. Despite her lifted chin and steel spine, he did not miss the goose bumps along her skin. Smug satisfaction filled him as he strode from the room and down the hall to his chambers.

Still, he didn't take a full breath until he was safely behind its locked door.

CHAPTER NINE

Only when Nathaniel was out of earshot did Clarissa release her held breath and allow herself to shuffle backward and plop down hard on the bed. She leaned forward, her head between her knees, swearing repeatedly under her breath. She'd wanted to call his bluff, to gain an inch of power in this situation by appealing to his desire for her.

She'd failed miserably. He'd rejected her outright, which meant that despite the heart-shaped smoke she'd seen at the bookstore and his physical response, he was well and truly over her. His negative emotions toward her must trump any physical attraction. Which meant any hope of reigniting the feelings he'd once had for her in order to make this experience easier was dead.

Probably for the best, considering she hadn't counted on his presence reigniting feelings in *her* instead.

When he'd walked into her room, for a second she was back in the quiet moments of their affair. Nathaniel stalking toward her was something out of a dream or a nightmare. Her body had betrayed her at the sight of his muscles rolling beneath his tailored suit, his sheer size radiating dominance across the room. Her stomach had fluttered. Heat had blossomed between her thighs. Her bra had felt suffocatingly tight.

Truly, some part of her had wanted him to take her when she'd removed her dress. Oh, she'd meant for it to come off as brave, a cynical jab at him for barging in on her without knocking, but feeling his heat against her skin, the smoky scent of his special blend of tobacco mixed with the underlying spice of dragon in her nose, she'd wanted him to give in to the fire that clearly still burned between them. She'd been stupid. She should have known he'd never have sex with her under such dubious circumstances. Nathaniel was many things, but he would never coerce a woman into his bed.

Too bad she'd lost this round. Her skin still burned from the memory of him. Her heart was a scorched wasteland from his rejection.

*Fuck.*

She set a timer on her phone. One hour. Sixty short minutes until she found out exactly what sort of punishment he had in store for her.

A thought niggled at the back of her brain and she pushed it aside. There was more to this than physical rejection, but she refused to examine those feelings. Hell no. She pushed herself up and stumbled to her suitcase, pulling on a pair of sweats and a T-shirt. Whatever Nate had in mind for this afternoon, she suspected his warning about her stomach wasn't an exaggeration. She washed the makeup off her face in the adjoining bathroom and pulled her hair into a ponytail.

Her black roots formed a stark halo around her face, blending into the platinum highlights toward a completely blond tail. She looked like hell. Along with a set of dark circles under her eyes, her skin appeared pale and lifeless in the bathroom light. The only ones who should see her like this were Ben & Jerry—and not the real people, but the picture on the side of the pint of Cherry Garcia she wished she was curled around right now.

All too soon, the timer on her phone went off. She swallowed down her apprehension and padded toward the ritual room on shaking legs. This was going to hurt in more ways than one. By the time she got to the secret door behind the kitchen, she was trembling everywhere and relieved he'd propped it open. She wasn't sure she could remember the procedure to trigger the lock in her current state.

He was there, waiting inside, seated at a table laden with jars and glassware, under a ceiling covered with dried, hanging herbs. With a wave of his hand, the door to the kitchen slammed closed and sealed behind her. The sound made her jump. She drew in a deep, fortifying breath and tried to relax.

Nothing about this room was calming. The walls were lined with shelves holding every manner of magical ingredient. Dried lizards and preserved eels. Animal skulls. Candles. Blood. The heady scent of magic filled the air, thick and vegetative, with the edge of smoke that always followed Nathaniel. This was the devil's workshop, and she had volunteered her soul to suffer his torment.

Bright amethyst eyes locked on her, their former gray color now purple with his use of power. He stirred a small cauldron on the bench in front of him and never missed a stroke as he commanded, "Please stand within the symbol."

Her gaze drifted to the floor. A triangle was sketched in chalk there with mystical shapes drawn at its apexes.

"Nathaniel, what is this symbol?"

"Ancient arcane magic."

"What does it do?"

"You're wasting time, Clarissa."

With one last tentative glance in his direction, she slowly and carefully stepped into the triangle. Power scraped against her skin. Experimentally, she reached her hand toward the chalk line, and her fingers bumped an invisible force. As she'd feared, once inside the boundaries, she could not exit the symbol.

"In order to solve your problem," Nathaniel said from his place at the workbench, "I need to know what caused it. I've prepared a series of potions. If one binds to a specific curse within your body, I'll know what type of magic was used to hinder your voice. The symbol will then reveal the curse's location inside you. Once we know both the magical origin and the placement, we can set about neutralizing it or removing it."

A chill traveled through her at the thought of Nathaniel removing her body parts to get at the curse. She closed her eyes to stop that train of thought. "All right. So I just stand here and drink what you give me?"

It occurred to her how vulnerable she was. He could do anything to her in this room and no one would know. Not even Tom. No one would ever find her. No one would hear her scream. She trusted that Nathaniel wouldn't hurt her on purpose—he couldn't, thanks to the boundaries of the blood bond and the magical contract of sanctuary—but accidents happened when it came to magic.

"Who do you know with motivation to curse your voice?" Nathaniel asked.

"The only one I can think of is Eva Hart. My latest single has been leaving hers in the dust on the charts all month."

"If memory serves, Eva is a witch, yes?"

She nodded once. Glass clinked against glass as he retrieved a vessel of questionable cleanliness from his collection and poured a finger's height of green liquid into the bottom. "This won't narrow it down to Eva, but it will tell us if it was a witch who cursed you."

He handed it to her inside the symbol. Apparently he could reach in even though she couldn't reach out. *Great*. "Ugh. It smells like..."

"Possum urine," he said. "I never promised this would be pleasant."

She breathed through her mouth to lessen the stench. "I drink this and then what happens?"

"As I mentioned, this potion will bind to the curse and show us where in the body the spell abides—at least if a witch is responsible. If I can see it, the shape and color glowing through your skin, I should be able to research its origins and find a cure."

She nodded. It sounded like a good plan despite the smell. She raised the glass to her lips but paused without drinking. "What happens if it wasn't a witch who cursed me?"

"If the potion doesn't bind, it will find its way back out of the body." He tipped his head as if his meaning should be obvious, then backed up and kicked a silver rubbish bin in her direction. It skidded to a stop at her feet.

*Great*. Taking one more shaky breath, she raised the glass in his direction. "Here's hoping that Eva is the culprit."

She tossed it back like a shot and swallowed it down. The taste that coated her throat made her gag, but the feel of the spell careening through her body was far worse. Worms, like giant, squishy caterpillars, crawled and writhed up and down each of her limbs. She screamed and clawed at her skin to no avail. The magic wriggled in her veins.

And then, when the worming had burrowed down to her toes and back again, it gathered in the pit of her stomach. All at once, it rose in her throat. She heaved into the bucket, her forehead breaking out in a dense sweat.

Although she hadn't drunk but an ounce of the brew, she filled the bottom of the bucket. Her head throbbed.

"Not another witch," Nathaniel said dryly, tapping his chin. "It's possible the hair had nothing to do with it. Perhaps when the woman touched you, she cursed you. Maybe a nymph or a sprite?"

He took the glass from her, strode to the bench, and returned with it a quarter full of glowing blue elixir.

"A little heavy on the pour, wouldn't you say?" she grumbled.

"The amount required for the spell is based on your weight." He arched a devilish eyebrow.

*Asshole.* She gave him her most stinging glare and tossed back the shot. This one felt like ice in her veins, and she shivered violently as it coursed through her body. It came back up her throat with force and swirled in the bucket like a blue whirlpool.

"No. No. That's not it either." Nathaniel took the glass from her sweaty hand.

Clarissa's head swam and her tongue went numb. She sank to her knees within the triangle. Her heart pounded like a restless prisoner against the cage of her ribs.

"Is there a problem, Ms. Black?" Nathaniel asked tersely. He'd returned with something purple and sludgy. Her gaze locked with his and she forced any weakness from her expression.

"No," she croaked defiantly. She took the glass from his

outstretched hand and tossed it back. It barely hit her stomach before her limbs turned to concrete. What poured out of her mouth a moment later resembled a giant slug. "What was that a test for?"

"A spell that involved vampire blood."

She leaned her hands on the bucket. "I need some water."

"It's better if you don't drink. It will dilute the magic. Besides, there are only two more." He left and returned with a fluorescent-orange elixir. Nuclear mango juice. "Fairy magic."

This time she had to pant to build up her courage. She tossed it back and forced herself to swallow. Instantly her entire body vibrated like it was filled with Pop Rocks. She waited.

When nothing happened, her eyes shifted to Nathaniel's. "I'm not throwing up. Maybe this is our answ—"

Vomit careened through her lips so fast and hard that she missed the bucket and slid backward on her knees. She fell forward, her hands landing in it.

"Water, please, Nate..." She was dying. Her mouth tasted like ash, and it was becoming difficult simply to remain upright. Every muscle in her body ached.

"Last one."

She thought concern flitted across his expression, but it was gone before she could be sure. He shoved a red elixir that reminded her of cherry cough syrup into the symbol.

"Can't we just assume this is it?" she asked through a raspy, sore throat.

"No. If this fails, it means this isn't a curse but something else. Perhaps you're legitimately sick. Some kind of witch disease."

Her hands were shaking so hard she had to use both of them to lift the glass to her lips. The syrupy red liquid smelled like sulfur. With every drop of willpower she had left, she forced herself to swallow. It burned going down.

The pain when it hit her stomach folded her in half and coaxed a scream from her lips. Her skin was on fire! She broke into a sweat and rolled onto her side, her breath coming in ragged pants. Tears streamed from her eyes. It hurt. It felt as if every drop of moisture had been wrung from her veins.

She waited and the torture gradually faded.

"By the Mountain," Nathaniel said under his breath.

Her hands glowed red. She tried to stand but failed. Her head was spinning. Still, it was impossible to miss the bright crimson lighting her from within.

"It's in my bones," she rasped. She wanted to ask him what had cursed her. What did the red mean? But black dots swam in her vision, and then her head cracked against the floor and everything went dark.

# CHAPTER TEN

"**D**rink. More. You still look green." Nathaniel struggled to keep his emotional walls up as he supported Clarissa's back and brought a bottle of sports drink to her lips. Seeing her pale and fragile against the white sheets, her limbs limp, her lips cracking, was almost enough to break his resolve.

At first watching her endure the effects of his test was cathartic. She'd hurt him in indescribable ways; it was her turn to hurt. He'd enjoyed it for about two minutes. But all too soon, the table-turning lost its appeal. Although the test had been necessary, he did not enjoy watching her heave her guts out or collapse on the floor. Carrying her to her room had proved a significant emotional hurdle. She'd draped almost lifeless in his arms, and the panic that rose at the feel of her against his chest truly was more punishment for him than for her.

"Orange. My least favorite," she mumbled before chugging the rest of the bottle.

He lowered her head to the pillow, took the empty, and

handed her another. "This isn't a hotel or an American restaurant. You can't have it your way."

"No." She shook her head. "You've made that perfectly clear."

He backed away from the bed and reflexively reached for the pipe in his pocket, then thought twice about lighting it in her presence and left it where it was.

"What did the red elixir test for?" Clarissa asked. "What type of magic cursed me?"

Waves of exhaustion washed over Nathaniel. He had to tell her although the thought disturbed him to his core. "You've been cursed by dragon magic."

"Dragon— How certain are you?"

"Absolutely certain."

Their eyes met. What little color she had drained from her cheeks.

"Do you have any idea who might have done this?" she asked him in an unsteady voice.

"No."

"Nathaniel... did you do this to get back at me?" Her last word was nothing but a breath.

"Give me some credit, Clarissa. I didn't even know you were in London until this morning."

Her lips pressed together, but she seemed to believe him. "Someone from the order?"

"Not that I know of. There's no love lost between you and the others though. I'm afraid you've thoroughly burned your bridges. Still, it's hard to believe anyone would bother with a curse now. Why not years ago? Why not when you first left us? I'm quite certain any animosity they might have held for you has only dulled with time."

"But they do hate me." She snorted. "My God, it's been a decade. That's a long time to hold a grudge."

"Is that what you think? You think this is a grudge?" He motioned between them, the muscles in his forehead tightening.

"What else would you call it?"

He growled. Why was he still in this room, rehashing ancient history? "Enough. Get some rest. Tomorrow we'll work on finding a cure, and before you know it you'll be off again and able to put this whole nightmarish event behind you."

Without another word or glance in her direction, he strode from the room to the sound of her quiet protestations.

The woman was infuriating. Having her here, talking to her like this, it was opening old wounds. He needed to fix her and send her on her way. Nothing would feel normal until he did.

Nathaniel strode into his library and nabbed his tarot cards from his desk. He'd always had an affinity for magic. While his brothers were busy training in the fighting pits, he'd often sneak off to watch his mother experiment with spells. By the time he was an adolescent, he'd practiced several with her, even created works of magic that she'd transcribed in her grimoire.

Dragon magic lived in his skin and in his scales, but aside from strength, speed, invisibility, and the ability to ward treasure, most dragons couldn't perform magic in the way a witch could. Most. He and his mother had found a way. Symbol by symbol and incantation by incantation, they'd discovered ways to use their own magic as a battery to fuel arcane rituals and potions. Witches drew on the elements, fairies drew on living things—dragons had to draw on themselves.

His mother had helped him develop the foundations of this magic, but over time he'd learned that combining his strengths with those of human witches and wizards greatly increased his effectiveness. With a few tools he'd developed with the help of the order, he could more easily focus his energy, the pipe from Warwick being a perfect example.

He fished it from his pocket and emptied it into the copper bowl on his desk. There was a package glittering on his ink blotter, next to the shadow mail candle he kept there. He turned over the tag.

*To dull the pain. Best, Warwick.*

He pulled the bow and unwrapped the brown-paper packaging. Inside, pipe tobacco with a lovely purple tint released its aroma into the air.

There was nothing he'd like better than to numb the pain right now. Numb the ache in his chest. He loaded up his pipe and took a few draws. The calming qualities of the tobacco kicked in quickly, thank the Mountain. Warwick's blend gave everything a nice rosy hue. Just the level of clarity he needed.

Clarissa had been cursed using dragon magic. It was the last thing he'd suspected. The only people he knew who practiced dragon magic in this area were in the order. He hated to believe that one of them would have done something like this without his consent, but she'd left them, abandoned the order and taken her magic with her, in the same way she'd left him.

He rubbed his chin. He had to admit it was possible that one of them heard she was doing a show in London and decided to mess with her out of some need for revenge or disjointed loyalty. That wouldn't do. If that was the case, the fastest way to be rid of her was to devise a plan to out the guilty party and force them to lift the curse.

He almost hoped the offender was among their ranks. The alternative was something he didn't want to think about. Nathaniel was one of eight dragon siblings on this, the third rock from the sun, and the other seven he hadn't seen in a very long time. He couldn't imagine why one of them would do anything like this, but if it *was* another dragon, that would be a difficult curse to break indeed.

Smoke from his pipe curled into question marks above his head. He wasn't a detective or a psychic, but that didn't mean he had no tools to divine the future. He shuffled his deck of tarot cards and squared them.

"How do I find who did this to her?" He flipped the top card.

*Temperance.* The card depicted Michael, the archangel of healing, straddling two worlds, water and earth in front of a long winding path. The angel was pouring liquid between two cups.

"Bloody hell." This was a card about unification. It symbolized harmony, grace, and forgiveness. Well, if the spirits were requiring him to welcome Clarissa back with open arms in order to find her cure, everyone would be disappointed. She could just live her life without her singing voice if it came down to that.

But as he stared longer at the card, he noticed the two flowers in the background. Iris flowers. They represented the goddess of rainbows. It was said that Zeus would sometimes make Iris go to the underworld to fill a golden jug from the river Styx and would require each of the gods to drink from it. If he or she had lied, they would fall over breathless for a year.

The card wasn't talking about him welcoming her back after all. This card was suggesting a test, just like the golden jug. A test of the Order of the Dragon. What he needed was a ritual that would draw out the guilty party.

A smile spread his lips. He tipped the card back onto

the pile. He knew exactly the ritual that would accomplish his goal, and it would have the delicious side benefit of making Clarissa very uncomfortable.

Clarissa couldn't sleep. Her insides ached as if she'd been turned inside out, scrubbed raw, and put back together. Not only did the remnants of nausea leave her tossing and turning in the cool sheets, but a gnawing hunger left her feeling hollow.

The half-moon bathed her room in ecru light. *Her room.* That was a slip of the mind. This room was no longer hers. It was the place she was staying, and as soon as Nathaniel broke the curse, a place she'd never see again. For some reason, that particular realization made her eyes prick with tears.

Her stomach growled. Nathaniel was probably asleep. She could sneak down to the kitchen and try to prepare something. Who was she kidding? Tempest would surely catch her and send her back up here without a bite to eat. She covered her eyes with her hands. What had she been thinking, forcing his hand and claiming sanctuary? Why would he be compassionate to her after what she put him through?

Nathaniel hated her and he was going to make this hell until she voluntarily left or her rights to sanctuary were fulfilled.

Worse, she deserved to be hated. He had bared his soul to her the last time she was here. He'd told her what it meant for his inner dragon to want her as his mate. If what he said was true, had she accepted the bond, he would go to his death loving her. She had no reason not to believe him.

He'd never lied to her. And the way he'd loved her had proven to be his singular focus. His loyalty and devotion to her had been unfailing over the year she'd spent here.

And his reward for the devotion was her leaving him without so much as a goodbye. Oh, she'd had her reasons. It had all made sense at the time. But she'd been brutal in her abandonment, telling herself that she wasn't doing anything to him that hadn't been done to her in the past. And wasn't it for the best? She'd been too young for a permanent commitment.

Only, her lack of maturity had caused her to end things in the cruelest way. Truly she regretted it now, seeing it through her adult eyes. And here she was, crawling back with her tail between her legs and forcing him to take her in.

Thirst left her tongue stuck to the top of her mouth. Were her tears making it worse? Everything in her neck and chest felt tight, as if a ball were lodged in her throat. The feeling only made her cry harder. She whimpered, unable to hold back her sobs.

The silver candle beside the bed flamed to life, and she clapped a hand over her mouth. Shadow mail. Nathaniel had invented the enchanted candles that could be used to exchange messages or even pass items between them. When she'd first come here, he used to use them to flirt with her late into the night. He must have heard her crying and was probably going to chew her out for it.

The shadows on the end table swirled and twisted, transforming from flat, two-dimensional gradients of black and ecru to three-dimensional charcoal curls. The individual strands braided and meshed into a dark cloud the size of a small box. When the smoke cleared and the candle blew itself out, there was a sandwich and a bottle of ginger ale in its wake.

Seeing the food was a relief and also made her tears stream faster. Nathaniel had sent this. The oreads did not use shadow mail. They had no need to. The thought that he'd put his animosity aside to provide her what she needed squeezed her heart. She didn't deserve it.

She moved the food to the desk to clear a spot on the end table, then opened the drawer. The box of matches was still there. With a flick, one blazed to life and she brought it to the candle's wick. She waited until the glow splashed across the wood.

Dipping her finger into the shadows, she wrote THANK YOU with her fingertip. She hoped and prayed the candle would still work despite her lack of magic. A sigh of relief broke her lips as the shadow writing coiled up and dissolved in the flame. A few seconds later, his response painted itself in wispy letters across the surface. STOP CRYING AND EAT.

The flame hissed and blew itself out.

She wiped her eyes and reached for the sandwich.

# CHAPTER ELEVEN

L ater that night, Clarissa finally slept, a deep,
dreamless sleep like she used to enjoy when she lived
at Mistwood full-time. She missed it. It was the kind of
sleep that only came from knowing she was perfectly safe.
After she'd eaten the sandwich Nathaniel had made for her,
she'd known that for sure. He wouldn't have fed her if he
truly loathed her and wished she were dead.

No. That wasn't exactly true. He likely did hate her, but
at least he didn't intend to torture her.

She dressed in a pair of sweats and a T-shirt and
grabbed her athletic shoes. There was one thing she had to
know, and a quick walk before breakfast would tell her what
she needed.

Tempest met her on the stairs, although he didn't reveal
himself to her. She heard his footsteps and smelled his eucalyptus scent. His disembodied voice was clipped when he
addressed her. "If you want breakfast, you can make your
own."

"I didn't ask you for anything," she replied firmly.

A current of air brushed her skin and she knew he'd

moved past. She descended to the main floor. It was late morning. Nathaniel would be gone by now, opening up Relics and Runes. It was the perfect time to find out how bad things really were between them.

She slipped on her shoes and jogged out the front door, her feet crunching on the gravel of the wooded drive and then the path that led to the orchard. The first trees were a half mile out from the manor, and by the time she reached the edge, her stomach was growling fiercely. She wished she'd thought to rummage in the kitchen for something before she'd taken on this quest.

The scent of blossoms met her nose. It was the middle of summer, and the trees were heavy with fruit and nuts. Nathaniel once told her that anywhere a dragon lived for an extended amount of time became infused with magic. It wasn't just the wards he'd placed around the property to conceal it from the world and protect it from those who would do it harm. Mystic energy oozed from his presence. It was in the air here. In the soil. In the water.

When she'd left, it had taken a full month for her body to adjust.

She followed the winding dirt path through the trees. Walnut, peach, olive, fig. She remembered the first time she was here and noticed that one particular tree seemed to be missing. She'd joked with Nathaniel about it, being an American and noticing the omission.

And then she'd bought him one as a gift.

She turned the corner and reached the center of the orchard. Breath whooshed from her lungs.

A mature orange tree spread its branches over a well-manicured circular mound of earth and mulch. Her tree. A citrus tree like this could not naturally survive in this climate. It took magic and care to keep it alive. Had

Nathaniel truly hated her, he would have ripped it out by the roots or cast a spell to deprive it of magic and let it wither and die. But he hadn't. The tree practically glowed and the branches bent, laden with fruit.

"The flesh is red."

Clarissa whirled to find Nathaniel behind her, dressed in jeans and a gray T-shirt that somehow managed to look sophisticated on him. His horse, Diablo, grazed along the trail. She hadn't heard him coming. Suspicious, considering his mode of transportation.

"I didn't hear you ride up."

His eyes narrowed, and the corner of his mouth quirked. "I can be rather stealthy when I want to be. What are you doing out here?"

She nodded toward the tree. "Thought I'd see what had become of it. The flesh is supposed to be red, you know. It's a blood orange tree."

Nathaniel's wings unfurled from his back with a snap, and he flew to the top of the tree to pluck two fruits from the branches. He drifted back down and tossed one to her. "I enjoy them occasionally, although most of what we grow in the orchard is donated to the local food bank."

A talon sprouted from the first knuckle of his right hand, and he peeled his orange in a few careful swipes, allowing the thick rind to fall to the pebbles near his feet. She noticed the path was littered with dried peels. Someone must partake of the fruit regularly enough.

"I thought you'd be at work by now."

He shrugged. "Have been and returned. It is almost noon, Ms. Black. The world still grinds along while you are sleeping."

"But... I thought the shop was open into the evening." Clarissa tried not to make her disappointment obvious, but having him here meant he'd probably want to continue his magical interventions for her problem. She wasn't ready to have her stomach drained of its contents again so soon.

"My protégé is working the rest of the day while I devote my afternoon to researching your ailment. It's best not to sit on problems like these. The sooner one can break a curse, the less time it has to take hold."

She nodded. "If it truly is dragon magic that was used to curse me, you should be able to neutralize it, right? No one knows this type of magic better than you."

He frowned. "Unfortunately, all the test tells us is that a dragon's blood, scales, or breath were used as a catalyst. The spell itself may be extremely complex. It would have to be considering it has taken root in your bones."

"So not an easy fix."

He shook his head. "Not unless we find the perpetrator."

"Warwick never enjoyed my company."

"Warwick would not curse you."

"You don't know what Warwick is capable of or the rest of the order. It has to be someone."

"Yes." Nathaniel scrutinized her as the silence stretched between them.

She dug her nails into the skin of the orange in her hands. "I wasn't sure my gift would still be here."

He lowered his chin, his brows becoming two dark slashes. "Why *wouldn't* it be here?"

She took a deep breath and shrugged her shoulders. "I thought since you hated me you might have torn it out by the roots or allowed it to waste away."

He considered that for a moment, tore off a section of orange, and brought it to his lips. "There was a time I thought I hated you."

She swallowed at the intensity in his eyes but remained silent.

"It started as fear. I thought you'd been abducted the day you disappeared. No note. No explanation."

"I'm sorry. I... I was afraid I'd chicken out and not go through with it if I had to face you... I—"

He acted like he hadn't heard her. "I called in everyone in the magical community, even supernatural acquaintances working for Scotland Yard. Then I received your letter and realized to my shock and embarrassment that you hadn't gone missing at all. You'd simply left me."

"There was nothing simple about it," she said softly.

The air in the orchard seemed to drop a few degrees. Unlike the night before when his anger had raised the temperature in the room, now he seemed to be putting off a chill. His gray eyes were cold as ice.

"After your letter, I explained to the order what had happened. We had to restructure several of the rituals we'd developed together while you were here. You see, I no longer had a partner. Our circle was out of balance. You can't blame them for hating you. They all took a hit to their magical reserves, not to mention the time and energy."

"I hadn't thought of that." Until now she hadn't thought much about the effects of removing herself from the order, but the blood bond they shared did fuel their magic. She winced as understanding sent a pang of guilt through her and twisted her stomach.

"My fear for your safety turned to anger. And I did hate you at first. But with time, my anger turned to sadness, then acceptance. I came to understand that your quest for fame was your number one priority, one for which you would pay any price."

*Not any price.* She kept the stray thought to herself.

Saying it would make it sound like he was something she'd been willing to sacrifice, a price easily paid. But it hadn't been easy, and there had been so much more to it than simply wanting fame. She glanced down at the path, focused on the dried remains of an orange peel.

"Never in all that time, Ms. Black, or in any of those stages of letting you go, did I think watching an innocent, healthy tree die would ease my pain." He popped another slice of orange in his mouth, his fingers red with the juice, red as blood.

"So then you don't... hate me?" She rubbed her palms together and lifted her gaze to his.

"No." He blinked. "I'm indifferent."

The word punched surprisingly sharp into her heart.

"I resisted your coming here because I worried it might rip open old wounds. But I'm pleased to inform you that it seems I've healed quite completely." He raised the remains of his orange, pointing to the tree with one finger. "The tree stays. You will go. Once I fix you, that is. And I find I'm okay with that." He inserted another slice between his teeth. "Enjoy your orange, Ms. Black."

He mounted Diablo and rode away.

IT TOOK EVERYTHING NATHANIEL HAD TO KEEP RIDING away from Clarissa and the orange tree. He thanked the Mountain she hadn't asked why he was there. The truth was, he liked to go in the morning, just as the sun filtered through the trees, and remember the day she'd given it to him.

They'd been lovers for a few months when she'd discovered that he'd never celebrated a birthday. Such a human thing, birthdays. When you were immortal, the number of years since one's birth seemed far less important. Besides, although he knew the day and year in Paragon, it didn't translate exactly to Earth years. The closest he could say was sometime in the summer.

So she'd chosen a day, and he'd come home from work to a dinner she'd made with her own hands: chops that could be used as hockey pucks, some undercooked red potatoes, and a paste she said was peas. It was the best meal he'd ever eaten. She'd followed it up with a lopsided chocolate cake with a single candle.

She stopped him before he cut into it. "Wait, I have to sing to you. There's a song."

"Ah, yes, the human birthday song. I have heard of it." He folded his arms and sat back in his chair.

The candle flickered to life with her first note. *Happy Birthday to you...*

The flame jumped from the wick and turned into a dragon. As she sang, her magic carried the tiny beast around the room, swooping and soaring, doing backflips for his amusement. When she finally reached the last note of the song, the dragon dove headfirst into the candle and turned back into a normal flame on a flickering wick.

She clapped.

"That was wonderful. Thank you. I see the draw of this birthday ritual," he said.

"Now you blow the candle out and make a wish." Her blue eyes danced over a bright and beaming smile.

"A wish?"

"Yes. You get a wish. Don't tell anyone or it might not come true. Actually, I wished for real parents when I was nine and I spent the rest of my life in foster care, so there are no guarantees here. Your chances are about the same as wishing on a falling star, but it is tradition, so give it a go."

The memory of the soft blush of her skin in the candle's warm glow warmed his heart. Everything about her seemed soft where he was hard, warm where he was cold. She'd been a powerful witch wrapped in the moss-and-lily-scented body of a goddess. He'd blown out that candle and wished for just one thing—*her*. Even back then, two full months before he'd offered her the bond, he'd wanted her to be his.

After cake, she'd walked him out to the orchard where Tempest had helped her plant the tree. It was only a sapling back then. Barely three branches on its skinny trunk. But with the help of his magic, it had grown into a beautiful, mature tree.

He regretted that no amount of magic could have done the same for their fledgling relationship. He ran his hand down his throat and headed for his study. One thing was for certain—he'd lied to her. Nothing about him was indifferent. Having her here had ripped the scab off his wound. Everything hurt. He needed to fix her magic soon and send her on her way. If he failed, her nearness might just destroy him.

# CHAPTER TWELVE

"Fresh rosemary!" Avery ran her fingers through the prickly leaves of the plant in front of the bookshop and brought them to her nose. "Mmm. I love the smell."

Rowan opened the door to the place and waited for her to enter. "I hear there is some sort of superstition about it keeping evil out. Not that I believe in human myths."

"Relics and Runes," Avery read off the window. "This sounds like the place to learn about human myths."

"It should be. Cecil Court is also called Publisher's Row. This street and this bookstore have been here since the late seventeenth century. Everything I've learned from my colleagues suggests that this is the premiere source for books on all things supernatural in London."

Avery stepped inside and gaped in wonder at the shelves of books on witchcraft and the occult. The city where she was from, New Orleans, had no shortage of references on the occult, but there was something different about this place. She walked deeper into the store and tried to put her finger on exactly what it was. And then it hit her. In

New Orleans, most of the shops seemed to cater to tourists with kitschy gris-gris bags prominently displayed to bring people riches or luck in love. This place was designed for practitioners, filled with thick textbooks and magazines, crystals, cards, and herbs clearly labeled but offered without explanation. This store wasn't about novelty but ritual.

"Welcome to Relics and Runes," a voice said from the direction of the register.

Avery turned to face a young man who was dusting something in the front window. "Hello." She narrowed her gaze on his nametag. "Albert."

He smiled at her and the faintest blush stained his cheeks. "Can I help you find something?" His voice cracked at the end of the sentence and ended in a bit of squeak.

"Actually, I was wondering if you had any resources on dragon myths and legends in the area."

"Oh, sure we do. Come, follow me." Albert led her around the counter and down a flight of stairs. "Actually, I wish the owner was here. He's sort of an expert in tales about supernatural creatures. Unfortunately, he's out indefinitely on personal emergency."

"Oh, that's terrible."

"Between you, me, and the lamppost, I think he might've needed a holiday to calm the nerves. Guy's a bit high-strung if you catch my drift."

She nodded.

"Here you are, right between the books on lycanthropy and spirit animals."

"Thank you. I can take it from here." She began perusing the books but felt him staring at the side of her face. She paused and turned her head slowly to look at him again. "Is there something wrong? Do I need to be supervised in this section or something?"

He laughed through his nose and ended in a snort. "Actually... uh... would you care to have tea? I mean, sometime, when you are available?"

Avery did a double take and noticed the interested look in the boy's eyes. He wasn't her type and seemed quite a bit younger than her, but she'd worked in the service industry long enough to have plenty of experience with unwanted advances. As they went, this one harmless.

"You seem like a nice person, but the truth is, I'm just visiting from America and my schedule is booked. I'm sorry."

He nodded quickly behind a toothy grin. "Well, all right then. Can't blame a chap for tryin'." He turned to go but paused to snap a selfie with her in the background. She caught a frame of herself staring stupidly in his direction on his screen before he jogged up the stairs.

She shook her head. *Men.* Turning back to the shelf, she ran her finger along the spines of the books in front of her. *Dragon Tarot, Dragon Meditations, Dragon Magic, Dragon Folklore.* That's it. She slid the hefty book on myths and legends of dragons in the United Kingdom from the shelf just as Rowan jogged down the stairs.

"Found it!" Avery said, holding up the book.

Rowan's eyes widened and roved around the basement room. There were as many shelves down here as upstairs, but the air was a bit stale, as if the room saw less use.

Avery reached out and rubbed Rowan's shoulder. "Hey, are you okay? You look sort of... distressed."

Rowan came fully into the basement and searched the rows of shelves. They were the only two customers down here, which was good because the level of agitation Rowan was putting off would make anyone nervous.

"Rowan? Rowan?" Avery's stomach dropped. Something had definitely rattled the dragon.

"Do you smell that?" Rowan wrinkled her nose.

"Smell what?" Avery balked at the intensity in Rowan's eyes. Their amber color seemed to darken with her mood.

"Smoky male. I think another dragon has been here recently."

Avery frowned. "Seriously?" She looked over both shoulders.

"Not that recently." Rowan rolled her eyes. "The scent is muddled by the herbs and tobacco residue. I could barely smell it upstairs. It's almost like he might have tried to cover it up."

"Do you think one of your siblings might have been here?"

Rowan planted her hands on her hips and shrugged. "Anything's possible." Her gaze flicked to the book in her hand. "Let's go pay for that. I need to talk to Alexander."

They climbed the stairs and Avery handed the book to the boy, whose cheeks reddened the moment he saw her.

"Good choice," he said, scanning the back. "That'll be nineteen quid."

Rowan handed him her credit card.

While he was ringing her up, Avery noticed a box of stones on the counter and ran her fingers over each of the different sections. Some felt hot, some cold, and some tingled where her skin brushed a smooth edge. She frowned, thinking of the orb Aborella had tricked her into wearing. Stones could hold curses and charms. She moved her hand away nervously.

"Who owns this store, Albert?" Rowan asked.

"Man's name is Clarke. He's off for a few days. As I

mentioned to your friend here, he's takin' care of some personal items." He bagged the book and handed it to her.

"Right. Thank you." Rowan sniffed as if trying to clear her nose to get a better whiff. She led the way toward the door.

"Call or stop by if there's anything else I can do for you," Albert called. "I'm at your service."

# CHAPTER THIRTEEN

*Paragon*

Whatever Aborella had done to Raven had drained her. Her limbs felt heavy, as if she'd been emptied of all her blood. The worst part was seeing Gabriel's face. He was bereft. She'd been mated to him long enough now to know that this was his personal nightmare. A dragon's heart beat to protect his mate, and this was completely out of his control.

"Raven, how do you feel?" Gabriel asked quietly.

She placed a hand on his cheek and lied. "I'm okay." With his help, she staggered to her feet. "I don't know how they got their hands on that spell or why it worked, but they took my magic. I've nothing left."

"Fuck." Gabriel's face twisted into a mask of rage. "If we ever get out of this, I'll kill her."

Tobias groaned. "Let's focus on the getting-out-of-this part. Killing her can wait for another day."

Raven stumbled to the pile of garments. She held up the smallest of the sets. The tunic and wide-legged pants were black with embroidered flowers and colorful dragons. "This feels like silk."

"Vilt, I'm sure. Mommy dearest wouldn't approve of anything less in her presence," Tobias said.

"What is this all about?" Raven asked. "I get why she took my power, but why dress us up if she plans to execute us?"

Gabriel sighed. "Mother has always had a yen for the dramatic. She'll want us looking our best for the Highborn Court before she beheads us."

Raven hadn't heard the name *Highborn Court* before, but the meaning seemed clear enough. "You think she'll execute us in front of the Paragonian aristocracy?"

"Not just Paragonian," Gabriel explained. "The Highborn Court is comprised of the wealthiest and most powerful families from the five kingdoms. Each of them also belongs to lesser courts in their own kingdoms, but the Highborns reign over them all. They are Eleanor's greatest supporters, the ones who benefit the most from her keeping her hold over the five kingdoms and the most likely to want to maintain the status quo."

Tobias gathered a cobalt-colored tunic and black pants from the pile and began to dress. "She wants something more than our heads. Call it a hunch."

Gabriel swore under his breath. "I don't know whether to hope you're right or wrong. I'd like us all to live to see another day, but if she's keeping us alive for a reason, her motives are surely nefarious." He snatched up the remaining pair of black pants and the emerald tunic. After dressing quickly, he spread his wings and wrapped them around Raven to give her privacy while she changed.

"Thank you," she whispered as she removed her dress. It was impossible to believe that she'd given birth only two days ago. She ran her fingers along the white scar that ran from her ribs to her hipbone. Although she'd been magically healed, it looked like she'd been disemboweled using a dull shovel. On top of loose skin and the added weight of a recent pregnancy, her abdomen sagged and rolled like something out of a horror movie. Even healing magic couldn't fix that. And her breasts hurt. Why did her breasts hurt? It wasn't as if she needed to nurse the egg.

"Beautiful," Gabriel said.

She raised her gaze to his and found nothing but warmth and more than a little male heat in his eyes. She pressed a kiss under his jaw, then dressed in the pants and hip-length tunic, which tied with a belt. There were no shoes provided. Well enough. The cool floor felt good in the hot room.

"It's best not to offer any information," Gabriel whispered in her ear.

She knew exactly what he meant. "I know."

A wave of heartbreak overcame her, and she swallowed the lump in her throat. He meant she couldn't talk about the baby. Words did not need to be spoken for her to know that denying the egg's existence was their best course of action right now. Aborella hadn't seen the egg. She couldn't prove Raven had given birth to a living heir. That meant silence was their best option, followed by a convincing lie that the pregnancy was unsuccessful. But she couldn't stop her heart from aching.

He wrapped his arms around her and kissed her temple. "Someday things will be as they should be."

She met his gaze, hers misty with unshed tears, and knew in her heart that if he had any say in it, they would be.

Four guards returned, opened the cell door, and ordered them to follow. Without another word, they ushered them down a lengthy stretch of hall and then up a round staircase. They'd been imprisoned three stories underground. Raven was relieved when the air grew cooler as they ascended.

She didn't miss how Gabriel and Tobias surrounded her, placing their bodies between her and the weapons hanging from the guards' hips. It was sweet how they protected her, not that it would matter in the end. If the empress wanted them dead, they'd be dead. Every single one of them. And without her magic, there was nothing she could do about it.

Finally the guards unlocked a door that opened into the palace proper and led them down another polished obsidian hall to a dining room that rivaled anything from Raven's experience or her imagination. The table was made of a single slab of deep red wood with an odd zigzagging grain that was both exotic and beautiful. The plates glittered solid gold, surrounded by silverware inset with multicolored jewels. At the center of the table, silver candelabra with white candles flickered in the soft light. Everything seemed to sparkle.

Somehow the combination, worth hundreds of thousands in the human world, came across as gaudy in this one. It was too much. Although she knew the glitz was real, there was so much of it that it looked fake. Along with the polished obsidian walls and the fire blazing in the gilded fireplace, it reminded Raven of a pirate's banquet, just over the top enough to look like it was a set created by a Hollywood studio rather than an actual dining room.

The guards who'd led them to the room gestured toward the table. "The empress requests that you wait here. Dinner will commence momentarily."

The four guards retreated through the side door.

As soon as they were gone, Gabriel tried the exit, but the door was locked. They weren't going anywhere. "Any ideas, Tobias? You were always the smart one, after all."

Tobias swaggered to the table and pulled out a chair. "We aren't getting out of here without playing Mother's game. My recommendation is that you choose a pawn."

Raven selected the chair across from him. Gabriel sat down beside her.

A chime rang and a voice announced, "All hail Eleanor, Empress of Paragon."

The door they'd entered through opened again. Two guards stood at attention as Gabriel and Tobias's mother walked in. She'd changed into a black gown with a full skirt and long puffed sleeves. Tall and dark, she stood ramrod straight, her perfect skin stretched over the sharp angles of her fine, delicate bones. The massive citrine jewel on her finger pulsed with magic Raven could feel across the room. She was undeniably beautiful but in the way of a wasp. Everything about her came across as deadly and cruel.

She strode to the head of the table. "It is customary to rise in the presence of the empress."

Gabriel glared at her. "What about when the empress is your homicidal mother?"

Eleanor ignored the barb and turned toward her guards. "Leave us."

Once the guards were gone, Tobias confronted her. "What do you want, Mother?" he asked in a tone dripping with annoyance. "If you intend to do to us what you did to Marius, you don't need to feed us first."

"You always were so impatient." She glowered at Tobias. "Even as a child. You could never wait for the end of the story. Always with the questions. Always with another book in your hands."

93

Gabriel crossed his arms. "Is that why you had Aborella bring us here? To reminisce about Tobias's reading habits?"

Eleanor raised an eyebrow. "No." She placed her hands on the back of the chair in front of her. "Believe me, had I wanted you dead, you would be. No, my children, all this time I've simply wanted you back."

Raven exchanged glances with Gabriel and Tobias. Thank the Mountain, they didn't seem to be buying it any more than she was. She placed her hand on Gabriel's thigh under the table and offered her support with a squeeze.

"Why?" Gabriel's voice sounded positively lethal. Every hair on the back of Raven's neck rose to attention.

Eleanor gazed down her nose at them. "Rebels are organizing. They call themselves the Defenders of the Goddess. We call them DOGs. My spies tell me each of the five realms has contributed to their membership. The basis of their objection to my rule is that they believe I murdered all of you and my claim to the throne is therefore illegitimate. You are going to show them they're wrong. By supporting me, your mother and your empress, you are going to prove to them not only that you are alive but that you approve of my reign."

Gabriel shook his head. "Why, by the Mountain, would we ever do that?"

She met his eyes with an unflinching stare. "Because if you don't, I will kill Raven, Gabriel. Why do you think her mortality was a priority?"

Gabriel clenched the edge of the table until his fingers turned white, his talons stretching from his knuckles.

"Don't. It won't help anything," Raven whispered.

"Listen to your mate," the empress said. "I can send Aborella to Earth to track down your young if Raven's life isn't enough of a motivation." She glared at Raven, whose breath hitched. "Yes, I know about the egg. Aborella is a seer, Raven, and a powerful sorceress. If I choose to send her, how long do you think it will take her to find your child? And if you and my sons don't return to the fold and play your parts, she will destroy it, your sister, and your family."

Raven's chest ached to the point she was sure her heart had stopped. Eleanor wasn't bluffing. Aborella would do it, and she was helpless to stop her. The smug look on the empress's face told her everything she needed to know. She would find her child. And she would use threats of violence against her baby or Raven to make them crawl on their knees if she wanted them to. And Avery, poor Avery. Her sister would defend her niece or nephew with her life, without a doubt. Raven couldn't risk Eleanor going after her.

Gabriel considered her, painfully remorseful. They both understood they had no choice. "What do you want us to do?"

The empress selected a bell from beside her plate and rang it longer than was necessary. A team of darkly clad servants swept into the room, one pulling out Eleanor's chair for her so she could sit down. The others swarmed the table with covered trays. Domes in hand, they left the room as fast as they'd come in, leaving behind a bounty of food, none of which Raven recognized. Their glasses were filled with water and wine.

"You ask what you can do," the empress said, running her nail along the lip of her glass. "For now I want you to eat. The rest you will learn soon enough."

# CHAPTER FOURTEEN

C larissa didn't see much of Nathaniel for the rest of the day. After a quick breakfast of her orange and some porridge that, to her surprise, was left for her in the kitchen by one of the oreads, she wandered the estate. Remarkably little had changed since she was last here.

Including what had once been her favorite room.

Over the centuries, Nathaniel had been a generous patron of the arts. She'd once called him her muse, but she certainly wasn't the only one he'd inspired. The gallery room contained the results of those relationships. Master painters, sculptors, composers, and musicians like her had gifted Nathaniel works over the years in gratitude for what he'd done for them either with magic or with money.

Mozart was once a member of the Order of the Dragon, and Nathaniel had on the wall a framed short composition by the man. There were works by Boucher, Goya, Blake, Gauguin, even one by Cézanne that always took her breath away. There was a Salvador Dalí she was sure few others had ever seen. Sculptures by Slodtz and Carpeaux also populated the room, including a haunting one of Nathaniel himself as a faun, wings out and with cloven hooves. She'd always hated that one. It made him look like the devil.

She'd forgotten how many originals he'd amassed. Each one represented a friendship, a person in whom Nathaniel had recognized raw talent and fostered generously. Clarissa used to think it represented the best of him. Certainly she had firsthand experience with his eye for talent and his generous heart. He'd plucked her out of total obscurity, hired her the finest voice coach money could buy, and funded her first demo. He'd introduced her to the order and taught her to use her magic. She owed him so much.

But there was a reason she hadn't sent him her first platinum record to hang on the wall. She'd lived here a year before she realized the significance of this room, and it was one of the reasons she'd chosen to leave.

She'd loved Nathaniel and he, to this day, had been the only one to ever make her feel loved in return. He'd wanted to mate with her, bond with her, marry her. He wanted her, permanently.

And she'd wanted to spread her wings. The studio had made her an offer no new artist could refuse. When she tried to talk to Nathaniel about it, he pressured her to accept the bond. That's when this room took on another meaning. Dragons collected things. Nathaniel wanted to collect her. Had she stayed, she'd be his bird in a gilded cage.

Her phone buzzed in her pocket and she took a peek. Tom. Again. She'd put him off all day. She fired off a hasty text.

*Can't speak. Resting the vocal cords. Procedure tomorrow.*

*Do you know the trouble you've caused? Everything's on fire.*

*Tell them all I have a rare acute infection. Refund their money. Handle it. This is your job.*

*They want pictures. They want to hear it from you. Rumors are flying. Have you logged on to Twitter? It's a social media shit storm!*

*Gotta go. Doctor wants to see me.*

She turned off her phone. This was only going to get worse.

Her stomach rumbled. She desperately wanted an omelet like the ones Nathaniel used to make her, with ham and vegetables and that cheese he imported from a village in France. She left the gallery with its complicated memories and jogged down to the kitchen.

She laughed when she caught her reflection in the stainless steel fridge. Thank God the paparazzi couldn't find her here. She'd dressed in her sweats and a T-shirt again and pulled her hair into a messy bun. Her face was washed, but she hadn't bothered with makeup. She'd turned thirty that year, ancient by pop-star standards, and the wrinkles at the corners of her eyes and around her mouth were growing more pronounced by the minute.

Aging did not go well with celebrity. Without her magic voice, she couldn't even hide the lines under an illusion.

"Indifferent," she said to her reflection. The word echoed through her head. Nathaniel was indifferent about her now. There was no longer any risk of him wanting to collect her. Even dragons, it seemed, liked younger women.

The frying pan was exactly where it had been before, and she placed it on the burner of the Viking range before digging in the fridge for the ingredients she needed. Eggs, milk, black pudding, lardoons, tiny sweet tomatoes... She opened all the drawers in the refrigerator but couldn't find the cheese.

She whirled when she heard footsteps behind her, then froze when she saw Nathaniel. There was no hiding what she was doing. Her arms were loaded.

"Busted," she said guiltily.

Nathaniel swaggered into the kitchen like sin personified in a pair of jeans that should have been a registered weapon and a tailored shirt and sport jacket. The light in the room seemed to grow darker with his presence. Not in a bad way. More like he brought the twilight with him. Everything went velvety and smooth jazz. If she glanced up, she might see stars.

"I can get Laurel to make you something," he said, glancing at the heap of goods in her arms. Fuck, he barely glanced at her face, instead frowning at the load. He really was indifferent. She bent over and ungracefully emptied her arms onto the counter.

"I'm craving one of your classic omelets." She didn't want to say it out loud, but the oreads never got it quite right. "I can make it."

His brows knit. "Then you'll need some Époisses de Bourgogne. There's a new wheel of it in the cupboard." He stormed over to the pantry and returned with the cheese. "Do you remember how to make it?" His expression turned stern. "Bother, I'd better do it. I have standards to uphold, and you always go overboard with the cheese."

"You can never use too much cheese."

She could have cried from joy as he pulled out the cutting board and drew a knife from the block. He started dicing vegetables like a veritable expert. She climbed onto the stool at the kitchen island and rested her head in her hands. She'd always loved to watch him cook.

"Would you care for wine?" he asked. "I recommend champagne or a sauvignon blanc with the eggs."

"I like red."

He raised an eyebrow in her direction. When he spoke, she sensed a tiny bit of venom in his tone. "Far be it from me to come between you and your every fleeting fancy."

Odd, she felt a flutter in her chest that she'd spurred that bit of anger in him. Anger wasn't indifference. She climbed down from her stool and found the wine in the wine cellar off the kitchen, exactly where it had been ten years ago. She selected a bottle. When she returned to the kitchen, she retrieved the corkscrew from the drawer where he kept it without even looking and popped the cork.

He scoffed. "It's like you never left." More bitterness. "I should have rearranged the kitchen."

"It's a perfectly appointed kitchen. Don't change anything just to spite me." She took down two wineglasses and poured the wine, then slid one over to him.

He took an unceremonious and rather large gulp. "There's a strange and uncomfortable déjà vu about this, don't you think," he said gruffly.

She sipped a bit of wine. "I don't know, it seems vastly different to me." She chided herself as soon as the words were out of her mouth. This was not the time for soul-baring honesty.

"How do you mean?" He glanced back at her, his face impassive.

She raised her eyebrows. "I'm older. More wrinkles. Less energy."

He didn't say anything but glanced at her quizzically.

"I have my own money, my independence. Yes, I need your help, but when I leave here, I do have a nest egg to fall back on."

He frowned, his spatula working overtime in the pan. "Are you sure that's true?"

"About the nest egg? Yes. Four double-platinum albums in ten years will do that for you. Plus you know me, I've always been careful with money."

"But why do you think you weren't independent when you lived with me?"

She snorted derisively. "I was barely twenty when I met you. I couldn't even drink legally in the States. I was literally singing for my supper in the tubes every evening before I leaned on your generosity. I slept in hostels half the time and on the couches of friends the other half. I use the term friends here very loosely."

He shot her a pointed stare. "And? You were kicked out of that horrible excuse for foster care in America at eighteen and not only did you survive, you made it to London on vacay. You did it all by yourself, Clarissa. When I met you, I was absolutely floored by how far you'd come on so little."

Her throat went tight at his words. Nathaniel wasn't the type to lie or hand out false compliments. She'd never known that he'd respected where she'd come from. Why would he, when he lived like this? "I was lucky. I was using the magic in my voice before I knew what I was doing. I could have hurt someone if you hadn't..." This was not the discussion she wanted to have.

He scoffed. "It's nice to know that at least my contributions to your magical education don't go unappreciated."

She didn't know what to say to that.

He turned the fire off beneath the pan and cut the omelet in half, then split it between two plates. She followed him to the small table in the kitchen by the window where the purple-streaked sky of twilight painted itself over the blooming beauty of the back garden. The oreads had set the table with water, tea, and buttered toast points. She grabbed one of the latter with her fingers, forgoing politeness to appease her growling stomach.

"Mmm." She closed her eyes as she chewed.

He placed the omelets down and pulled her chair out for her. "Sit," he ordered.

She did and started in on the omelet without another word. It was so good she thought she might orgasm at the table in her own *When Harry Met Sally* moment.

"We need to discuss next steps," he said tersely. "Neither one of us wants you here any longer than you need to be."

She lowered her fork. "What do you have in mind?"

"A ritual." He swirled his wine.

"What type of ritual?" Why did she feel like whatever he was considering would be painful? *All we need is your pinky finger ground up and cooked into a cracker, Clarissa.*

He stilled. She had the faintest feeling he was taking her in, calculating the risk of something.

What he said next was measured, each word carefully chosen. "You have claimed sanctuary because you are bonded by blood to the order. You and I know your curse was rendered using dragon magic. I believe if you participate in the *Exosculatus* ritual with the members of the order, the temporary magic it imbues you with might be enough to... prime your pump, so to speak, give you just enough magic to allow you to expel the curse from your body."

Despite the delicious food in front of her, Clarissa lost her appetite. She stared at her plate. Exosculatus meant kissing in Latin, a fitting name for the ritual whose purpose was to share magic among the order. Witches and wizards of various levels of expertise and strength made up the membership of the Order of the Dragon. When Exosculatus was performed and the group "raised the circle," an expression that conveyed the moment the magic gripped and lifted everyone at once, a great balancing took place. Nathaniel, as a dragon, was an almost limitless source of power, and performing the ritual with him at its center charged everyone's magical batteries to maximum capacity.

After she'd been inducted into the order, she'd performed it with them twice, once to introduce her magic to the group and another time to welcome a new member named Fiona. But she was aware that it could also be used to bolster someone's magic when they were drained due to illness or accident. It wasn't a cure-all, but Nathaniel was right, it had the potential to flush out many underlying problems in the participating witch or wizard.

The problem was, Exosculatus lived up to its name. The ritual was performed naked. It had to be to allow for the maximum flow of magical energy. Raw and passionate, the movements were more like a dance, and the effects were nothing short of intoxicating. She remembered the orgasmic rush of Nathaniel's strength as it had entered her body the first time she'd performed it. Back then, the ritual had ended with them making love, not because it was necessary for the magic to work but because when the magic *did* work it exaggerated every desire, every emotion, every need.

Be it lust or love or anything else, the spell brought it to the surface. She took a sip of her wine. Nathaniel might be indifferent, but she wasn't. She wasn't sure exactly what to call her feelings for him. There was attraction for sure, but also something deeper, a sense that, despite his anger with her, he would always be there for her. It was a complicated tangle of emotions. If she took part in this ritual, she wasn't sure she could control herself. What if they made love? What if he rejected her again? What if his indifference was more than she could bear? Whatever happened in the grips of magic, it would complicate everything.

"Clarissa? You know this is the only way," he said through his teeth.

His full meaning clicked and her eyebrows rose. "You think it was someone in the order and that performing the ritual will call them out. They'll be moved to attack me when our emotions are joined."

He nodded once. Of course! Her focus had been much too narrow. This wasn't about her and Nathaniel at all. She'd been cursed using dragon magic. Besides Nathaniel, the only ones strong enough to levy such a curse were members of the order. Exosculatus made member emotions accessible to everyone. If someone in the order hated her enough to curse her, the ritual would expose it like nothing else could.

"It's a good idea, but..." She watched him over her plate, the way he curled his long, tapered fingers against his jaw when he was studying her, the strange gray hazel of his eyes that appeared amethyst when his magic flared, the short, well-tamed coffee-ground-colored hair that was a bit spikier on top than it used to be. It all came together in a man whose fierce presence filled the room. He was a coiled spring, a jack-in-the-box one crank away from flying out of himself, a barely contained storm.

"But what, Ms. Black?"

She leaned back and allowed her gaze to pass over him. "Won't it be difficult? I mean, given our history?"

He folded his hands and stared at her as if she were a bug he was considering crushing under his heel. "Was it hard yesterday when I left you in your bedroom?"

*Yes*, she thought.

"No." She pictured him walking out the door, leaving

her mostly naked and definitely wet. God, she'd thought he'd been tempted too. Now, she realized, whatever he'd done to break the connection he'd had with her had been real and permanent. God, she'd been stupid. "That's right, you're indifferent."

He gave her a curt nod, his gaze as cold as ice.

It was time for her to face facts. The man she'd always secretly thought loved her like no one else ever had or would didn't love her anymore. It was what she'd thought she wanted.

So why was she finding it hard to breathe?

# CHAPTER FIFTEEN

He saw the moment he broke her heart, and it didn't make any sense to him. He was as concerned about the Exosculatus ritual as she was. It was going to be harder than hell to keep his hands off her once the ritual began. But he was sure that as the most powerful member of the group, he could conceal his ongoing love and longing for her. To find the one who'd cursed her, he'd happily give it a try.

He'd expected performing the Exosculatus would be difficult for *him*. But the moment he denied it, her face had fallen as if she was absolutely crushed. He thought back to the night before, to the moment she'd pulled her dress over her head and offered her body to him in exchange for his help. At the time, he'd thought she wanted to use sex to reignite the unfinished bond between them and use it to control him.

Had he been wrong about her motivation? Was there a partial truth to it? No doubt she'd wanted to control him, but maybe there was more to it. Maybe, in her deepest subconscious, she wanted to be here. Perhaps the curse happened to be a convenient excuse.

She'd mentioned her wrinkles. A fear of aging might be another reason to try to get back in his good graces. He could make her immortal if he fed her his tooth. But he'd never told her as much. He'd carefully withheld the information, wanting her to love him for him and not some hope of eternal youth. She couldn't know; therefore, perhaps it was a lingering affection?

No. No. He couldn't afford to think that way. If he dropped his guard for even a second, the love for her he so carefully kept walled off inside himself would come through, and once she left again he'd be ruined. It had almost destroyed him the first time. This time would absolutely wreck him.

"What's wrong, Clarissa? Does something about performing the Exosculatus spell concern you?"

"I don't want to hurt you." Was that pity in her eyes? That wouldn't do at all.

He stood and leaned across the table until he could feel the warmth of her breath on his face. In a low voice, he said, "The only one you should worry about getting hurt is you."

Her face paled by several shades and her eyes focused on his lips.

"Be ready tomorrow by twilight. I'll have Laurel find you a robe." He strode from the room, the sound of her pounding heart music to his ears.

It was easy to be smug at first. He had her right where he wanted her. Tomorrow night by this hour, he'd know what she was feeling. He had magic. She didn't. He'd be able to read her like an open book. But in the quiet of his office later that night, fear entered the equation. He'd pretended not to want her anymore, but nothing could be further from the truth.

When dragons mated, they did so for life. It was always

so with his kind. And although he'd slept with many women over the years, he'd only offered the mating bond to one, to Clarissa. The night before she'd left, he'd admitted that his inner dragon wanted her, wanted to mate with her in a way that was forever. A mating bond was more permanent than a marriage. For him, once the mating was in place, he would love her and only her for the rest of his immortal life.

Dragon mating bonds were so strong that in Paragon, it was not unheard of for a dragon who had lost his or her mate to request a mercy killing. But a mating bond that strong required two things—a dragon must offer to mate and his potential mate must accept. Consent to mate was everything. A dragon could have sex without triggering a mating bond, although once a dragon offered the mating, it was often painful to continue a physical relationship without it.

On the other hand, dragons could bond without mating. Nathaniel had bonded with his driver, Emory, in order to impart his longtime servant and friend with immortality. It had required feeding the man his tooth. That sort of bond was also permanent but by no means as strong as a mating bond. And although he'd been tempted to offer that sort of gift to Clarissa in the beginning to lure her back into his arms, he'd known that it would be torture if she never accepted his invitation to mate and the bond sentenced him to pine for her for eternity.

The worst part about what had happened between them was that she'd never told him a definitive no. She'd just left. He'd delivered his heart to her on a platter, and she'd simply walked away from it. And so the mating bond was never accepted or declined. She was not his, and he was not bound as to a mate. But that didn't mean his feelings for her had died. The thread he had offered her was still there, waiting for her answer. She'd never given him the closure of an outright refusal. And so even now his dragon wanted her. And if she asked for the bond, if she said yes to his proposal, he might be helpless to refuse it. The level of control it would take to keep his inner dragon at bay would be more than he could muster.

He lit his pipe and poured himself two fingers of scotch. Raising his glass, he toasted Warwick for the welcome effects of the numbing tobacco. He was going to need all the help he could get.

HE AVOIDED HER THE FOLLOWING DAY. WITH THE ritual close at hand, he couldn't risk further igniting emotions he'd long worked to suppress. He spent most of the day in his dragon form, curled under a mountain of treasure in his treasure room. Every dragon had one. The vibrations from the gold and jewels were healing to his natural form and soothing to his soul. He'd need soothing if this was going to work.

When he wasn't resting, he was smoking, puffing on Warwick's tobacco like his life depended on it. Maybe it did. If he failed to suppress his feelings for Clarissa, and she rejected him again, he'd most certainly want to die. Still, he knew this was the only way to help her, and helping her was the only way to be rid of her. He filled a vial with blood and used shadow mail to deliver it to Warwick. At the rate he was smoking, he'd need more tobacco ahead of schedule.

As the sun descended, he donned the hooded black silk robe he used for this ritual. He wore nothing else, not even shoes. The silk brushed his naked legs and ankles as he walked. Already it felt like a caress. He thought of her.

He'd reached the foyer when he saw her at the top of

the stairs. Dressed in red silk that clung to her curves, she descended the stairs, her blond hair drifting out from her shoulders. He missed how it was before, all dark and silky. The blond gave her appearance a sharp edge. Like the colors of a bright spider, it was a warning that she had grown into a deadly adversary. Something to be feared.

"Ready," she said, her bare feet landing on the cool marble beside him.

He tried not to notice the way her nipples strained against the silk. *Bloody hell.*

He forced his mouth into a firm line and raised his chin. "The order should be convening now."

He led her out the back door of the house, past the pool, and into the dark forest beyond. Deep inside the woods, he reached the order's most sacred space on Mistwood grounds. The clearing, carpeted with wild violets, had been their gathering place for centuries. A ring of smooth black stones marked the perimeter.

Warwick was already there, standing in a black robe beside his wife, Victoria, whose petite stature left her red robe dragging on the ground. They greeted Nathaniel affectionately with hugs and vigorous pats on the back.

"Thank you for the tobacco," Nathaniel mumbled in his ear.

The man's graying eyebrows bobbed and his pug nose wrinkled. "You're welcome. I hope it helps." Warwick nodded coldly toward Clarissa.

Victoria glanced briefly in Clarissa's direction, then pivoted away with her nose in the air. Nathaniel frowned at the snub, hoping Victoria was not the one responsible for Clarissa's state. His list of possible suspects grew as the rest of the coven seemed to share Victoria's sentiment.

Calliope and Fergus arrived next, followed by Aiden

and Jane, Finn and Bronwen, Willow and Percival, and Fiona and Steven. They all embraced him, one by one, before backing into the circle with varying degrees of obligatory greeting to Clarissa. Even Fiona, who had been inducted by Clarissa, was markedly cold. He almost felt sorry for her. Almost.

"What do we do with her?" Victoria asked him bluntly. "Since Jane joined, we'll be fourteen all together. Not an optimal number for the ritual."

Clarissa's gaze darted to the other members. All of them had daggers for her, and he could see her squirm under their judgmental glares. An uncomfortable tug worked its way through his chest. He'd led her to do this. He owed her some support.

"Clarissa and I will both play the role of Puck in the ritual."

All eyes snapped to him.

"A dual role?" Willow said in alarm. "You'll be too strong. You'll overflow the cup."

Nathaniel shook his head. "No. She's cursed. She has no power. She'll be going through the motions in the hope the ritual will drive the curse from her, but she won't be contributing any power." He wished he could share the true reason for the ritual with the order, but he didn't want to risk anyone refusing to participate. If one of them had cursed Clarissa, it would be all too easy for them to conveniently excuse themselves.

The couples murmured to each other.

"Is it safe?" Jane asked, her soulful brown eyes glinting in the growing moonlight. "We shan't catch it?"

"It's safe. As safe as magic can be," he said. But the truth was, he'd be hard-pressed to prove it. "I need your help, all of you. Clarissa has claimed sanctuary and called on our order for protection against whoever did this to her. I believe flooding her with our magic will help cleanse her of whatever dark spell plagues her. This is the only ritual that can do so. Do I have your cooperation?"

He watched the group carefully. If one of them was responsible for the curse, they'd most likely refuse his call. But one by one, each agreed and a couple of them—Jane who was new and hadn't been hurt directly by her, and Aiden because he loved Jane—patted her on the shoulder and said they'd do their best to help her.

"Then if everyone would join me, we will begin."

The other twelve circled, toes outside the ring of stones. He held out his hand to Clarissa.

"We've never done it this way before," she said. "Are you sure?"

Their eyes met, and he knew instantly he was in over his head. He'd be forced to touch her. He'd be forced to share energy, space... heat with her.

"Yes, I'm sure," he said. Burn it all down. In for a penny, in for a pound. Whatever happened tonight, he was in. Besides, it wouldn't be the worst thing to lose control. Just one more time.

# CHAPTER SIXTEEN

What Nathaniel was trying to do was admirable. Clarissa could see the wisdom in it. The Exosculatus ritual was designed to make the coven more powerful. Nathaniel as a dragon was a source of almost unlimited magic, but his power was latent. He was a magical creature with only limited access to wield the energy found within his scales and flesh. But combined with witchcraft, his abilities became much more effective.

Witches and wizards, on the other hand, had control over the elements but limited inherent power. Every spell they cast must be fueled by something, the elements themselves, or blood, or some other catalyst. Tonight, and all nights for the Order of the Dragon, the group would draw power from Nathaniel, their limitless magical battery, and in return, they would share their power over the elements with him. Everyone involved would get a boost, including her.

And hopefully, with that power, she could drive out the curse. To make that happen though, the ritual had to invoke open connection among the group. All barriers to sharing energy had to be stripped between them.

She slipped her hand into Nathaniel's and allowed him to lead her into the center of the circle. He turned her around until her back was pressed against his chest. All at once, the entire coven untied their belts and dropped their robes. She dropped her own, feeling the warm night breeze caress her skin. Behind her, the brush of silk told her Nathaniel had dropped his as well. She didn't turn around, but the thought of him naked and close behind her made her heart beat faster.

Nudity was nothing compared to the intimacy they were about to share. The six witches and six wizards around her were about to act out a fairy gathering. Fairies, as a species, often shared magic with the most powerful faun among them, the puck. Just like Puck, immortalized in Shakespeare's *A Midsummer Night's Dream*, the character Nathaniel played in the ritual was mischievous, shrewd, and would call upon the enchantment of the forest around them to feed the order with its wild energy.

Nathaniel's amethyst ring glowed to life as he passed his hand over the earth beside them. The violets and moss rippled and the dirt turned itself over. Two stag horns rose from the ground, attached to a golden crown that followed them to the surface.

Nathaniel dusted off the excess dirt, raised the crown to the cheers of the order, and placed it ceremoniously on his head. "I am that merry wanderer of the night. Awake. Let us dance our ringlets to the whistling wind."

The ground beneath Clarissa's feet began to vibrate. The members of the order joined hands and slowly began to circle. The air around her grew warm and thick with magic, the night folding in on them like a velvet blanket. Her breath hitched as Nathaniel's large hands landed on her hips and lifted her onto his feet, her naked flesh pressed against his. His arms stretched along hers.

"Follow along with me," he whispered.

The heat of his breath against the shell of her ear sent a stroke of anticipation through her. His body was warm and hard behind her. She wanted him. She wanted him inside her, and they hadn't even begun. Oh God, she was doomed.

Nathaniel began to move and she moved with him, the dance telling a story although no further words were spoken. The rambunctious puck motioned to the sprites in his employ. They were playing a trick on the night, swapping identities with each other to hide from the gods and goddesses of the woods. As the twelve circled, Clarissa bent, crept, and reached toward them, Nathaniel's limbs working as one along with hers.

The circle rose. Raising a circle had to be experienced to be truly understood. It felt as if gravity ceased to exist. Her feet lifted from the earth. She was light as a feather on the wind. She still danced, moved, stomped, but everything was easy, vibrant, weightless. Magic rushed into her like a warm breeze. It tossed her hair. The tingle of energy flowed through Nathaniel's skin and into hers, and God, the feel of it awakened her. Her body grew warm and wet and ached with need. The teasing touch that brushed her backside caused her blood to burn. Her breasts grew heavy, her nipples hard.

All the desire, all the sexual energy building within her, she threw it into the dance. She knew when the order felt it because the couples turned their heads to look at each other with giggling lips and eyes flashing with lust. And then, like a withdrawing wave, it came back into her. She'd never played this role before. The sexual need that returned to her was what she'd put out times twelve. It settled like a heavy weight between her legs. *Oh God.*

She could see it all in her head, every step, every move that Nathaniel made. They were one in this dance. A drum began to beat. Magical creatures in the woods, the earth, inside her head, or perhaps the air itself, bore witness to their ritual. Summer lightning rumbled across the sky. Their dance was suddenly accompanied by a symphony of flashing light and whirring insects.

More magic unraveled from Nathaniel and poured out to the edge of the circle, only to be thwarted by the dancers and forced back to the center. There was a rhythm to it. Wave, contraction. Wave, contraction. Each one stronger than the last until her skin vibrated with mystical energy. She could feel it in her bones.

In the blink of an eye, daggers appeared in each of the hands of the twelve and a chalice arose from the earth in front of them in the same way the crown had. Nathaniel guided her hands down to lift it, his own supporting the cup under hers. One by one, the witches and wizards sliced their skin and dribbled blood into the cup. Her blood was next. Nathaniel helped her, using the sharp tip of his talon. Nathaniel's blood splashed in last. When all was inside the belly of the cup, the blood turned into wine, swirling red and smelling of ripe red currants and raspberries. She inhaled the heady scent. Wrapped in a cocoon of magic, she took the first sip.

Stars above, the rush was like riding lightning across the sky. She passed it to Nathaniel, noticing every perfect line of his face, the chiseled, corded muscles of his arms, the scent of dragon in her nose. It was overwhelming. She longed to meld with him, touch every inch of him, taste him.

As the others drank, the last barrier between them was

shattered. The first had been their clothing, the second had been the divide between them and the natural world, and this third one was the boundary between their minds. All the thoughts and feelings happening in the circle crashed into her with the next wave of magic. The ritual was complete.

Now, connected to their thoughts, she tried to detect who might have cursed her. But no hate flowed in her direction. Although there was a short lick of sadness, confusion about her leaving, anger, and then of missing her, those feelings resolved quickly. What remained was an overwhelming feeling of love, belonging, acceptance. It crashed into her and lifted her feet a quarter inch off the violets.

The connections between the other couples tickled her. They broke from the circle, pairing off and running into the trees, giggling and joining together in the shelter of darkness. Metaphysically connected now, as the first couples began to make love, their passion flooded her in the same rhythm. Wave, contraction. Wave, contraction.

She whirled to face Nathaniel. There was so much power between them her hair floated from her shoulders as if she were underwater. Darkness rubbed like velvet against her skin. Nathaniel's normally gray eyes glowed bright, fluorescent amethyst in the night. He truly looked like a puck— his face had become more supernatural than human. She wanted him desperately.

She reached for him but he caught her wrists.

"I feel no hate for you in this circle," he said.

"No." For the love of everything holy, how could he remember their quest to find the one who had cursed her among the coven? All she could think about was him. "No. It's not them," she said. "I would have felt it."

He glanced away and shook his head. "Are you able to use your power?"

She sang a few notes and they danced on the air around her. "I think so. But it's weak. It doesn't feel the same yet."

His glowing gaze raked over her. "Give it time."

She stepped closer, her skin alive with the prickle of anticipation, the bubbling moans of lovers floating around them. The drums beat. Fireflies called to each other in the darkness. Heat bloomed low within her—desperate, carnal need.

"I'm sorry," Nathaniel said. "All this, and we didn't find who cursed you."

Sweat broke out on his forehead. He was holding back. Guarding something carefully behind a mental wall. *Whoa.* The power required to resist the circle's influence was absolutely mind-boggling. But what was he guarding? She desperately wanted to know.

"I'm not," Clarissa said. "I'm not sorry we did this at all."

Using all her strength, she drew Nathaniel to her and kissed him. His lips were warm and soft. His hand rose and grabbed her upper arms like he might push her away, but he only pulled her tighter to him. At his coaxing, she opened for him and his tongue thrust and stroked against hers.

The last of his resolve crumbled, and the feeling that rushed out from behind his mental walls sent a shiver through her. He was not indifferent. He wanted her. Wanted her more than anything else in his life. The sheer strength of the wanting was almost frightening in its complexity. But there was more.

Wrapped inside the lust was his desire to protect her, then his need to cure her of her curse, and under it all warmth that could only be love. She had to guess the feeling was love. She'd never known love from anyone else but Nathaniel and had nothing to compare it to. But what struck her then was the absolute power of the emotion. It had grown stronger with her absence, despite his outward desire to push her away. Despite his lie that he was indifferent.

His mouth did wicked things against hers. The kiss had grown rough, claiming, its rhythm a pulse she could feel between her legs. Stars above, she never wanted to stop. His fingers dug in her hair, and she slid her palms around his rib cage, scraping her nails gently up his back to the base of his wings. He unraveled them for her, their flesh brushing the tips of her fingers.

She stroked along the webbing, and any emotions she'd felt before were replaced with a feral, predatory lust. Lust that left her like she was a fish out of water, gasping for the sea. The sheer need crashed into her, overwhelmed her. That was the thing about this ritual. When you took the barriers down, you had to be ready for the deluge that came through. She'd thought she was prepared, but by God, the feelings coming off Nathaniel shook her to her core. She'd never before felt that level of need. He wanted to mark her. He wanted to make her his.

His trill rumbled in his chest.

His arms wrapped around her, his body large enough, hot enough for it to feel like he completely enveloped her. His erection pressed hard and hot against her lower belly. Their mouths melded in a wild and fierce dance that was all too familiar. Easy. Her hands stroked along his lower back and clawed his ass. Ten years hadn't been anything, had it?

All she'd have to do is wrap her legs around him, allow him to lift her a few inches, and he'd be inside her. The memory of the pleasure he could produce in her body almost made her cry from need. But it was that steady protective warmth woven through the lust that almost broke her.

It was love. It had to be love.

Without a doubt, if she allowed herself to return that love, if she expressed her true feelings physically with him now, she'd destroy both of them. She'd only ever been good at one thing—singing. Together, they were a disaster. Either he'd need to give up his life to indulge this fire between them, or she'd need to give up hers. What type of love destroyed you? Theirs was a fire consuming itself. What would happen if it burned itself out?

# CHAPTER SEVENTEEN

Mountain help him, Nathaniel had not expected the ritual to show him this. Clarissa loved him still. The emotion beat against his senses like a shower of hot rose petals. But there was something else braided with that affectionate feeling. He sensed fear, longing, anxiety. Was she afraid he'd reject her?

He tried to pour everything he could into the kiss, his mouth, his body, showing her what he couldn't say in words. He shouldn't need to say it. With the ritual in full motion, she could easily read him if she tried.

A flood of apprehension hit him like a bucket of ice water, and she broke from his embrace and backed away. Her tears glistened in the moonlight.

"Clarissa..." Her name was warm honey on his lips.

She turned and ran for the house, her skin flashing silver in the moonlight. Watching her run, feeling her unresolved lust in his veins, ignited his inner dragon's fire. A growl percolated up his throat. A smile spread his lips. He could play this game, predator and prey. He gave chase.

Nathaniel blinked and the landscape turned hazy

purple. She was a sprite and he was the puck, the crown of horns still heavy on his head. Her scent tingled like heaven in his nose, and the lure of her flesh made his breath come in pants. Dragons were exceptionally fast. He could have her if he wanted to, but he was enjoying the chase. He waited until she was near the pool, almost to the door.

He passed her and stopped abruptly. She ran right into him. Right into his arms.

"Nate. We can't," she said, her hands forming to his ribs in a way that brought out his mating trill. She closed her eyes at the sound. "God, I want to. You must know I want to."

"Good." He pulled her closer and placed a kiss on the pulse of her neck.

"It will only hurt worse when I have to leave."

He stopped, his lips hovering over her skin. Nothing had changed. She loved him. He could feel she loved him. But she still planned to leave. As soon as he fixed her magic, she'd go again. That could be tomorrow if the power of the order flushed the curse from her blood. Or it could be weeks from now. But she was leaving. She loved him, but she was leaving.

He drew back and looked her in the eye. "Why? You can't lie to me now, Clarissa. I can feel what you're feeling. You love me. I know it as well as I know the sun will come up over that horizon in a matter of hours."

Her shoulders sagged and the tears he'd seen in her eyes flowed faster. "Of course I love you. I've always loved you. You're the only family I've ever had!"

"Then why? Why won't you be mine?"

"My career isn't here, Nathaniel." She spread her hands as if it were the most obvious thing in the world. "I tour constantly and when I'm not traveling, I'm in a studio in LA or filming videos. Your life is here. Our lifestyles are incompatible." She turned from him and hurried toward the door.

"Incompatible? We aren't electronic devices, Clarissa. We can make choices." Anguish crushed his chest. This couldn't be happening.

She looked at him over her shoulder, wiping under her eyes. "I already have. Singing is the only thing I've ever been good at. It's been the only constant in my life since I was five. All those years in foster care. All those years hopping from family to family. All I had was my voice. I need my career. I need it to feel safe and stable, and I need my audience to feel wanted. Is that enough honesty for you?"

He stepped in closer until there was only a breath between them. He desperately wanted to touch her, but he didn't. When he spoke, his voice was low and menacingly soft. "Your voice wasn't a constant. It did fail you. Your audience and, I suspect, your manager are turning on you because they only love what you give them. They don't even really know you. When you lost everything, you came to me. Do you know why, Clarissa?" He paused and noticed she was shivering and it wasn't from the cold. He was a fucking bastard. A selfish fucking bastard who wanted her and he couldn't stop himself. "You called me because I *do* know you. I knew you before you were a brand or a star. I knew you when you were a struggling street musician who was so poor you didn't have a bank account. I loved you then and I love you now."

She took his face in her trembling hands. "If love was enough, we'd have it all, baby." She kissed him firmly, turned, and disappeared inside the house.

Nathaniel moved to follow her but encountered resistance as he tried to enter the door. All at once, he remembered the ritual. The puck belonged to the wild and could not go inside. He removed the crown of horns from his head and raced back to the circle, placing it at the center and watching the ground swallow it along with the chalice. By the time he'd returned to the house, she was locked inside her room.

"Damn it all." He strode down the hall to his own chambers and reached for his pipe. The ache in his chest festered like a burning sore. He packed the pipe with Warwick's numbing tobacco and fired it up.

Still, it was hours before sleep carried him away.

# CHAPTER EIGHTEEN

Clarissa was too wired for bed. Everything Nathaniel had said to her seemed to rattle around her brain, demanding her attention. He loved her. He still loved her. The moon shone through her window and she stared out into the night pondering this revelation. In the distance, Jane and Aiden staggered from the woods, leaning against each other, laughing and kissing. She lowered her gaze. Her presence here was torture for both her and Nathaniel. What she needed was to drive out this curse so she could go back to the way things were.

She took a breath and sang.

*Your night, it crawls to meet*
*the darkness inside me.*
*Don't you know*
*that your energy*
*is the thing making me me?*

She was on pitch and the sound was good. Good but not great. Despite having the order's power still pinging around inside her, her own power had not come back. Her voice was her magical instrument. Without it, she had no way to wield what Nathaniel had given her.

With a sigh, she pulled on an oversized T-shirt and climbed between the sheets. Her body still hummed from the ritual. The feel of the cotton against her skin teased her and sent a throb of need from the tips of her breasts to her core. The deep ache she felt for Nathaniel was so intense she considered taking care of things herself. She smoothed her hand down her stomach to between her legs. But if past experience was to be trusted, pleasuring herself would only make her want him more, like an appetizer before the main event.

She rolled over onto her stomach and tried to think of nonsexual things. Bunnies. No. Rabbits fucked, well, like rabbits. Ice cream. A vivid image of the frozen delight melting down her torso to where Nathaniel lapped it off her belly filled her mind. She grabbed a pillow and pressed it over the back of her head.

Why couldn't she just have had sex with him? People had casual sex every day. It didn't have to mean anything. It wasn't a proposal of marriage.

But she knew why. If she allowed Nathaniel to make love to her, it would tear him apart when she left, and she couldn't do that to him. She couldn't hurt him more than she already had. Even asking him for help was something she'd sworn she'd never do out of respect for what they'd had, and she'd already pushed things to the limit. Already kissed him. Already allowed him to know her true feelings. His mental health was more important to her than her body's pleasure or her heart's desire. But she was dancing too close to the flame. Her body burned. Oh, how it burned.

She released the pillow and gasped for breath, then flipped over onto her back and forced her eyes closed. Sleep evaded her, and after tossing and turning for what seemed like forever, she eventually rose from her bed and decided a cold shower was in order.

Silver light already glowed through the window. The sun was rising and she hadn't slept a wink. Physically, she felt both wound up and exhausted. Overcaffeinated even though she hadn't had tea in more than twelve hours.

It was with some sense of horror that she realized this wasn't the end. After last night, Nathaniel would be more motivated than ever to break the curse and send her on her way. He would want to try something else today. Likely something even more risky and painful. And she'd be required to go along no matter how tired she felt or how painfully horny it made her.

She groaned.

Her phone vibrated on the nightstand and she looked down to see a text from Tom.

*Please tell me the therapy is working. The O2 is sold out and the tabloids are boiling over. Take a look.* He included a link to a story in the *Daily Mirror*.

She did not click the link but left the phone right where it was. Instead, she slipped into the shower, ran the water cold, and tried to wash Nathaniel from her mind.

# CHAPTER NINETEEN

## *Paragon*

Everything Eleanor had wanted was coming to fruition, and Aborella had been the one to deliver it to her. The high sorceress and fairy of Paragon sat in a seat of honor in the great hall, the fuchsia silk of her gown draping beautifully over her dark purple skin. Her complexion was nearly as dark as it had been before Raven had drained and almost killed her. A few more sessions among the forests of Paragon and she'd be at full strength.

Thankfully, Eleanor didn't need Aborella's abilities right now. Her plan was going smashingly. The band began to play, and the empress appeared at the head of the aisle, dressed in a regal black-and-diamond gown that brought out the glow of the citrines and diamonds crowding her ring, crown, necklace, and scepter.

Everyone who was anyone was in attendance, the entire Highborn Court as well as all the most important families in Paragon. Dressed in their finest vilt gowns, they stood from the rows of chairs brought in for the occasion and then knelt before her. Aborella noticed some of their jewels had been enchanted by local witches and wizards to give off their own light. None shone so bright as Eleanor's however, but then Aborella had spelled those herself.

The empress climbed onto the dais and lowered herself to the blood-red velvet of her throne. Brynhoff wasn't with her today. Now that Aborella thought of it, she hadn't seen Brynhoff in a number of days. Was he ill or something else? No matter—she'd never cared for him anyway.

"You may be seated," Eleanor commanded in her sharp nasal tone. There was a rumble as their guests rose from their knees and sat. "As your invitations suggested, I have an exciting announcement to make. Many centuries ago, my son Marius was killed in what we all thought was a traitorous uprising by my other children. That night was every mother's nightmare. My remaining children disappeared in a clash of swords and magic. All of us believed the Treasure of Paragon were either dead or in hiding after what they'd done. Not only did it break my heart that my own children could do such a thing, their absence left no choice but for me and my brother, Brynhoff, to remain on the throne to lead our kingdom.

"We have spent significant resources trying to track down those responsible for Marius's death. Justice, after all, must be served. But we were thwarted by a side effect of the sorcery used that night to distract us from the attack. No one who attended the coronation remembered exactly what had occurred. No one, as you will recall, except Brynhoff, who accused my other children."

Aborella smiled at the lie. Oh, Eleanor remembered everything, as did Aborella. She'd helped Eleanor design the spell to poison Brynhoff's mind so he'd kill his own nephew and then planted the memory of the uprising by the other children. It was Aborella who was responsible for the fact that none of the guests could remember a thing about the event. She proudly raised her chin at the importance of her magic to the crown.

"Recently, thanks to the work of Ransom and the rest of the Obsidian Guard," Eleanor continued, "the truth has been revealed! It gives me no pleasure to divulge to you that Brynhoff, not my other children as was formerly believed, was responsible for the coup. Brynhoff, not my children, was the true traitor."

Aborella's jaw dropped at the invented revelation, and the hall erupted into murmurs and loud gasps. Surprising—Eleanor hadn't mentioned her plan to place the blame on Brynhoff. She narrowed her eyes on Ransom, the new captain of the Obsidian Guard. He'd risen to power months ago after Captain Scoria was murdered by Eleanor's wayward children. Aborella watched him cross to her now, a fine-looking male dragon with full chocolate-brown hair, a square jaw, and dimpled chin. In his black-and-red uniform, he looked younger than Scoria but also a bit naive. Still, Eleanor seemed to favor him, to the point Aborella felt a pang of jealousy. How was it that she had not been included in the scheme?

"Fear not. Due to Ransom's dedication, we have brought Brynhoff to justice."

Ransom stepped onto the dais and drew a draped piece of black cloth off a small table. All the air seemed to rush from the room as the silver agate heart that once was Brynhoff's was revealed. Aborella scanned the stunned faces behind her. It was as if everyone in the crowd was holding their breath.

So Eleanor had assassinated him. Aborella squelched

another grin. The empress was now the ultimate power. Brilliant plan, regardless of how she chose to execute it.

"What evidence did you have against him?" a man yelled from the back, breaking the silence. Aborella couldn't see who it was, but the accusation in his voice was unmistakable.

"I'm glad you asked." Eleanor raised her chin. "Gabriel, Tobias, please join me."

Aborella stiffened. Eleanor was taking a great risk trusting her older children to play this part when they knew the truth. Yes, Raven's comfort was a valuable carrot and her life and the life of their child was a brutal stick, but all it took was one wrong word to be the spark that started a revolution.

Aborella watched as Gabriel stepped out from the staging area, dressed in a royal tunic and sash, an emerald crown upon his head. Darkly handsome, he took his place on his mother's right side, although not a hint of a smile crossed his lips. Tobias followed, looking just as princely in his attire and sapphire crown. He took his place on her left, folding his hands and staring at the audience in a way that made his blond hair and blue eyes take on an icy quality.

The moment of truth. Would they go along with the plan for Raven's sake? Or would Aborella be allowed to kill the witch tonight?

The murmurs rose to a deafening pitch as their guests processed that the two eldest living heirs to the kingdom of Paragon were back. They only quieted when Eleanor raised her hand.

"As you can see, Captain Ransom has recovered two of my sons, who were tortured and held captive by Brynhoff. The rest are still missing. But the important thing is that Gabriel and Tobias remember what happened that night.

They were able to identify Brynhoff, and I took decisive action against him. I am more than pleased to welcome them home."

A louder rumble began as guests began to discuss the implications.

A woman in the front, Lemetria—Aborella recognized her as the wife of the wealthy doormaker, Darium—stood and asked in the pretentious tone of the aristocracy, "Will Gabriel, now that you have cleared him of the accusations of treason, take the throne per Paragonian tradition?"

The empress smiled up at her son, and Aborella held her breath.

"No," Gabriel said. "Not at this time." The whispering among the crowd rose to a roar. Gabriel spoke over it. "Our abduction was difficult. My brother and I are still recovering and applying ourselves to the task of educating ourselves on what has happened in Paragon during our absence. Until we do, we feel it is in the best interest of our kingdom for our mother to continue ruling as she has."

The murmurs started again. Aborella watched a look of disgust pass through Tobias's features before disappearing behind a carefully impassive mask. His eyes glossed over, but from her seat in the front row, she could see his jaw work as if he was grinding his teeth.

"My sons will rule by my side for the foreseeable future. You will treat them as full princes of Paragon, and they will have full privileges and security from the Obsidian Guard. Please act accordingly."

What she meant was the guards would be enforcing their silence and cooperation. Aborella loved every minute of it. She only wished she'd succeeded in bringing Alexander back as well.

"Now, if you will join us for refreshments in the grand

ballroom, Gabriel, Tobias, and I will be available to discuss matters of politics."

Everyone stood and was ushered into the next room by the servants. Aborella rose to follow but soon found Gabriel glaring down at her, his gloved hand on her shoulder.

"Where is my wife?"

She narrowed her eyes on him. "Comfortable, alive, and safe, thanks to your wise cooperation."

Eleanor stood from her throne and raised an eyebrow in their direction. Aborella gave her a reassuring nod. "Come, Gabriel. It's never a good idea to keep your mother waiting."

# CHAPTER TWENTY

When Nathaniel woke in the morning, the memories of the night before came crashing back into his head. Warwick's tobacco had saved him from a night of tossing and turning, but its numbing effect only lasted so long. Now his emotions were all on the surface again. Clarissa loved him. It wasn't enough. The dichotomy made him want to tear down the walls.

He needed to do whatever was necessary to recover Clarissa's voice and get her out of here. He couldn't stand much more of this. Every moment with her here was like having his heart in a vise. He tapped the heel of his palm against his forehead. *Think, Nathaniel. Who could wield a dragon curse other than you or the order?*

The phone rang, distracting him. He glanced down at the caller. Professor Wallace. A friend. A colleague. He'd been a member of the order at one time, until a bout with cancer moved his heart close to home and he simplified his life.

Nathaniel answered the call, curious why he was phoning at the early hour.

"Nathaniel, I'm so glad I caught you."

"Peter, you sound distressed. What can I do for you?"

"Oh dear, I'm afraid I have some disturbing news. It... it might be nothing, you understand. Just a coincidence. But it was odd, I tell you. So odd."

"What are we talking about?"

"A few days ago two young women brought me a book. The owner of a gallery in New York and her assistant. The book is in perfect condition, late seventeenth century. Written in a combination of ancient Greek and Latin. It's about the order, Nathaniel. You are mentioned in its pages."

"Hmm. I remember we made a few manuals back then, mostly books of medicinal healing for the locals. It's incredible one survived."

"There's more."

He waited. Judging by the long pause, Wallace was concerned about telling him this part. "What is it, man?"

"The assistant... She... I was taken aback when I saw her."

"Why?"

"She, um. Do you know that American singer you used to have a relationship with ten years ago, when I was part of the order?"

"Clarissa?"

"Yes... Well... This assistant could have been her twin. It flustered me, her having the book. I thought Clarissa was posing as this person for some nefarious reason, and I'm afraid I consequently treated her quite badly. But then I remembered your Clarissa is blond these days. I just thought it was odd, magically odd, to see a doppelgänger show up at the university with a book connected to you."

"You don't know the half of it." Nathaniel felt a chill work through his body.

"Huh?"

"She's here. Clarissa is here. She lost her power Friday night. It looks like a curse."

"This woman came to see me Saturday afternoon."

"Who knows anything about doppelgänger magic? Who can I call in on this?" he asked, his mind racing. Doppelgängers were rare and their magic was innate, metaphysical. He wasn't sure exactly how Clarissa's double might be involved in the curse, but it couldn't be a coincidence that she was interested in dragon magic.

"The only one I can think of is the Cornish pixie queen. Pixie genetics produce a pair of doppelgängers with every one thousand births. I've read they have mystical properties. Perhaps she could help you sort out the dynamics."

Nathaniel rubbed his head. The memory of what Clarissa had told him flooded back into his thoughts. Someone had taken her hair. "What if she's not a doppelgänger but a skinwalker?"

"Do you have reason to believe someone got hold of her genetic material?"

"Hair."

"Good heavens, Nathaniel. This is complex magic. Very complex. There's only one creature in all of England who can help you if that's the case."

"Don't say it."

"You need to consult an oracle."

He grabbed his head. He knew a creature that could answer all their questions, but the price of her abilities was higher than he was willing to pay. "Thank you, Peter. I must go now, but I appreciate your letting me know. I'll be in touch."

"Absolutely. But Nathaniel?"

"Yes?"

"Be careful. My sixth sense is buzzing on this one. I consulted the cards and pulled the Tower. Something is coming for you. I don't know what. I don't know who. I can't say how the girl or the book ties in. But change is coming. You must beware."

"I understand, and your warning is fully heeded."

"Blessed be."

"To you too."

Nathaniel frowned as he disconnected the call. This was getting weirder and weirder.

He showered and dressed, then went to the kitchen where Tempest had prepared porridge and bacon. He tried to eat, but his mind spun around what he'd learned.

"Porridge again? What, are special omelets only for dinner?" Clarissa stood at the end of the dining table. She was smiling, but there were dark circles under her eyes.

"You look exhausted." He stood and poured her a cup of tea.

She dropped heavily into the chair across from him. "I don't suppose you read the *Daily Mirror* this morning?"

He shook his head slowly, sat back down. He hated the tabloids, and he dreaded hearing what she was about to say.

"Well, I'm the cover story. It seems the general consensus is that I had a nervous breakdown and can no longer perform. People are taking bets whether I cancel my O2 concert. They think I'm going to go full Britney and shave my head."

"The tabloids exaggerate the truth and invent lies regularly." He waved a hand dismissively. "You can't take it personally. We will break this curse, and you will be on that stage as planned."

She folded her hands on the table and rested her head. "Isn't this when you tell me I told you so?"

He frowned and sipped his tea. "Why on earth would I do that?"

"Last night you said my fans didn't really love me, only what I do for them. There was no concern in the comments of the article, Nate. I'm tabloid fodder, and the only thing my *fans* care about is if I'm going to fulfill my obligation to them as ticket holders. If I were sick, no one would be sending me flowers except maybe Tom, and he'd make his secretary do it."

Nathaniel lowered his cup to the table. "It gives me no pleasure to be right about that. I wish I were wrong. But you see, as we established last night, I do love you, and it's easy to tell the difference from this side of the fence." There was no point in denying it. He was done hiding his feelings for her comfort.

"Nate..."

"Aww, Clarissa, are you suddenly unwilling to pay the price of fame? Should I break out the world's smallest violin to play you a melancholy song to go with your melancholy circumstances?"

"I think my mood is completely valid given what's happening," she snapped. "I'm witnessing the death of a career I've worked hard for, all because someone had it out for me for reasons beyond my control. I am nothing without my voice."

Fury had him out of his chair, his dragon rolling through his body like a freight train. He bound around the table and lifted her to her feet, grabbing her by the chin like a child. "You are everything. Everything. You lost your magic, not your voice. You can still speak, you can still sing, you still participated in that spell last night. You have arms that move and legs that make me weak. And when you smile, I see the woman who found a way to do what she wanted to do when she had far less than you have now. You are everything to me, just as you are and for always. But if you can't see your own worth, no one else will either."

He placed a rough kiss on her mouth, then let her go. She dropped back into the chair.

He strode toward the door.

"Wh-where are you going?" she asked after him.

"I have to check on the store. Get some sleep, but be ready by noon. We're going to try something else, and you'll need to be rested when we do."

WELL, SHIT. THE KISS HAD LEFT CLARISSA COMPLETELY boneless in the dining room chair. Meanwhile, Nathaniel strode toward the door unaffected, his suit a physical love letter to the corded muscle beneath it. How was he still walking after that? All she could think about was all that coiled power wrapped around her last night in the woods. He'd feel so good in her bed, like the world's best electric blanket.

And he loved her. Nathaniel Clarke, the high priest of the Order of the Dragon, had admitted his love for her. After ten years of her abandonment. Even without her magic. Even with dark circles under her eyes, hair that desperately needed the loving attention of a hairdresser, and the fine lines and wrinkles that seemed to have formed the moment she'd turned thirty. He loved her.

The temptation to give in to the feeling, to stay here and play house and let him take care of everything, was almost overwhelming. It was a temptation greater than her physical desire for him, even though that burned bright within her.

Nathaniel would keep her safe always. She'd always have enough to eat and a place to sleep.

And that was absolutely terrifying. Everyone she'd ever allowed herself to love had abandoned her. He would too eventually. He'd collect her and then become bored with her, and she'd have nowhere else to go. There wasn't another family waiting for her or even a foster system to catch her if things turned bad. If she trusted Nathaniel, she'd be walking the high wire with no safety net.

She finished her breakfast and then went straight back to her room, feeling even more exhausted than before. A text from Tom blipped on her screen.

*Hope progress is being made. Text me an update when you have a chance.*

She turned off the phone, crawled into bed, and curled on her side. Pulling the covers over her head, she allowed herself to slide into an uneasy sleep.

"CLARISSA? CLARISSA?"

Clarissa desperately wanted to remain unconscious, but Nathaniel's commanding voice forced her eyes open. His stern face stared down at her. She yawned and stretched. "Hmm?"

"You've overslept. Get ready. We need to leave soon."

She blinked up at him. He was phenomenally attractive. She'd read somewhere that gray eyes were a mutation between green and blue. His were the color of stormy skies right now, although they became magnificently purple in the throes of magic. With his complexion and dark hair, they were positively stunning.

"Where are we going again?"

He huffed. "To consult with a supernatural being who will know how to break your curse."

"Who? I thought you said the curse used dragon magic as a catalyst." She rubbed her eyes with both hands. "Who knows more about dragon magic than you and Warwick?"

He scowled at her. "For once in your life, just do as I ask, Clarissa."

All softness had bled from his expression, and she climbed out of bed to escape his prickly exterior. "Fine. You don't have to get snippy with me."

He glanced toward the ceiling as she unceremoniously undressed and reached for a change of clothes. After last night, she wasn't going to pretend to be bashful.

"There's something I need to tell you. I wanted to tell you this morning, but I didn't get the opportunity," he said.

"Sounds serious. What's going on?"

"A friend contacted me early this morning. It seems there is someone in London who looks exactly like you." Everything about his expression seemed to indicate this was horrible news, although Clarissa didn't understand why.

"I'm a celebrity, Nate. People try to imitate my appearance all the time. There was a woman in Russia who paid tens of thousands of dollars to have plastic surgery in order to look like me." She shrugged. "It's weird, I admit, but not the end of the world."

He cleared his throat. "Do you remember Peter Wallace?"

"Of course. Is he still teaching history at Oxford?"

Nathaniel nodded. "This woman who looks like you brought him a manuscript... that was written by the order. He said she was your doppelgänger."

She shook her head. "What? What does that mean?"

"I wasn't that concerned at first. Even Wallace said it

could be a coincidence. But this morning, after I left you, I went to Relics and Runes. I have a new worker named Albert. He doesn't know what I am. He showed me a picture, a selfie he took with a woman he claimed looked exactly like the famous Clarissa. Now, Albert has no idea you and I were ever an item. He doesn't know anything about me. He's new and he's barely more than a boy. But he found this woman attractive. Asked her out."

He pulled his phone from his pocket and brought up a photo.

"What the fuck?" Clarissa was looking at a picture of herself in the lower level of Relics and Runes, only her hair was its natural shade of black and she didn't own that dress. "It's uncanny. It's like looking into a mirror."

"I thought so too. But the really unsettling part is that she was buying a book on dragon magic."

"Hmm?" Clarissa stared at him with total disbelief. What did it mean? This was too weird to be a coincidence.

"A natural doppelgänger is a very rare magical occurrence. Extremely rare among humans. She could be yours. If so, I have no idea why she's here. Perhaps she's tapped into my magic or the magic of the order somehow for some nefarious reason we have yet to understand."

Clarissa stared at the picture of her double. The woman didn't look evil. If anything, she looked normal, more normal than Clarissa herself. She was definitely younger, now that she inspected the face more closely.

"We know that whoever did this to you took a strand of your hair. Perhaps this isn't a doppelgänger at all but a skin-walker. The magical possibilities are dark, and this thing seems to be working its way closer to home."

Dressed now, she ducked into the bathroom and

squeezed a blob of toothpaste on her toothbrush. "So what do you think we should do?"

He appeared in the doorway. "I need to know exactly what we are dealing with. We might be able to use Wallace to lure this thing to us, but without knowing what it's capable of it's just too dangerous. We could be walking into a trap. We need help. We need more information, someone to tell us what it is and why it might be interested in you."

Clarissa swished and spat. "Who could know that? We'd need a seer or an oracle."

Nathaniel nodded. "There's only one creature in the United Kingdom that sees all and knows all."

"You can't mean..." Clarissa knew of only one such creature, and it was a horrible abomination.

Nathaniel confirmed her greatest fear. "Grindylow. Hurry. I want to make it to Lancashire before nightfall."

# CHAPTER TWENTY-ONE

He had to be out of his mind. As Nathaniel thought about what he'd have to do to get Grindylow to answer their questions, he experienced true fear. The creature was unlike any other, a water demon as ancient as the water itself. Even when Nathaniel was in the area, he stayed as far away from her lake as possible.

But Grindylow was an oracle. He had to try.

"I thought Grindylow required the sacrifice of a child in exchange for answering any questions? I'm telling you right now, I'm not murdering a kid for the sake of my magic," Clarissa said.

"It's good to know you have a line you will not cross."

"So then what's your plan?"

"I'm still working it out."

"We have four hours in the back of this car. Work it out with me."

Nathaniel looked out the window. The funny thing about dragons and immortality was this: he could be killed. No, he would never die of natural causes, and he was very difficult to kill. Decapitation was the only reliable way to inflict permanent death on a dragon. Clarissa understood that, and if he told her his plan in advance and gave her too long to think about it, she might attempt to talk him out of it. He couldn't have that. This was a necessary risk.

He'd have to change the subject.

"What have you told Tom about your time here?"

"I'm in a spa in Switzerland, undergoing experimental therapy for my strained vocal cords."

She leaned back against the seat, and he was struck by how graceful she was. She held herself like a queen, not an orphan who'd grown up with foster carers, some of whom had made it a habit to slap her around and underfeed her. She'd never had a dance class as a child. Nor a voice lesson. But whoever her ancestors were, her real ancestors, they'd given her something. Something a hard life couldn't take away.

"However will he survive without you?" Nathaniel had never liked the bastard.

"Oh, you know Tom. I'm not his only client, but if my career went under, he'd take a hit."

"Financially or personally? I always wondered if he fancied you back in the day."

She snorted. "Oh, he did. Tried to get in my pants on a number of occasions."

Nathaniel's dragon twisted, and a growl rumbled through his chest before he could do anything about it.

"Easy," she said and laughed lightly.

Nathaniel rubbed his chest and cleared his throat. "Apologies. It's instinct."

"Still?" She gave him a soft, curious look.

He hated himself for tipping his hand once again, but he nodded. It was the truth. His dragon desperately wanted her and would likely have done nightmarish things to Tom if ever given the chance. "Still."

"I don't owe you an explanation, but if it makes you feel better, it never happened. Tom is... not my type. Plus I know exactly what he is. I know he'd use me. I'm his client, not his doormat, and I'd like to keep it that way. I have some self-respect."

A smile stretched his lips. "Good. You should be with someone who truly adores you."

"What about you? You must have had a long parade of lovers over the past ten years." Her gaze darted to her tangled fingers.

"No," he said evenly.

"No?" She studied his face. "Why not? There was always someone interested in the high priest of the order— witch, fairy, druid, or human."

He rubbed his hand over his mouth. "I am a man of particular taste. A busy man. I'm fine on my own."

She frowned and looked out the window. "You always are... fine, I mean. I have this memory of you from when we were together. It was the first time I really understood how old you are."

He laughed darkly. "Ancient compared to you, I suppose, but I will remind you that I do not age like those of your species. My body is no more than thirty by your standards."

She raised an eyebrow and a blush stained her cheeks. "Oh, I know. I saw for myself, up close and personal, last night. I'll look older than you in a few years."

"Never," he said quietly, admiring the way the light from the window backlit her profile.

She rolled her eyes at him. "I'd just started staying with you because you said you couldn't bear to know I was sleeping in the hostels. We hadn't even, you know..." She lowered her chin. "...become a couple yet. But I was staying at Mistwood and this man came to your door with horns growing out of his head."

Nathaniel laughed. "I remember that. Alisdair. Poor Scot didn't know he had fairy blood and tried to do a transfiguration spell. Got stuck halfway."

"Anyway, he came in and fell to his knees. He was shaking, trembling from fear. And it took me a moment to realize he was afraid of you."

"Well, he should have been. It's against the code of the order to perform that type of magic without permission. Not to mention, his motives were sketchy. The man was attempting to turn himself into a goddamned ram. He said he wanted to spy on his neighbor about a land dispute, but really, what a strange way to go about it."

She giggled. "I agree. And he was a sight for someone like me who wasn't familiar with magic. But I remember thinking that you must be extremely powerful for him to fall on the floor, shaking like that. Were you a gangster? A killer? The head of a cult? Why was this man, who was just as big as you, with horns growing out of his head, so afraid of you that he was practically wetting himself?"

Nathaniel snorted. "You must have assumed I was a monster."

"I wondered, for a moment. But then you told him to get up, blew some sort of powder into his face, and made the horns go away."

"I also gave him graveyard duty for a month."

"Graveyard duty?"

"In decades past, it was common for magical folk to sit in a graveyard at night and speak to the dead on the rare chance one of them should have any warnings or suggestions for us. Truthfully, the dead will speak to anyone who will listen. They like to hear themselves talk. Self-importance doesn't die with the body. We stopped doing it because we'd often get inundated with stories and questions about people's descendants. It wasn't as useful as it was time consuming."

"You made him sit in a graveyard and talk to ghosts for a month?" She smiled wickedly.

"No better way to teach someone to respect magic." He gave her a wink. "Did it scare you? Seeing me like that?"

"No. It made me... admire you. You could have handled that situation in many ways, but you showed compassion. I've known men who would use any excuse to flex their muscle, but I've never seen you abuse your power. Not ever."

The corner of his mouth quirked upward. "One who knows their power has no need to prove it."

She snorted. "See, human men don't go around saying things like that unless they're a yogi or Russell Brand."

He waved a dismissive hand in the air.

"And then the first time I saw you shift... When you took me to your treasure room to show me... I really under-stood. You are a dragon. A massive purple dragon with claws and teeth as long as I am tall. You can take anything that you want, but you don't. For as long as I've known you, I have never seen you use what you are to your advantage unfairly." She sighed. "Do you know how unusual that is? To have the power you do and no ego to go along with it?"

This conversation was making him uncomfortable. He pulled his pipe from his pocket and lit up, thankful for the familiar numbness of Warwick's tobacco. "I can't have everything I want. I can't have you. Even if I took you, you wouldn't be mine."

She sighed and met his eyes. "I'll always be yours, Nathaniel," she whispered. "But if you had me, if you kept me like all the gold and jewels you have in your treasure room, you'd notice I wouldn't shine as bright. You wouldn't want me anymore if you had me. I'd just be another thing you'd already collected."

His eyes narrowed and his inner dragon chuffed. She was serious. She turned to stare out the window, and it occurred to him that this was it. This was the truth. She'd never told it to him straight before. She'd said she wanted to strike out on her own. She'd said it was because she couldn't stand the thought of losing her singing career or her audience. But the truth cut deeper. She'd never had a real family. No one had ever loved her the way she should be loved. And so she didn't think it was possible. She honestly believed he'd grow tired of her. She'd grow old and he'd lose interest. And if she'd given up her art for that, she'd truly have nothing left when it happened.

"Clarissa," he said softly, "that's not how a dragon's bond works. When we mate, we mate for life, and life to an immortal dragon is a very, very long time."

WHY ON EARTH HAD SHE TOLD NATHANIEL ALL THAT? By God, she might as well cut open her chest and show him her still-beating heart. She'd never been so forthcoming or vulnerable about her deepest fears before. Maybe she'd never realized exactly what had motivated her to leave back then until now. Or maybe...

"Did Warwick add some kind of truth spell to that smoke?" She stared at his pipe. "I shouldn't have said all that."

He shook his head. "Same as always." He blew a smoke ring, and it turned into a bright red heart above her head.

"Oh."

"I'm glad you told me. Now I can tell you how utterly full of crap you are."

"Excuse me?"

He leaned toward her. "You are full of shit, Clarissa. You can't possibly believe that to be true. Not anymore."

She shrugged. "Why not? Because you say dragons mate for life? People will say anything to get what they want."

"Do people usually wait decades? Do people...?"

"What?"

"Never mind." He looked away from her and smoked his pipe. When he spoke again, his voice was fire and brimstone. His gray eyes flashed. "You underestimate me, Clarissa. You shouldn't."

A chill crept along her skin although the temperature in the car had actually risen a few degrees. That was his inner dragon speaking. Nathaniel was the dragon and the dragon was him. He was a shifter. But the part of him that slept when he was in his human form sometimes woke up. She'd seen the dragon last night when he'd hunted her after the ritual. And now the beast was right there on the surface.

It was a humbling thing to look into the face of a dragon, especially when you didn't have any magic of your own to protect yourself. She watched the hills roll by and didn't speak again until the driver, Emory, did.

"Almost to the lake, Mr. Clarke. Where would you like me to park?"

"Close enough to the water that you can help if need be. You have the weapon?"

"I do. Practiced a bit with it beforehand."

"What weapon is that?"

"Crossbow," Nathaniel stated. "Holy-water-soaked bolts."

"What exactly is the plan, Nate?"

"We offer Grindylow a child and then ask her questions."

Clarissa inclined her head. "And where do we get this child?"

Nathaniel wiggled the fingers of his right hand where a large amethyst ring resided. Clarissa knew few specifics about how dragon magic worked, but she knew the ring was the closest thing to a magic wand that dragons possessed.

"Explain."

The amethyst flashed and Nathaniel changed. His body folded in on itself in a way that made Clarissa profoundly uncomfortable. It was too angular. There were too many folding joints and protruding bones. The transformation was physical, not mystical, and coupled with the slurp of bodily juices and the crunch of grinding bones, it was truly disgusting. She had to turn her head away. When the noise stopped, she tentatively glanced back at Nate. A twelve-year-old boy was in his place, dressed in a child-sized pair of jeans and a T-shirt he'd procured somewhere.

"Holy fuck! Where did you put it all?"

"Dragons are masters of illusion. I can look any way I desire. Although, I must say going any smaller than this would be astoundingly tight." He rolled his shoulders as if his current shape and size wasn't exactly a walk in the park.

"So what's the plan? We ask the questions and then you get into the water with her and pull the old switcheroo back into the dragon?"

Emory opened her door, and she got out in the middle of nowhere at the edge of a misty body of water. Nathaniel crawled across the seat after her. It was so strange for him to only come up to her shoulder. He looked exactly like a skinny grade-schooler.

"That's not how this works," he said. "Grindylow will want her payment first before she gives you any information."

"But... how will that work?" Suddenly her stomach felt sick. Muscles in her chest tightened.

"You will feed me to the demon. You will ask your questions. When you are done, you'll call my name and I will shift and rise from the water." His voice was painfully low.

A lump formed in her throat. "No, you can't do that. It... that thing could chew you up and hold you underwater."

"I can't die from drowning."

"But you won't be able to breathe. You'll feel it. You'll suffer. What if it rips you apart? I've read this thing wants blood."

He said nothing. So then there was a chance. There was risk. Even an immortal dragon wasn't invincible. "You can't do this."

"It's already done." He started walking toward the water.

"Nathaniel, please!" She didn't even know what to say, only that every cell in her body knew that this was the wrong thing to do. It wasn't worth it. "It's not..." Her voice gave out as he reached the water's edge, his little-boy body a slight, pale thing before the dark water.

"Call to her, Clarissa," he said over his shoulder. "And please, ask your questions quickly."

All the muscles in her body locked with fear as a dark mat of hair crowned at the center of the water, and then two bulging dark eyes, and pale, waterlogged cheeks.

"Clarissa," he said between his teeth. "Don't let her have me for free."

"Grindylow!" she called. "I have brought you the sacrifice of this child in exchange for questions answered."

Long limbs rose from the water, each with an extra joint that ensured there would be no confusing her with human. Her ribs protruded under grayish-white skin like a set of sickening gills. Her nostrils flared.

"How old is the boy?"

Clarissa glanced at Nathaniel. He looked twelve at the least, but Grindylow loved children—the younger, the better. "Eleven."

"Three questions," she said, licking her lips.

"Five," Clarissa shot back.

Nathaniel was silent. He stood at the water's edge, looking terrified. His knees shook. She hated this.

"Three, girl. This is the way it has been and always will be." Grindylow's voice warbled as if she were speaking underwater, but she was exposed from the waist up now, aquatic plants draped across her grotesque and twisted body.

Clarissa stared at Nathaniel and hated this, but some part of her knew there was no going back. If she tried to back out now, Grindylow would attack. Nathaniel had chosen this. He hadn't told her until the last second for precisely this reason. He knew she wouldn't be comfortable with his choice, and he wanted to do this for her.

Her heart broke as she said, "Okay. Three."

Those multijointed gray limbs shot out and tore through Nate. Clarissa didn't even see what happened. There was a spray of blood, a splash of water, and then he was gone. Desperately, she wanted to cry, but anything she said from here on out could be considered one of her three questions, and the longer she took to ask them, the longer Nate was under that water.

But Nathaniel had put her in a terrible position. She hadn't had time to think of how to phrase her questions, and she doubted Grindylow would be forthcoming if she needed clarity. There was, however, one obvious place to start.

"Who caused the loss of my magic?"

The beast spread the thin flaps of skin that served as lips and exposed rows of black teeth. "The dragon queen and her fairy liege caused what vexes you."

Dragon queen. Clarissa knew of no dragon queen. The Order of the Dragon had one high priest, and it was Nathaniel. He'd told her once that his mother had been queen of Paragon, but she'd died in the bloody coup that brought him here.

"How do I get my power back?" she yelled. It was a broader question than how to break the curse. If her problem didn't stem from a curse, she'd learn nothing with that question. But this one should gain her the answer she wanted.

"Rebind thee to thy sisters." The empty pits that served as Grindylow's eyes narrowed on her.

"Liar!" she yelled. "Return the child. I have no sisters!"

The pale limbs thrashed, and Clarissa was doused with murky water. "Insolent witch. Grindylow does not lie. Grindylow cannot lie. Ask thee thy third and then run from my sight or I will punish thee for thine insult!"

Well... that wasn't the reaction she'd expected. She pushed the answer out of her head and focused on her last and final question. But what should she ask? None of this made any sense.

"How do I find these sisters?" she spat out.

Grindylow shifted. "One is near. She will come to you. The other must be retrieved from her obsidian tomb before the queen finishes what she started."

"Obsidian tomb? Where is that? Is she dead?"

Grindylow retreated into the lake, her dark head sinking toward the surface. "Three were asked. Three were given. Now we eat."

"Nathaniel!" she screamed.

Emory was by her side in an instant, crossbow raised. But Grindylow was gone. She disappeared below the dark surface. Emory grumbled and aimed the crossbow at the ripples that signaled her departure. He couldn't fire, not without risk of hitting Nathaniel. The water turned as smooth as glass.

Clarissa rushed toward the lake, her toes slapping the edge and spraying mud up her legs. Emory grabbed her around the waist so she could go no farther.

"Nathaniel! Nathaniel!" She screamed with all the air in her useless, magicless lungs.

A bubble rose and popped. She held her breath. With a thrash and spray, a dark wing broke the surface, and then Nathaniel in his human form, wings spread, rose partway out of the water, his fist driving into Grindylow's gaping maw over and over.

"Why isn't he transforming?"

"Wing's broke," Emory said as if no further explanation was needed. He fired the crossbow.

The arrow pierced Grindylow's shoulder, and she dropped Nathaniel before sinking into the bubbling, dark deep. Nathaniel took a few swimming strokes toward her. Fuck, he was pale, and one wing definitely wasn't working.

Clarissa pushed out of Emory's grip and waded waist

deep into the water, reaching out and grasping Nathaniel's fingers. She hauled him to shore.

"Help me," she cried.

Emory waded in ankle deep and grabbed Nathaniel's other arm. "Hurry, miss. That arrow won't kill ol' Grindy, just give her a sore shoulder and a sore disposition to match."

Leveraging every ounce of her weight, she squatted down and with Emory's help heaved Nathaniel out of the water. She landed on her back with him lying in the grass beside her. He was barely conscious.

"Nathaniel, can you walk to the car?"

His eyes fluttered, and then he turned his head away and spewed a fountain of dark, frothy water.

"Bloody well not okay yet," Emory said. "Let 'im rest a bit."

Nathaniel turned back to her. "Hurt."

"Why didn't you shift into your dragon form?"

He groaned. "Wing broke. Treasure room."

Emory sighed. "I thought that might be the case. Changin' into a kid like that uses a ton of magic. He doesn't have enough left to heal himself fully, and if he shifts here and now, he might make things worse. Help me get him back to the car."

She was soaked to the bone and covered in mud, but together, they were able to move him in short bursts. Unfortunately, the broken wing dragged painfully on the ground. Nathaniel couldn't retract it, and she couldn't figure out a way to cradle it while she helped carry him. She gave a relieved sigh when they finally reached the car.

With one last, massive effort, she dragged him into the back seat. She ended up leaning against the far window and coaxing his back against her chest with his body between her legs. Her thigh gave some support to the wing, and in this position, she could keep him from rolling off the seat. Although he dwarfed her frame, she was strong enough to hold him, especially after what he'd done for her. She'd hold him until her arms gave out.

"Ready, Emory. Get us home."

# CHAPTER TWENTY-TWO

Everything hurt, yet at times Nathaniel thought he might be in heaven. He was surrounded by Clarissa's scent, cradled in her arms, between her legs. She felt warm to him, which was odd. Usually he ran hotter than her 98.6. He supposed the loss of blood accounted for the change. He wasn't healing.

He glanced down at his ring. Its normally amethyst stone was almost completely black. Grindylow had bled him and drowned him. His magic was drained. He'd live of course. His head was still attached to his shoulders, but this was as close to death as he'd ever come.

"What did you find out?" he asked, but only the last two words actually projected from his lips.

She kissed his temple. "Shhh. We're almost there."

They were not almost to Mistwood. A quick peek out the window told him they had hours yet to go. Even that quick pop of his eyelid hurt. He closed it again. "What did Grindy tell you?" he asked more clearly.

"Maybe we should wait to talk about this later."

He gently squeezed the arm that was wrapped around him.

"Okay." She pressed her lips against the top of his head in an easy kiss, and he felt a little warmer for it. "I asked who stole my magic and, get this, she said, and I quote, 'the dragon queen and her fairy liege.'"

He stiffened in her arms. He only knew of one dragon queen, his mother, and she was dead. But she did have a fairy who performed magic with her, Aborella. That couldn't be right. Even if his mother had lived, she'd be in a dungeon in Paragon. She wouldn't even know Clarissa existed. Unless Brynhoff had replaced her. Was there a new queen of Paragon?

He squeezed her arm again.

"Nah. You need to rest, Nate. Just don't worry about anything right now."

Unease suffused her voice. Whatever it was that Grindylow had told her must be upsetting to her. He sensed she was holding back out of fear for him, that whatever she'd learned would upset him and slow his healing. He squeezed again, now even more curious to know.

Her lips landed near his ear. "I said no." Her warm breath brushed his cheek. "I'm still angry at you. You should have told me what you planned to do."

He sighed. His back hurt, but when he tried to adjust in her arms, he couldn't move his wing.

"Try not to move," she said softly. "That wing doesn't look good. Maybe Tempest can set it when we get home."

He settled against her in absolute agony. "Talk to me." He needed the distraction. She didn't disappoint.

Her lips brushed his ear again. "I would never have let you do that if you'd given me a chance to refuse." Her voice was stern, and he lay perfectly still, hoping she wouldn't yell. He was in too much pain for that. "It wasn't worth it, Nate."

Something hot and wet hit his cheek. He cracked an eyelid and watched her wipe a tear away. Another tear hit his jaw. He squeezed her arm again and shook his head. The small movement made his brain boil, and he settled against her chest.

"Don't cry," he rasped.

"I'd rather live without my voice than live without you." This time when her lips pressed against his ear, his heart leaped. Had he heard her correctly?

Her cheek snuggled in against his, and her warmth ushered him into oblivion. He must have slept hard, because the next time he opened his eyes, they were pulling up to Mistwood and Tempest and Laurel were rushing toward the car door. To his dismay, he was pulled from Clarissa's arms. Oh, how he would have protested that if he could, but he really wasn't well, and when Tempest straightened his wing and rebroke the bone so he could set it properly, Nathaniel growled straight from his inner dragon.

"Treasure room," Tempest ordered. "Emory, help carry him."

"I'll help," Clarissa said.

"You are not going into his treasure room," the oread spat out.

But Nathaniel reached out and grabbed her hand. "Yes."

Tempest grumbled. Hands lifted his body. She was there, right beside him. Minutes later, he landed on a pile of gold and jewels. The feeling was heavenly. The cold metal, the vibration of the stones beneath his back. He felt the power flow into his cells. His spine lengthened and he stretched and folded, flapped his wings. His bones cracked more than usual, and the transformation was slower than any he'd made before. But when it was done, he could open his eyes again.

She was there, watching him, small now that he was in his dragon form. She grabbed his nose and planted a kiss on his snout.

"Show me you can use it," she said, glancing at his wing.

He obliged with an experimental stretch and flap. He groaned a little from the pain, but it was working.

"Good." She stroked his face again. "See you in a few hours?"

He inclined his head, then backed into his pile of treasure, closed his eyes, and rested.

Clarissa was pretty sure that no amount of scrubbing would ever free her from the stench of Grindylow's bog. She reeked of it. There had been blood in her hair. Either hers or Nate's, she didn't know. Her mind replayed the moment the monster had sliced through his twelve-year-old body, and she turned up the hot water to combat the chill that ran through her.

Eventually her hands started to grow pruney, and she decided she was as clean as she was going to get. She turned off the water and drew a fluffy white towel from the rack. Her legs shook as she walked to her bedroom.

She was physically tired from dragging Nate to the car and holding him through the long drive home, but the mental fatigue from the painful regret rattling through her brain was far worse. Everything felt heavy. What she'd done to Nathaniel was wrong. She realized that now. If he'd shown her anything today, it was that his heart was true.

And she had walked away from it, not from indifference but out of fear.

All this time, she'd believed the lie she'd told herself, that this was about her career and independence. But it wasn't. This was about fear. She'd feared Nathaniel would change his mind about her, so she'd ended things to beat him to the punch. It was a coping technique. A way to avoid the pain of abandonment she'd all too frequently experienced.

But today... today it had all become too clear. He was more important than her voice. If given the chance, she would have refused his plan. She would have done anything to avoid watching Grindylow hurt him. Even if it meant disappointing every one of her fans and Tom. Even if it meant canceling the O2. She couldn't picture a world without him in it.

She brushed out her wet hair and tossed the towel on a chair, then crawled into bed. There was only one choice to make now that she realized her true feelings. She couldn't be without him. She couldn't pretend for a moment more that she didn't need him as much as she needed the air she breathed.

When he awoke, she would tell him. It was time for her to say yes and to mean it.

# CHAPTER TWENTY-THREE

"Clarissa?"

The sound of Nathaniel's voice entered her dreams and called her out of sleep. When her eyes fluttered open, he was there, shirtless and in a pair of loose-fitting sweats. She stared at his chest. He was a masterpiece of long, lean muscle with a set of abs that made her long to stroke their hard peaks and valleys. She could stare at that chest all day and never get tired of it.

"I can dress," he offered. "I was just concerned. It's been hours. It's the middle of the night. Tempest said you hadn't eaten."

She sighed. "I'm sore and very hungry." She ran a hand through her hair. It had dried while she slept and fell loose and wild around her shoulders.

"Let's make you something." He held out his hand to her. "A proper special omelet."

She slipped her hand into his and sat up, allowing the blanket to fall from her naked body. It wasn't a mistake. She'd been thinking of him when she crawled between the sheets, and she was thinking of him now. She wanted him to see her.

He sucked air through his teeth. "Shall I fetch you a robe?"

"No."

"I know I told you there was nothing I hadn't seen before the first night you were here, but there is only so much a man can take." His voice was coal and grit. "You have to get dressed, Clarissa. I can't..." He shook his head and turned his gaze away.

She climbed from the bed and placed her hand on his cheek, feeling the stubble against her palm. Bracing her thumb on his chin, she turned his head to face her. "Be mine, Nathaniel." Her voice was so weak she could hardly hear herself.

His gray eyes turned hard and cold in an instant. "Careful, Clarissa—this isn't a game. If you're playing with me, you won't like how this ends."

She searched his face, craning her neck to see him better in the dim light from the door and the moonlight streaming in the window. "Today, when Grindylow grabbed you, I didn't care if I ever sang again."

His brow furrowed. "You don't mean that. You've said over and over again how important it is to you."

She shook her head. "All I cared about was getting you back. All I felt was regret for not forcing you back into the car once I understood the scheme. What sort of horrible person sacrifices someone she loves for... for a song?" She felt nauseated just thinking about it.

"Love isn't enough, remember?" he said cynically. He tried to take a step back, but she moved right along with him.

"I thought that was true when I said it, but I was

wrong." She frowned. "Love was enough today. Enough to make me realize that I cannot live in a world without you. All these years, somewhere in the back of my mind, I assumed... No, I knew down to my soul that you'd take me back whenever I was ready. It made me confident, this secret I had in my subconscious, that I held the love of a dragon. Oh, I thought you'd take other lovers, sure, but no one, no one would ever touch what we had."

"I'm not a toy you can take out of the box when you want to play with it." He narrowed his eyes on her.

"I know. I was wrong. I realized today that I can live without my voice, I can live without my magic, I can live without a family." Her voice cracked. "But I can't live without you. Please forgive me for taking so long to decide. But if you want me still, I am yours."

The look he gave her was nothing short of mystified. It was like she was speaking a different language. For the longest time he just stared at her, face impassive, body tense. Minutes passed and she felt truly naked, exposed in a way she'd never been before.

She looked away and laughed under her breath. "It *is* too late, isn't it? You don't feel the same way as before."

His hand landed on her arm. "No. That's not it."

Her eyes met his. "Then what is it?"

"You're still Clarissa. The Clarissa. You have a concert at the O2 in a week."

"I know."

His eyes grew dark and stormy. "The extreme circumstances of today have heightened your emotions. It's quite possible you're in shock. When the sun rises, or the next time Tom calls, I fear you'll change your mind."

She shook her head. "Not about this."

"I need you to listen to me. Really listen. If I take you as my mate, if you agree to be mine, I cannot break that bond, not ever. I could hold you at arm's length before because you did not agree. Once you give yourself to me in this way, I can't go back. The love we felt before will be a shadow of what will exist in its place."

He'd told her that before about the mating bond, that for dragons it was akin to a marriage that could never be dissolved. She wasn't sure she could fully understand what that meant as a human. Could anyone who wasn't immortal wrap their mind around it?

"I think I understand. I mean, as much as I can, not being a dragon."

He let her go and paced the room, clearly agitated. When he turned back to her, his eyes were glowing amethyst and it was his dragon that spoke. "If you change your mind, I will come after you. I won't be able to abide your distance."

She crossed her arms. So it had come to this—he'd expect her to live here with him, which meant severely limiting her career. Of course, without her magic, her career would be limited anyway. The chance that she could decipher what Grindylow had said to her and get her magic back seemed distant. Sisters? Dragon queens? It hadn't been what she was expecting.

And then there was the emptiness that she felt when she thought about going back to her old life. That was something she couldn't deny. She'd been lonely before and hadn't even realized it. But being here, being with Nathaniel, the old spark was back. For him. For life. She might have lost her voice, but she'd found again her reason for wanting to sing.

She looked straight into the face of the dragon and her

throat caught as she said, "Don't you know, Nathaniel, I'm already yours."

*MINE.*

Nathaniel could smell it. Her love for him, her wanting, filled his lungs. He took a step toward her, then another. She did not back away although he must have been terrifying with his dragon so near the surface. He could feel it burning in him, its desire to complete the bond so intense he could think of nothing else. Still, some part of his logical mind expected her to run. Expected her to turn him away, the same as she had the night of the ritual.

She didn't. And the look she was giving him pushed all the right buttons. It was total surrender. Unlike the night of the ritual, he wasn't hunting her. She was an active participant in the electrical charge building between them. She met him halfway, slamming into him in the middle of her bedroom.

He wrapped his arms around her as her mouth crashed into his, returning her kiss with all the intensity that had built inside him for a decade. She melted against him. He teased her bottom lip until she opened for him, then licked and thrust into her mouth until she moaned.

By the Mountain, she smelled of lilies and sex, her need blooming between her legs and kindling his dragon senses. He was hard in an instant, almost painfully so. He swept her into his arms.

"Where are you taking me?" she asked as he strode from her room.

"My room. The bed is bigger, and I intend to use every inch of it."

He watched an intoxicating pink creep across her cheeks. Silently, he reveled in it. She may be older now, more sophisticated, but he could still make her blush. He entered the master bedroom and lowered her to the black silk of his sheets while he shimmied off the sweats he was wearing. She stretched like a cat, her creamy skin a delicious contrast against the dark fabric. She was spilled milk he intended to lap up.

"God, I missed this bed," she said, doing a snow angel against the fabric.

He grabbed her ankles and slid her to him, spreading her legs wide. "I missed you."

His lips found her ankle and teased along the bone and along her calf. She writhed. Her fingernails dug into his hair.

"So impatient," he murmured against the inside of her knee. He slowed, creeping along her thigh. His mating trill started in his chest, and she moaned as the vibration tickled her skin.

"That sound. I could listen to that all day." She arched herself toward his lips, and he flashed her a self-satisfied smile, then trailed closer to her center. She closed her eyes. "Your mouth is... so... hot."

"Open your eyes. I want you to watch me, Clarissa."

Her eyes popped open, that arresting blue sending a ripple of anticipation through him.

"Good." He held her gaze as he spread her ankles wider and licked up her center. Her whole body shivered. "I want to know that you're here with me. That you want this."

"Oh... Nate. I do." She spread her arms wide and clawed the sheets.

He started working on her properly, his tongue flicking along her delicate flesh. He could feel the tension building within her, hear her breath coming in pants. He rested one of her ankles between his wing and shoulder and slid his fingers into her slick heat. She came apart under his tongue, her entire body trembling. Her gasp of pleasure filled the room.

Wings unfurling, he stretched over her, supporting himself on his elbows. A satisfied female sigh brushed his cheek.

"I want you in me."

"Mine." He raised his hips, positioned himself, and entered her.

Nathaniel had been with women before Clarissa, and he'd been with her before they were mated. But nothing compared to this. As he slid into her slick heat, the mating bond snapped into place and everything changed. Every cell in his body aligned with hers, and when their eyes met, he could see she felt it too.

"It's... oh... it's like..." She couldn't finish. Her hips rose to meet his, finding an easy rhythm.

He leaned back, spread his wings, and lifted her.

"So deep," she crooned, bracing herself on his neck.

She moaned as he thrust inside the deep vee of her legs. On his knees like this, with her suspended in his arms, he had everything he'd ever wanted. Everything made sense. And he realized he would always feel this way. All the pieces fit. He moved with her until she grew tired and let go, flopping onto her back on the mattress and pulling him on top of her.

"More. Faster," she said.

He stretched on top of her, gave her what she needed, pistoning into her until she shattered around him once again. He found his own glorious peak, and everything in the room melted away. All that existed was her. Her moans of pleasure. Her body writhing gently beneath him. The soft mounds of her breasts against his chest. The long thin stretch of her waist.

When he finally came back down to earth, she had his face between her hands. "I love you, Nathaniel. I love you so damned much."

"I love you too, beyond limits." He rolled onto his back, taking her with him, and reveled in the feel of her weight over him. He stroked her hair down her back. "Now, my mate, tell me everything Grindylow told you. We're getting your magic back."

# CHAPTER TWENTY-FOUR

Every part of Clarissa's body felt deliciously exhausted, as if her bones had gone liquid and she was melting into Nathaniel beneath her. But then he looked at her and asked her about Grindylow.

The truth was, at the moment, she didn't care if she ever got her magic back. All she wanted to do was enjoy more of this, more of being this dragon's mate. She could spend days in this bed as the object of his affection. But there was more to her hesitation. What Grindylow had told her about having sisters had rocked her to her core. It couldn't be true of course. There had to be some explanation. Perhaps she'd used the term *sister* symbolically.

"You said in the car that Grindylow blamed the dragon queen and her fairy liege for what happened to you. Am I remembering that right? I was out of it."

She rested her chin on his chest. "Yes. Exactly what she said. Do you know who she might be talking about?"

"Only my mother and her fairy-sorceress sidekick. Her name was Aborella. But that couldn't be it. My mother is dead."

"Did a new queen replace her?"

"Even if one did, why would she be targeting you? She's in another world. No one in Paragon has even met you." He threaded his fingers behind his head.

"I don't know."

"What was your second question?"

"I asked how to get my powers back."

"And what did she say?"

"Yeah, get this... She said I need to rebind myself to my sisters."

His eyes narrowed. "I didn't think you had any sisters."

"I don't. I was told my real parents died in a car crash. I had no biological siblings. The Blacks adopted me, but they died in a freak accident when I was five. After that, I was raised in the American foster care system. None of the other children I ever lived with felt like sisters. It's total BS." She'd already shared her personal background with Nathaniel, but it bore repeating after all this time.

He seemed to turn that over in his mind. "So what was your third question?"

"I asked how I find these so-called sisters. I thought maybe she was using the term metaphorically and that her answer would help me figure it out."

"What did she say?"

"She told me one was nearby and would come to me. The other, and I quote, 'must be retrieved from her obsidian tomb before the queen finishes what she started.'"

He raised his head off the pillow and frowned at her. "Did she actually use the term obsidian?"

"Yes."

"Not dark? Not black?"

"No. Obsidian."

"Hmmm." A muscle in his jaw began to twitch, and she could feel his entire body tense beneath her.

"Why does that bother you?"

"The palace where I grew up was called the Obsidian Palace for a reason. It was built into the side of a mountain and was made entirely of the stuff. Floors, walls, ceilings... dungeon. Polished to a shine. We used to call the dungeon the obsidian tomb because if you were sentenced there, it was usually a life sentence. The conditions were bleak and no one could hear you scream."

"So... according to Grindylow, someone I am somehow related to is in a dungeon in Paragon?"

He shrugged. "It fits the picture. If the dragon queen is truly to blame, then it's possible that this other piece of the puzzle, this symbolic sister, is also Paragonian." He scoffed and shook his head.

"I know, ridiculous, right?" She sighed.

"I was just remembering that our bond would be illegal in Paragon. Relationships between dragons and witches were forbidden."

"Oh? Why?"

"There's a story from where I come from. It's part of our history. Centuries ago, a witch from the kingdom of Darnuith fell in love with a dragon and tried to overthrow the kingdom of Paragon. The coup was stopped and the witch and dragon were killed, but afterward it was determined that the combination of the two supernatural creatures was too powerful. Witches control the elements, but they are mortal. Dragons have limited powers but an infinite source of magic. Together, it was feared the right union might be unstoppable. And their offspring... the fear was they would be an abomination, a dragon shifter able to compel the natural elements independently. Theoretically, they would never tire. Never run out of power and never die."

"Hmm. So what we just did is breaking the law?" She laughed and bobbed her eyebrows. "Criminality has never been so delicious."

He gave her a slow, masculine smile. "They'll have to lock me up to keep me from you."

She kissed him softly.

"It's a good thing we aren't in Paragon. Nothing to worry about here."

"Good thing."

"But there is this bit about your 'sister' being near and finding us." He rubbed his chin.

"Do you think there's something to it?"

His gaze shifted to hers and he ran his finger along the edge of her hair, then tucked it behind her ear. "What if— and hear me out on this—she's referring to your doppelgänger that Wallace told us about?"

Clarissa blinked. With all the excitement, she'd forgotten about the look-alike who'd tried to sell Peter the book on dragons. "You think by sister, she meant someone who looks like me?"

He nodded. "Perhaps the reason this woman is searching for more information about dragon magic is that she knows it was used to neutralize her magic as well. Perhaps she's a witch."

A tingle crawled up Clarissa's neck. "A magical sisterhood, like a coven. It's possible. How do we find her and ask her?"

"I'll call Peter. He can make up some excuse for the sellers to come back for the book. When they do, we'll be there."

# CHAPTER TWENTY-FIVE

*Paragon*

Raven wallowed in a pool of her own sweat. The Obsidian Dungeon was hot as hell, the polished stone offering no solace from the unrelenting heat. In fact, the stone only seemed to act as an oven. She missed her magic. She'd have loved to make it snow. Even the water the guards gave her in a trough in the wall would only stay cool for a matter of minutes. It tasted of sulfur, but she'd drank as much as she could before it became the temperature of hot coffee.

There was no comfort in her cell. No window. No breeze. And she wasn't alone. She shared the water trough, a wooden bucket surrounded by a basket weave of metal, with a prisoner in the cell next to hers. If she squinted through the squares of the grid and the break between the bucket and the metal, she could just make out a man in the neighboring cell. *Not a man*, she thought. Likely a dragon. He'd finished the water she'd left behind, not seeming to mind the temperature.

She paced in front of the bars of the cell. Gabriel must be beside himself. He'd do anything to get her out of here. All she had to do was wait. If they expected him to act his part, he'd demand she be treated humanely.

"If you keep pacing, you'll dehydrate faster. They only bring water twice a day." A voice came from the cell beside her. A male voice, smooth and melodious.

"You're probably right. It's just so insufferably hot."

"The coolest place is the back corner, near the trough. It's hotter near the bars."

She moved to the back corner and slid down the wall. It was slightly cooler. Still not comfortable, but better. "How long have you been down here?"

"A few weeks."

She sloughed sweat off her forehead with the back of her hand. "*Why* are you down here?"

"The same reason you are."

She laughed. "You have no idea why I'm here. Why would you think that?"

"Everyone in the dungeon is here for the same reason. We pissed off the queen. Oh, excuse me, the empress. See, it's mistakes like that that earned me this cell."

"What's your name?"

She heard him shift positions on the other side of the wall. "No names. It's better that way."

Raven frowned, although she understood the sentiment. He had no reason to trust her, just as she had no reason to trust him. "Okay."

"So what did *you* do to end up here?"

"Pissed off the queen, I mean the empress," she said dryly. Like she was going to offer him more than he was willing to give.

The man laughed. "Right. Your accent is foreign

though. You're not a Highborn, that's for sure. You must be an outsider. From one of the other kingdoms?"

Raven traced a pattern against her palm and had a change of heart. There was one thing she wanted others here to know, because it was clear Eleanor intended to hide it. If that weren't true, Raven would be with Gabriel now.

"I'm Gabriel's wife," Raven said softly.

"Gabriel? The heir? He's been gone for centuries."

"He's back. We're back."

There was a long pause. "I heard a commotion at the other end of the dungeon, but the sound was muffled. I couldn't make out words."

"That was us."

"You and Gabriel? I thought I heard a third."

"Tobias is with him."

The stranger shifted, bringing his mouth closer to the grate. "Are they here, in another part of the dungeon?"

She blew out an exhausted breath. "No. They're upstairs at some sort of banquet."

The stranger scoffed incredulously. "If you truly are mate to the heir, why are you in the dungeon if he's being welcomed back like the prince he is?"

Feeling exhausted, Raven wiped the sweat from her forehead. She was so hot she could hardly think. It felt like her brain was boiling.

"Eleanor knows if she keeps me here, Gabriel will do anything she asks. He would never cooperate with her otherwise."

"I see. So you're a dead woman walking."

Raven shook her head. "No. Gabriel will come for me. He'll make sure she treats me well or he won't do what she wants."

He gave her a pitying laugh. "Maybe, at first. But she'll find a way to keep you from him."

"You don't know that. Gabriel will never allow it." She closed her eyes. Her head pounded.

"It's clear to me that you aren't from here, so let me explain something to you. Gabriel is the eldest heir to the throne of Paragon. Eleanor enjoys her seat on the throne and will not give it up. A rebellion is rising among the kingdoms. Eleanor's best bet to stay in power is for Gabriel to entertain suitors. An alliance by marriage with one of the other kingdoms could stave off the rebellion and give her an excuse to appoint him ruler of another court and save her seat. She needs to use him, which means she'll use you."

"Gabriel will only cooperate so long and so far. We're bound. He'll burn the place down before he takes a second mate."

The dragon snorted. "You're not understanding this, are you? Gabriel will do it for you. All Eleanor has to do is keep you alive. He does what she wants, you get fed. He refuses, you don't. A dragon will do anything for his mate. Anything. At first he'll do it for a chance to see you. Those visits will grow longer and longer apart. Then he'll do it for simple proof you're still alive. Then he'll do it for her word she will not harm you. Soon you'll be as good as dead, locked in a coffin of stone with just enough to keep your heart beating while Gabriel plays out her wicked scheme."

An invisible vise clutched her torso and squeezed. He was right. If Eleanor had any intention of being remotely kind, she wouldn't let her bake in this dungeon. A chill slicked over her sweat-drenched skin.

"You understand now," he said. "You see what I'm telling you is true."

"*Fuck*," she whispered. She was tired and her head was

throbbing. "Every time I think I understand the level of evil Eleanor embodies, I'm proven wrong. She soars right past it."

He laughed a deep, rumbling chuckle. There was the dragon. Up until then, she might have mistaken him for human based solely on his voice. But that laugh, that was the laugh of a beast biding its time somewhere inside.

She closed her eyes and leaned her aching head against the wall. "Come on, Gabriel," she said under her breath.

"You may get one chance, maybe two, to get out of this cell," the dragon said. "Eleanor may entertain the idea of letting Gabriel see you at first, the better to string him along."

"I'm counting on it."

He lowered his voice. "It will be soon. He'll want to see you before he sleeps."

Raven wondered how he could tell the time in this dim pit of obsidian.

"When they take you upstairs, you need to do something for me. For us."

Raven narrowed her eyes. "Us? I don't even know your name."

"No, but you already know we are on the same side when it comes to Eleanor."

She rubbed the back of her neck. "So?"

"Listen to me very carefully. I am going to tell you a story about Eleanor, and if you want to survive this thing she has planned for you and Gabriel, you'd better listen."

A BLOND GUARD DRESSED IN A RED-AND-BLACK TUNIC with a braided gold sash across his chest slid a key into the lock of her cell. Raven remained perfectly still, her body weak and thirsty from the heat, until the door was completely open.

"Come with me," he said. "Now."

She rose and followed, glancing back to get a glimpse through the bars of the neighboring cell. A flash of pale skin and chestnut hair caught her eye before the guard tugged her elbow and thrust her toward the door.

"Where are you taking me?" she asked the guard, her throat cracking from thirst.

"Silence."

The sheer pleasure as they climbed the circular staircase and the temperature dropped had her breathing more deeply. When the guard opened the doors to the palace proper and a cool breeze wafted over her, she almost moaned.

He half dragged her down the hall and thrust her into a room. The door closed and locked behind her. Well, this was far more comfortable than the dungeon. A bed was situated at the center of the room, swathed in white linens and facing an open window with a view of the stars. But it was the door to the right that drew her. A bathroom.

She turned on the faucet and lowered her lips to the flowing water. It was cool and sweet. She drank until her belly could hold no more, then filled the tub. She stripped out of her clothes and got in even before it was full. In a small ceramic indent in the side of the basin, there was soap and what she assumed was shampoo, although she couldn't read the labels. She lathered her skin and then her hair, rinsing away the caked sweat and grime.

She'd just finished washing when the sound of footsteps in the adjoining room sent her reaching for a towel. She wrapped it around her body and crept behind the door. It opened toward her nose and she held her breath. Gabriel stepped into the bathroom.

"Gabriel." She blew out a relieved breath.

Gabriel whirled and took her in his arms.

He kissed her and cupped her face. "I was so afraid. I didn't know what she'd done to you," he said breathlessly. "This... this doesn't seem so bad."

She closed her eyes. "They didn't keep me here."

When she opened them again, his held the intensity of an angry dragon. "Where did they keep you?"

"In the dungeon."

Gabriel cursed and backed away, shaking his head.

"It's hot there. Dreadfully hot. And they didn't feed us all day."

A heinous curse flew from Gabriel's lips, and he charged from the bathroom to the door. "I want food in here now!" he yelled to the guard in the hall. The growl that followed rattled the walls. The man bolted for places unknown.

She pulled him back into the room. "We need to talk."

He closed the door. "What is it? Is there more? Did they hurt you?"

"No. Listen. There's a man in the cell next to me. A dragon. He told me that if they allowed me out tonight, there was something I should do, something that could help us."

Gabriel narrowed his eyes. "Who was this dragon? What was his name?"

She shook her head. "He didn't tell me his name. He said there's a magical object hidden in the library behind a book called *The Saddle of Arythmetes*. It's a box with something inside that he says will help us escape, and if I can get my hands on it and bring it to him, he may be able to break us all out of here."

The growing scowl on Gabriel's face told her what he thought of the idea. "Raven, you have no idea who this man is. If he's in a dungeon in Paragon, he is no friend of yours."

She hugged the towel tighter around her. "I can't explain it, Gabriel. I trust him. He... he reminds me of someone."

"You were hot and tired and starved. This person offered you some comfort. But you have to realize this is likely a trap. Why do you think they put you in that cell next to him? Odd, don't you think?"

Raven furrowed her brow. She hadn't thought about it at all.

"This dragon tells you to steal something from the library and bring it to him. What then? I'll tell you what will happen, Raven. He'll turn you in, and then Eleanor will have a reason and an excuse to keep you down there permanently."

The truth behind his words fell heavy on her shoulders. He was right; she wasn't thinking clearly. If not for Gabriel, she might have made a terrible mistake. There was a knock on the door. Gabriel opened it and rolled in a tray laden with food of a type she'd never seen before.

When the door was closed again, he took her by the shoulders. "Come, let's find you something to wear."

He led her to a closet filled with lustrous fabrics.

"Wow. This is all gorgeous."

"This was my old room. They've replaced the clothes with things that are fashionable now. Unfortunately, it's all for men. Here. This should work to sleep in." He handed her a pair of stretchy tights and a soft shirt that would have likely been formfitting on him but hung on her like a tunic.

"Thank you."

"I think you'll like this meal. It tastes a bit like your pork, but spicy and with more of a tang."

He loaded her plate and she sat down in front of it. In minutes, she'd inhaled half of it while Gabriel sipped a glass of wine across from her. She supposed he'd already eaten. It had to be late. Paragon's two moons were high in the night sky.

"Something else the prisoner said is bothering me," she whispered.

Gabriel leaned forward, all his attention on her. If he thought she was stupid for listening to the man in the dungeon, he gave no indication. Her mate was fully attentive with nothing but concern in his eyes.

"He said that Eleanor would want you to entertain a union with royalty from one of the other kingdoms. He said she needs it. She needs to use you to buffer relations because there is a rebellion rising."

Gabriel leaned back in his chair and threaded his fingers over his stomach. "Hmmm."

"That sounds ominous."

"Eleanor hinted as much tonight. She introduced me to several women from royal families across the five kingdoms."

Raven dropped her fork. "Then maybe this dragon is right. He says Eleanor will slowly try to distance me from you in an attempt to coerce you into playing the bachelor and smoothing over political turmoil."

Gabriel rubbed his face. "I don't know, Raven, but I won't allow them to send you back there. If Mother wants my cooperation, she'll allow you to stay here."

She scoffed. "This is just a different type of prison."

Tension crackled between them. Neither option was

ideal, and they both knew it. Eleanor had the upper hand. Gabriel rubbed the back of his neck in exasperation.

"Tell me about today. What happened?" Raven asked.

"Eleanor executed Brynhoff and blamed his dead heart for everything that happened at Marius's coronation. She told the Highborn Court that Tobias and I were 'recovered' by Ransom, Scoria's successor and the new head of the Obsidian Guard. She basically absolved herself from all responsibility for Marius's murder while simultaneously forcing Tobias and me to support her as empress while we recovered from our prolonged absence."

"Fuck. She's brilliantly evil. Now whatever rebellion is stewing, they can't use Marius's murder or your disappearance against her to gain favor with the populace."

He nodded. "She has all of us right where she wants us."

Suddenly Raven wasn't hungry anymore. She leaned back in her chair and toyed with her food, twirling her fork. "So what do we do?"

"We bide our time. We do what we have to do. And we pray."

Raven thought back to just a few days ago. After she'd delivered their baby, she'd died. She'd lost too much blood and her heart had temporarily stopped beating. In that dark moment, she'd had a vision that the goddess Circe had come to her. She remembered the goddess, her creamy olive skin, dark hair, and eyes the color of molten gold. She'd seemed so kind.

Raven raised her chin and said, "I think prayer is an excellent idea."

# CHAPTER TWENTY-SIX

**Paragon**
**A long time ago**

Nathaniel peered around the corner into his mother's private parlor and spotted her inside, the yellow silk of her floor-length dress bunched in her hand. His scrawny body was slight enough she didn't notice him at first, which was exactly what he wanted. She was doing something strange, something he'd never seen a dragon do, and he wanted to watch.

Mother had drawn a symbol on the obsidian floor in chalk, a strange symbol like the ones he'd been taught in school that only the witches of Darnuith used. His schoolmaster said witches were evil, filthy creatures that couldn't be trusted, which made the fact that the symbol was here, drawn by his mother, all the more odd. On one side of the symbol was a bowl of water. On the other side, a white bird. The bird's feet and wings were bound, and it writhed helplessly in its spot.

Mother paced around the circle, her citrine ring glowing

gold on her finger. "*Fitzucalcula,*" she said. Nothing happened. "*Fitzucalcula!*" she said again, louder.

"It needs fuel," Nathaniel said.

His mother's eyes snapped to his. She was so beautiful, a dark, red-lipped queen whose eyes turned soft and loving when she saw him.

"What are you doing up, Nathaniel? Isn't it past your bedtime?"

"I felt it," he said, pointing to the circle.

She tilted her head. "What's that? You... felt the symbol?"

He nodded. "It's whispering to me. Not in words exactly." He shook his head. "But I can sense it. It's telling me what to do to make it work."

"Well, come in. If the symbol is speaking to you, you must help me with it."

He jogged to her side and she squatted beside him and kissed him on the cheek.

"Can you tell what Mummy is trying to do?"

Nathaniel concentrated on the things in front of him. "It's a spell like witches do."

"Ah, ah, ah." She wagged her finger. "It is a spell, but it's a new kind of spell. One that dragons do, or will do when I figure it out. I have a friend from the fairy kingdom who is teaching me, only I can't get it to work."

"What's it supposed to do?"

"I'm trying to make this bird look like a narwit. Dragons can use illusion on themselves, but we can't change how other things appear. If I can learn this spell, I can learn to extend my illusion beyond my body."

Nathaniel narrowed his eyes. "It needs fuel."

"I heard you say that before. How do you know that?"

"I can feel it." He pointed at the symbol. "That's the

magic—it's like the gears for grinding flour." He pointed to the water. "That's what you are grinding." He pointed to the bird. "That's what the magic will act upon. The illusion will wrap around the bird."

"What do you mean when you say it has no fuel?"

"There's nothing to turn the gears." He looked up at her. How could he make her understand?

"Ah, but the magic word is supposed to turn the gears. *Fitzucalcula.*"

Nathaniel shook his head. "Dragons don't have magic in their words." He laughed.

Her eyes widened, and he could tell the moment she understood. "You genius boy. Of course we don't. We have magic in ourselves."

He nodded.

She hugged him around the shoulders. "Would you like to do the honors, or shall I?"

He gazed up at her with such love he thought his heart would explode. "Can I, Mummy?"

"Oh yes, dear boy. You are very good at this. Let's see you make it work."

He extended a talon from his left hand and pressed it to the skin of his right index finger. A bead of blood formed there, and he held it over the circle. Three fat drops slapped the floor.

Immediately the symbol glowed to life and started to spin, lifting off the floor and taking the bird and the water with it. It was a whirlpool. A hurricane. A blur of feathers and rain.

It all crashed to the floor and broke apart rather abruptly, the magic dissipating like clearing smoke. There in front of him was the cutest pink narwit, wiggling its four ears at him and grunting softly. His mother squealed.

"Very good. Very good, Nathaniel." She hugged him tight.

He smiled so wide his cheeks hurt.

"I have an idea."

He widened his eyes expectantly. Perhaps they'd do another spell.

"How would you like to skip fighting in the pits for a few weeks and instead work with Mummy to write her new book on dragon spells?"

Nathaniel jumped up and down. He hated fighting. If he could, he'd never go to the pits again. "Oh yes, Mummy, please."

She kissed his temple. "Done. Now go to bed. Tomorrow we'll experiment with something new."

He obeyed, so excited for this new adventure.

### Mistwood Manor
### Modern day

NATHANIEL WOKE WITH A START AND WAS PLEASANTLY surprised to find Clarissa still curled into his chest. She was his. Finally. Just the thought filled him with warmth and a seemingly bottomless well of love and protective instinct. He kissed her on the top of her sleeping head, drawing the scent of warm, sex-exhausted woman into his nose. A dragon could live on that.

So why, after such a perfect morning, had he dreamed about his dead mother?

It had to have been Grindylow's suggestion that the dragon queen was to blame for Clarissa's curse. Nathaniel had wonderful memories of his mother. Together they'd filled her spell book with magic adapted to a dragon's abilities. It was groundbreaking, and he had come to practice magic with her on a regular basis. It was that magic that had saved them all.

When Brynhoff had murdered Marius, his mother had safely transported them to Earth, using the very magic he'd helped her develop over the years. He'd understood it better than any of his siblings. And she'd likely been murdered by Brynhoff for protecting them. That was three centuries ago. He didn't even know who the queen of Paragon was now, but if it would help his mate, he would find out.

He carefully extracted himself from under Clarissa and reached for his phone, moving into his library and closing the door before placing the call so that he wouldn't wake her. When his friend answered, he got straight to it.

"Wallace, I have a favor to ask." He explained how he wanted to meet the doppelgänger.

"I'll get them here. I'll be in touch with a place and time," Wallace said in his typical no-nonsense tone.

Once his old friend ended the call, Nathaniel reached for his tarot cards.

"Tell me about the queen of Paragon." He dealt his usual spread. The ten of wands stood out immediately. "Oppression," he said, and it was related to the four of swords. The card could have many meanings, but the one his mind attached to was coffin or tomb. Perhaps his mother's death, the literal oppression of her life. The other cards in the spread seemed to enforce something more though. Oppression *due* to her death? Perhaps the new queen was exceptionally cruel. The last card in the spread was the Wheel of Fortune. He sat down hard in his chair. Were the cards suggesting it was his destiny to set things right? He swept the cards back into his hand.

He was getting ahead of himself. One step at a time. He would meet this doppelgänger and see if she could provide clarity in the interpretation of Grindylow's words.

His phone buzzed in his hand. A text from Wallace.

*My office. 1 pm.*

After a glorious breakfast, most of which was spent with Clarissa on his lap, Nathaniel explained his plan to his new mate. She enthusiastically agreed it was the best place to start.

Several hours later, he escorted her to Peter's office. The warm wood paneling and heavy mahogany desk was as welcoming as the man who greeted them both with a tight hug. "My dear friend, it is a pleasure indeed to see you again."

"You too, Wallace."

"And you, Clarissa. I hope you don't mind my saying so, but I'd wondered if you'd return to us. I am relieved to see you back in the fold." He embraced her with a steady thump to her back before releasing her.

"No offense taken. I'm glad to hear you're in good health."

Nathaniel took a seat with his back to the door, Clarissa next to him. "So, where is this mysterious book and the owners you mentioned?"

"On their way," Wallace said.

There was a knock on the open door and they all turned. Nathaniel almost fell out of his chair when he saw who stood in the doorway. His dragon twisted. His senses snapped to attention, his nose attempting to confirm what his eyes were showing him. It had been centuries, but his sister hadn't changed all that much.

"Ms. Valor. Thank you for coming," Wallace said.

Nathaniel's jaw worked uselessly, his gaze locked with

the dark-haired woman in the doorway. Finally his voice gave way with one breathy word that escaped his lips. "Rowan?"

"By the Mountain!" She ran to him and hugged him as hard and as certainly as she had when they were kids. She kissed him firmly on the cheek. "Nathaniel!"

When the hug broke, he looked at her in confusion. "What are you doing here?"

She opened her mouth to speak but paused when another woman appeared in the doorway. Nathaniel's voice failed him again. It was Clarissa. Younger than she was now and with the natural black hair she once had as a young woman.

The newcomer's gaze darted between each of them and then locked on Clarissa.

"Oh my... You're Clarissa. Like *the* Clarissa! I have all your music!" She held out her hand, and Clarissa shook it robotically, staring at the woman with an expression of shocked silence. "Believe it or not, people say I look like you."

Rowan turned to the young woman, "This is my associate, Avery Tanglewood."

Clarissa finally found her voice. "It's nice to meet you. You, uh, you do look..." She trailed off, her lips parting.

Rowan grabbed Avery's elbow. "Avery, this is my brother Nathaniel."

Peter Wallace straightened. "Brother?"

All Nathaniel could do was repeat himself. "What are you doing here?" He felt like someone had pulled the rug out from under him and he was falling fast and hard toward the floor.

Rowan grabbed his hands like an anchor in a tumultuous sea. "We were wrong, Nathaniel, about everything.

We don't need to stay apart. So much has happened. Please, come with us. There's something we need to show you."

Nathaniel didn't understand, but he nodded his head. He reached for Clarissa's hand. She was still staring at Avery like she was entranced. Shocked silent, he moved to follow Rowan from the small office.

"B-but what about the book?" Wallace asked before they could leave.

They all turned to him for a beat. Nathaniel had to blink a few times before he remembered what his friend was talking about.

He exchanged glances with Rowan before admitting, "I am fairly sure I wrote it."

Rowan gave Wallace a warm smile and shrugged. "Keep it."

# CHAPTER TWENTY-SEVEN

Clarissa tried to concentrate on what Rowan was saying but her mind kept fading in and out. This was important. Nathaniel's mother was still alive and ruling Paragon. The queen now called herself empress and had masterminded the coup that had exiled the dragon siblings.

They'd returned to a flat in London where Rowan claimed she had something Nathaniel had to see. That something was actually a someone. Clarissa met Rowan's mate, Nick, who was a giant of a human and greeted her with a warm hug and a thick New York accent. She'd also met Nathaniel's brother, Alexander, who was thin for a dragon and whose rumpled T-shirt and jeans told her he was possibly less refined than his siblings. He'd introduced his mate, Maiara, whose quiet disposition left Clarissa with more questions than answers.

But as they all gathered around a table in the dining room, it was Avery she couldn't stop staring at in absolute wonder. It wasn't just that the woman looked like her. Clarissa felt the strangest sense of connection, like she'd known her for a very long time even though they'd just met.

"Here's a picture of Raven," Avery said, holding out her phone.

Clarissa perused the screen. Raven's build was less curvy than her own and Avery's but she still looked enough like Clarissa one might assume they were related. Sisters. Was this who Grindylow had been referring to?

"Where is Raven now?" Clarissa asked in a whisper, not wanting to interrupt the conversation between Rowan and Nathaniel.

Avery threaded her fingers. "She's a prisoner of Paragon. Aborella abducted her along with Gabriel and Tobias the day after the baby was born. She's been gone two weeks now."

"Baby?" Clarissa asked.

"Yes." Avery smiled. "Gabriel and Raven have a child."

Clarissa's hand shot out and squeezed Nathaniel's arm. He'd just discussed with her how the mating of a dragon and a witch was illegal in Paragon and how the greater fear there was that the offspring of such a union would be too powerful to allow to live. A sick feeling wormed its way into her gut. Gabriel was a dragon. Raven was a witch. Had Avery really just said they'd had a baby?

Nathaniel turned narrowed eyes on Avery, and the dining room went eerily silent. "Did you say *baby*?"

Nick chuckled. "I never get tired of the look on people's faces."

Rowan gave him a hard nudge.

Avery stood and motioned for them to follow. She led them through the kitchen and into the living room where a fire burned in a sleek, modern-looking fireplace despite it being a warm day in summer. There, in the fire, was what Clarissa could only describe as an egg, although it was unlike any she'd ever seen before. Slightly bigger than her head, it had a bumpy exterior as if it were made from a wound string of pearls interrupted by a ribbon of smooth shell that spiraled from top to bottom. The entire thing pulsed with teal light.

Clarissa placed her hands on her hips and opened her mouth to speak, but the words caught in her throat. Her hands slid off. She planted them again. They slid off again. "Is that... a ... um?"

Nathaniel held her by the shoulders. "It's a dragon egg."

"Half witch, half dragon," Rowan said, "to be exact. We don't know if it's a boy or a girl, so we're calling them Li'l Puff."

Nathaniel's eyes widened. "And Aborella captured Gabriel's mate, who is a witch?"

Rowan nodded. "Along with Gabriel and Tobias."

"Does Mother know about the baby?" Nathaniel asked. Clarissa didn't miss the ice that had slid in behind his gray eyes or the menace in his tone.

"We don't know," Rowan said, her fingers finding Nick's beside her.

Behind the two, Alexander wrapped Maiara more tightly in his arms. The sick feeling was back, and Nathaniel confirmed her fears.

"It's forbidden," Nathaniel mumbled to her. "They are all in great danger, and if Mother finds out about this baby, so are we."

The fire danced around the egg. Through the smooth strip of shell, Clarissa glimpsed a silhouette shift inside. A baby, by a witch and a dragon, just like her and Nate. Her heart ached. She had to protect this little one. She squeezed Nathaniel's hand.

"Grindylow mentioned three sisters," she mumbled, thinking about Raven. Nathaniel focused on her in that intense way that always made her feel like the center of the universe.

"It has to be you, Avery, and Raven," Nathaniel said. "Avery found us. Just as she predicted."

"Who's Grindylow?" Rowan asked.

Nathaniel raised one finger toward his sister. "What is it, Clarissa?" He must have noticed her frown.

"I was just thinking about what Grindylow said... Raven was captured two weeks ago. My power was taken after she was captured." Clarissa turned toward Avery. "Did you lose your power too?"

All the light drained from Avery's eyes and she shook her head. "I was never a witch. I have no power."

Clarissa looked at Nathaniel in confusion and he shrugged. "Well, I am..." Clarissa corrected herself. "...I used to be a powerful witch until someone stole my magic. A strange redheaded woman plucked a hair from my head just before it happened."

Avery bristled. "What did the woman look like?"

"Tall, sophisticated."

"Did she seem too perfect? Like she'd had extensive plastic surgery?"

"Yes, now that you mention it."

Avery lowered herself to the sofa. "That's Aborella. The same illusion she used when she was controlling me."

Rowan moved closer to the fire. Nick didn't seem happy to let her go, and Alexander's and Maiara's expressions were murderous. Whoever this Aborella was, she was hated among this crew. "Nathaniel, you've always understood magic better than the rest of us. What do you think's going on here?"

Nathaniel reached into his pocket and pulled out his pipe, lighting it up and sending a ring of smoke toward the fireplace. "Clarissa, Avery, and Raven don't just look alike." Nathaniel cast her a glance and Clarissa nodded, reassuring him it was okay to share. "Clarissa and I visited an oracle recently. A very dangerous but very powerful demon oracle. It is known her words are never untrue, although they're sometimes open to interpretation."

Avery was rocking slowly now, her arms wrapped around her waist as if bracing herself for something horrible. "What did she say? Is my sister d-dead?"

Clarissa shook her head. "No. I don't think so."

"She said the three of you are sisters and that Mother and Aborella took Clarissa's power and presumably Raven's by unbinding you from one another."

There it was. Clarissa hugged herself against the tension that rose in the room.

"Sisters?" Avery said, spreading her hands. "Raven and I are sisters, a year apart. Clarissa just looks like us."

A ring of smoke blew over their heads, two smaller rings poking through its center. "I think it might be a metaphysical sisterhood. You are practically doppelgängers. Perhaps Grindylow was referring to a sisterhood in the magical sense rather than true heredity."

That seemed to unsettle Avery, and she stared at Clarissa with a strange sort of wonder. "How old are you, Clarissa?"

She balked. "Rude!"

Avery blushed and shook her head. "Raven and I are twenty-three and twenty-four. I was just wondering if there was any chance... You see, our father is kind of an asshole."

"Thirty. And no. My parents were killed in a car accident when I was baby. I don't know much about them, but I was told I was their only child."

"Oh, I'm sorry."

Rowan ran her hand along the mantel, frowning. "Nathaniel, what makes you so sure Raven is still alive? I want to believe they are, but after what Mother and Brynhoff did to Marius..."

"Grindylow told us Clarissa could get her power back if we bound the sisters again. If that's a possibility, she must be alive."

Rowan let out a relieved breath. "Then Mother probably hasn't killed Gabriel or Tobias either."

"Who knows how long that will last?" Avery said, becoming agitated and pacing behind the sofa. "If Raven is still alive, we have to get her back."

"I agree," Nathaniel said.

Rowan's gaze grew hard. "You do? But there's not enough of us. We can't take on the Obsidian Guard. Even if we find Xavier, Sylas, and Colin, we'll need help on the inside to free them."

Nathaniel leaned an elbow on the mantel and stared into the fire. "No, we can't take them by force. Thankfully, we won't have to."

"What are you talking about?" Alexander's interest in the conversation seemed to have grown.

"I know Mother's magic. With some planning and stealth, I can get us into the palace unseen. I am the only one who can slip through the wards. The guards won't expect it. They don't staff the interior of the palace like they do the grounds. With any luck, we can slip in, find them, and get out before anyone knows they're missing."

Alexander scratched the side of his jaw. "When you say you know Mother's magic? What exactly do you mean?"

With a wave of his hand, Nathaniel disappeared and reappeared across the room. He took a puff from his pipe and blew out a smoke ring that expanded and dropped down the walls. A second later, they were all standing in a dark wood. The couch had become a log and the fireplace a campfire. Nick swore, and Maiara said something in a language Clarissa didn't know.

Tiny bugs bounced off her skin. Clarissa smelled pine and smoke from the campfire. An owl hooted in the distance. And then with a wave of his hand and a flash of his amethyst ring, it was all gone.

"I mean that while you all were learning to be warriors or princesses"—he looked pityingly at Rowan—"Mother was teaching me magic. I helped her write her grimoire. And if what you say is true about her..." He looked at Clarissa. "...and she's actually behind what Aborella did to my mate, she should be very afraid of me. I know her vulnerabilities, and I will exploit every one of them."

Nathaniel Clarke was a dragon, a dark menace of power and magic, but Clarissa had rarely seen this side of him. Until now. His eyes were burning purple, and she thought in that instant that if she were Eleanor, Dragon Queen of Paragon, she'd be very afraid. Very afraid indeed.

"Now, as pleasant as this flat is, I'd like to invite you all back to Mistwood Manor to stay until we can make a plan for retrieving our brethren. It will be safer there." His gaze fixed on the egg. "For all of us."

THE RAGE WELLING WITHIN NATHANIEL WAS ALMOST impossible for him to contain. He hadn't believed Rowan at first. Their mother was still alive? How could that be? But his sister wasn't given to speaking untruths. And once he'd seen Alexander and heard their story, it was clear that everything he'd believed about Paragon the past three hundred years was a lie.

The hardest part was thinking the worst of his mother. She'd been kind to him, always. He was her favorite. They'd spent hours together in his youth, perfecting spells. Part of him still hoped that maybe there had been some mistake or she'd been compelled to do the things she'd done.

Grindylow didn't lie though, and the oracle had specifically implicated the dragon *queen* in her answer. If his mother was still alive and she was still on the throne, she was queen no matter what she called herself. Considering his mate had lost her magic soon after Gabriel, Raven, and Tobias had been captured, it was relatively clear his mother was responsible. She'd survived the coup that resulted in Marius's death and had intentionally never contacted any of them. She'd been involved in cursing Clarissa. There was no scenario where Eleanor was still in power, responsible for what happened to his mate and his siblings, and somehow was the same sweet woman who'd taught him magic.

Although he would love a proper explanation for all that and desperately wished he could confront his mother and Brynhoff about it all, he understood this wasn't the time. His first priority was his mate, and rescuing Gabriel, Tobias, and Raven was the first step to making her whole.

"Welcome to Mistwood," he said to his siblings. "Rowan and Nick, my oread Tempest will show you to your room. Alexander and Maiara, please follow Laurel."

The oreads blinked into sight and led their guests toward the second floor.

Nathaniel turned toward Avery. "If you'll follow Clarissa and me, your room is across from ours." He didn't miss how Clarissa beamed up at him when he said "ours."

Did she think he'd tolerate her sleeping in her old room now that they were mated? Not likely.

Clarissa's phone buzzed, and she withdrew it from her pocket. "It's Tom again. I need to respond or he won't stop texting me."

"Take your time." He kissed Clarissa's temple and watched her stroll off toward the library. Once she was out of sight, he turned toward Avery and lifted her suitcase. "This way. I'll show you to your room."

She was still holding the egg in a portable incubator. Nathaniel reached for it to help her, but she shook her head. "I've got it."

"All right."

Avery was clearly protective of her niece or nephew. He led her up the stairs and to the end of the hall. The guest room he'd had prepared for her was the closest to his room and had the biggest fireplace in the house. Nathaniel started a fire for her while she retrieved the egg from its heated carrier.

"Allow me. I am impervious to the flames." He reached for the egg, but Avery jerked back and hugged it to her chest.

"I'm sorry, Nathaniel. I know this is coming off as rude, but honestly Li'l Puff doesn't like to be handled by other people," she said. "Both Tobias and Gabriel got knocked on their asses trying. I'm the only one who can touch them."

"The egg knocked Gabriel and Tobias on their asses?" Nathaniel grinned. The thought was delightful.

"It produces a purple electric charge that shocks people when the baby's scared. I remind him or her of Raven, so it hasn't happened with me."

She donned a pair of fireproof gloves and placed the egg on the grate.

"So that's why you take care of the egg and not, say, Rowan."

Avery chuckled. "Honestly, even before we knew about Li'l Puff's zappy-zappy powers, Rowan resisted the idea of fostering the egg. She's really bitter about motherhood. I don't know what life was like for you in Paragon, but she for one seems fairly scarred by the experience."

Although Avery said it lightly and he had no doubt it was true, Nathaniel frowned at the notion. He'd enjoyed his youth. Maybe it was because there was little chance he'd ever sit on the throne. He wasn't a threat and he wasn't valuable enough for his future marriage to be used for political positioning. He was simply Nathaniel, a dragon prince with a secret, natural talent for magic. He'd always been treated with respect by his mother and indifference by his father and uncle, which was fine by him. It saddened him though that Rowan's experience was so different.

"Well, if you need anything, call for Tempest or Laurel. They don't like to appear physically to strangers if they don't have to, but they'll get you what you need." He stood and turned for the door.

"Why don't I have any magic?" she blurted.

He stopped and pivoted back to her. "I have no idea."

She extended a hand toward him. "But you understand about magic. You must have some theories. Raven is younger than me by a year, and she's this powerful witch. We have the same genes. The same parents. You say I'm part of some magical sisterhood with your girlfriend, who is also a powerful witch. So... what's wrong with me?"

A tear slipped from the corner of her right eye, and Nathaniel's heart melted. She wasn't Clarissa, but she looked too much like her to think of her as a stranger or to not be affected by her emotions. He sighed and motioned for her to have a seat. He sat down across the fire from her.

"Magic isn't linear," he said. This was a lesson he usually gave new witches or wizards in the order, but he thought some knowledge might give her comfort. "It doesn't flow in conjunction with time. It ebbs and flows with intention. You mentioned to Clarissa you're twenty-four, correct?"

"Yes."

"Clarissa's magic appeared when she was twenty, but it took practice to tease it out of her. She had symptoms but had no control over what would become of her abilities until she met me."

Avery rested her elbows on her knees. Her fingers threaded and she rubbed her palms together slowly.

"Do you want to have magic or does it scare you?" Nathaniel asked softly.

Avery sighed and leaned back in the chair, the firelight dancing across her cheek. "I'm not sure if it's magic I want exactly, I just want to be something more." She shrugged. "I'm a waitress. I can't even say that I work at a fancy, exclusive restaurant. I sling beer and bar food at my parents' pub. Didn't even have to apply for the job. I was never much good at school. I didn't go to college. I don't sing or play an instrument. There is literally nothing special about me."

"That's not true," Nathaniel said immediately.

She laughed. "You've known me for a few hours. Believe me, it's true."

He crossed his arms. "Yes, I have known you for only a few hours and already it's clear to me you are an important part of a magical trio of powerful witches. As for your own power, I've already seen a hint of it."

She shook her head. "What are you talking about?"

"You are the only one who can touch the egg. You told me yourself."

She rolled her eyes. "That's not a big deal. It's just because I look like Li'l Puff's mother."

He narrowed his eyes at her. Nathaniel had a hunch about something, and he was rarely wrong when it came to magic. "If that's the case, then Clarissa should be able to handle the egg. You look almost identical aside from a little blond hair dye."

Avery's face fell. Just as he thought. It was an element of pride that the baby had chosen her, and she actually thought she had nothing to do with it. "That's true."

He took out his phone and fired off a text to Clarissa. She appeared in the doorway a few moments later. "Sorry about that. Tom wouldn't stop about the $O_2$. We're going to have to come up with something... Oh, what's going on?" She glanced between them, clearly noticing the look on Avery's face.

"Do you mind acting as our test subject?" Nathaniel asked.

Clarissa raised an eyebrow. "What do you want me to do?"

"Just take the egg out of the fire."

She gave him a quizzical look. "You want me to reach into the open flames?"

He took out his pipe, lit it, and blew a smoke ring that morphed into a wave symbol. He pushed it toward the fire. The flames died.

"It needs to stay warm!" Avery said.

He raised a hand. "I'll restart the fire as soon as we're through with the test. Clarissa, the shell will be cool to the touch." He inclined his head in the direction of the fireplace.

Clarissa stepped to the egg and gathered it in her hands. "It is cool," she said, "And bumpy." He had a single breath to believe he'd been wrong before a purple electric storm of magic brewed around the egg. "Ouch!"

Before she could drop it, Avery had it in her hands. "It's okay, Li'l Puff. You're safe," Avery whispered to the egg.

"What the hell was that?" Clarissa asked, shaking her hands like they hurt.

"Avery thought the reason she was the only one other than Raven who could hold the egg was because she looked like her sister. I was simply proving to her she was wrong."

Avery set the egg back in the fireplace, and Nathaniel lit it back up.

"I guess it is just me. What does that mean?" She looked between him and Clarissa.

"I'm not sure yet. Your magic was taken from you when you were unbound from each other. Even if you had had magic before, it would be gone now. What you do have is a natural ability, similar to Clarissa's voice. Clarissa can sing beautifully, with or without magic. When it comes to her voice, the magic is the rose on the already iced cake. You have... something else. You are a comfort to this child. Perhaps your magic will be related to that, a balancing force."

"So I might have magic."

"Yes. We won't know for sure until we reconnect you three and are able to test you," Nathaniel said.

Avery's attention turned back to the fire, and he could have sworn the hint of a smile flashed across her lips.

Clarissa's hand landed on his arm.

"Well then, it's time for bed," Nathaniel said. "Please help yourself if you need anything." He took Clarissa by the arm and led her from the room.

"That was kind of you," Clarissa said as they entered their own room and closed the door.

"What was kind? Suggesting she might be more than she gives herself credit for? I had to. She reminds me too much of you to let her wallow in self-doubt."

"Actually, I meant what you said about my voice. There really isn't anything special about it without my magic, but I appreciate that you said there was."

He stopped and turned to her, unable to keep the surprise from his expression. "You can't believe that. Clarissa, your talent is not reliant on your magic, only enhanced by it."

She turned away from him and snagged her nightgown from the corner of the bed. "You're an easy audience."

He took off his suit jacket and started unbuttoning his shirt. "Hardly. Sing for me," he said. "Now."

# CHAPTER TWENTY-EIGHT

Clarissa stopped what she was doing and regarded Nathaniel. He was shirtless, wearing only the slacks he'd dressed in that morning, and the sheer masculine energy he was putting off made her blood surge in her veins.

"Now," he said again, in the low gruff voice of a man who was used to having his way. "Sing for me." His eyes were locked on her, acutely focused as if she were the only one in the world. It was a heady thing being the center of a powerful dragon's attention. It made her want to obey. Made her want to please him.

"You're not the boss of me," she said, flashing him a snarky smile.

He lowered his chin. "Please."

How could she refuse such a gentle and pleading dragon? She opened her mouth and sang the song she'd written about him.

*Your night, it crawls to meet*
*the darkness inside me.*
*Don't you know that your energy*
*is the thing making me me?*

*I was once a dying thing.*
*You helped me find my wings.*
*Now I fly among the stars,*
*free from you, free from us.*
*But it's cold without your fire.*
*It's cold without your fire.*
*If I could take the blame*
*and lure back your flame,*
*I'd hold you once again*
*And it would never be the saaaaame.*

He had her in his arms before she could finish the last note of the refrain. "Still magical," he said into her mouth. His fingers flew down the front of her blouse, and he pushed it from her shoulders. Her pants were next, his movements fast and precise. He tasted of tobacco and desire. She tried to respond, reached for the buckle on his belt, but he came at her like the ocean, his hands and mouth everywhere at once, overwhelming her senses, and she found it was impossible not to simply move with it, like jumping into the wave and allowing it to carry her in the swell.

In a heartbeat, he had her on the bed, both of them naked. He rolled her on top of him and stared up at her like she was his own personal goddess. "Tell Tom you're ready to sing at O2."

She stopped. "Isn't that risky? The concert is Saturday night. What if you can't bind us before then? I won't have my magic."

"Then sing without your magic. Tell your audience you've recovering from... whatever you told Tom you're having fixed. Your voice is incredible, Clarissa, just as it is. You are enough as you are. They will love you, not like I do, but enough for you to continue doing what you love while we figure this thing out."

She rose up on her knees, vividly aware of their nakedness and the fact he was pressed between her legs in the most delicious way. She wanted to feel him inside her, wanted to ride him and be ravished by him until she was spent and sated. But her mind fought against her body. This was important. This conversation was long overdue.

"But what's the point, Nathaniel? I told you I'm yours. I gave myself to you. What meaning would that have if I left again? My career takes me all over the world. I'm touring right now and for the next year. We'd be apart more than we'd be together."

"Only if you don't take me with you."

A lump formed in her throat. "Your home is here. So is your business."

"And they'll still be here when I return. Albert is proving a worthy apprentice, and I can help him from afar. Tempest and Laurel will take care of this house while I'm gone. Warwick can run the order."

She lowered her body flush with his. "You're serious. You'd do that for me?"

He took her face in his hands. "I'm too old a dragon to waste time worrying about geography. Call me your lover, your husband, or say nothing at all. Make me your bodyguard or personal assistant. I don't care. Just say we'll be together, and I'll follow you anywhere."

The warm flood of emotion that cascaded through her was overwhelming. She knew what this was. She'd seen it before. Been close to it before. But never allowed it in before. This was love. Unconditional love. "Yes. Oh yes, Nate."

Her lips crashed into his and her hips rose to position him under her. His mating trill vibrated against her lips as he slid inside. Oh, the feel of him. He stretched and filled her, lighting up every pleasure sensor in her body at once. The tips of her breasts brushed his chest, her hands braced against his ribs, and she started to move. He matched her thrust for thrust, their movements a dance of increasing need. Her skin tingled.

Nathaniel's hand brushed hot against her throat and skimmed down between her breasts. He lifted from the bed and caught one of her nipples in his mouth, flicking the tip with his tongue. Heat trailed around her ribs up her spine. His fingers were hot velvet.

Moving above him like this, on top of him, she could almost pretend she could contain all that power between her thighs. But his magic was a formidable thing. She felt it build in the air around her. Tendrils of dragon enchantment enfolded her, sinking into her flesh. She had none of her own magic now, but she could feel his pulsing inside her. The air was thick with it. It zinged along her skin, plucked at her nipples, circled her clit. Sweat broke out along the base of her neck and she tossed her head back and allowed the orgasm to crest, her inner muscles working overtime on his cock.

He growled and fisted her hips, finding his own release and shuddering beneath her. His pleasure fed hers until she collapsed on top of him, tucking her face into his neck.

When she was able to form words again, she whispered, "Will it always be like this?"

"Always."

"When will you go to Paragon to help Raven and your brothers?"

"Tomorrow."

"Do you want me to come with you?"

"No. It's too dangerous in your current state. But don't worry about me. I know what I'm doing. You stay here and do what you need to do to get ready for the show. Trust me, I'll be back in time to watch you take the stage."

"Will you take me someday?" she whispered. "To Paragon. I'd love to see where you grew up."

That seemed to sober him and she watched ice creep behind his eyes. "Maybe, if it's safe."

She kissed him on the cheek, climbed off him, and headed for the shower. She didn't allow herself to slump until she was safely on the other side of the door. She did trust him. Nathaniel was perfectly capable of taking care of himself. But anxiety wormed through her torso. It had been three centuries since Nathaniel had been to his home world. She didn't fully understand the politics, but she understood the danger, and once he left, she wouldn't take a deep breath again until he was back home.

# CHAPTER TWENTY-NINE

**Paragon**

Once they finished their meal, Raven was too tired for anything more, as was Gabriel. She thought she'd suffered in the dungeon, but Gabriel seemed exhausted. He hadn't shared many details about what the empress had made him do that night, but it was clear she'd worn him down. Raven and Gabriel crawled into bed together, and she drifted to sleep almost instantly in the shelter of his arms.

All too soon, a pounding came on the door. Raven opened her eyes, her lids feeling like sandpaper. Paragon's suns had begun to rise. There wasn't a clock in the room, but by the low placement of the suns in the sky, she knew it was very early. Her head told her she'd had less than four hour sleep. Beside her, Gabriel groaned.

The pounding came more persistently. "Prince Gabriel, I will be forced to enter if you don't respond."

"What do you want?" he growled.

"Empress Eleanor requests your presence in the dining room for breakfast."

"Tell her I need my rest. I can't support her agenda if I'm exhausted." Gabriel stared at Raven as he spoke and brushed his fingers along the side of her hair.

The door opened, and Raven tugged the blanket to her chest although she was fully dressed in the tights and tunic Gabriel had given her to wear last night. It was more for a sense of security than anything else. Gabriel, on the other hand, was out of the bed so fast the breeze from his wings spreading blew back her hair.

"Get out," he growled to the guards. But the two men in red-and-black uniforms weren't the only ones at the door. Eleanor herself strode in, wearing a red-and-purple gown that Raven thought belonged at a Met gala. It looked like it was constructed of woven, velvet-covered wire that formed a sort of cage around an underdress of silky material. It matched the red of Eleanor's lipstick. Blood red.

"What do you want?" Gabriel asked her.

"I want your compliance," she hissed. "I want your subordination! We start our day early in this kingdom, Gabriel. I can't help that you stayed up late entertaining your..." She waved her hand toward Raven. "Whatever this is."

"She's my wife!" he yelled. "My mate."

Eleanor rested her hands on her hips. "Impossible. Dragons are forbidden to mate with witches." Her gaze coasted down her nose at Raven in disgust. "With or without their power."

"She is my mate and she will always be my mate," Gabriel snapped. He lowered his body into a crouch and the temperature in the room rose several degrees.

Eleanor inclined her head and stared at him with feigned pity. "Take her back to the dungeon."

"No!" Gabriel's wings extended with a snap. He intercepted the first guard and slammed him into the wall. The man dropped into a heap like dirty laundry. The second guard stopped short, eyeing Gabriel tentatively.

Eleanor's ring glowed to life, and Raven watched a pulsing, magical shield expand between the guard and Gabriel. His talons bounced uselessly off it.

"Careful, Gabriel! If you want Raven in your bed tonight, you will follow my commands. Privileges are only given to those I can trust."

Gabriel looked back at Raven with desperate, frantic eyes, the muscle in his jaw working overtime. Raven feared he might crack.

"It's okay," she said, although she dreaded what would happen next. She couldn't watch Gabriel tear himself apart trying to protect her. "I'll go. I was fine yesterday. I'll be fine today." She pushed off the blankets and rose from the bed.

"See. Your pet understands."

"She's my mate, not my pet," Gabriel said through his teeth.

Eleanor raised her chin. "Get dressed and meet me in the dining hall. There's much to do today."

"What about Raven? She needs breakfast too." Gabriel gestured toward Raven.

With a sway of her chin, Eleanor said, "I'm not a monster, Gabriel. She will be fed. Now move."

The guard took Raven by the elbow, and with one last glance back toward her husband, she was ushered from the room and back to hell.

She didn't think it was possible, but her cell felt even hotter than before. She returned to the far wall, back into the dark corner that seemed minimally cooler than the rest of the cell. Despite Eleanor's promise, she was offered no breakfast, but there was water and it was still cool when it flowed down her throat.

"Did you get it?" the stranger asked through the iron grid between them.

"No. I was never allowed to leave my husband's room."

He growled. "You must try harder. If they let you out tonight, do whatever you need to do, but get that box. Without it, we are both doomed."

"How can I trust you? You could be working for her, trying to get me to do something that would land me in here permanently. She'd love the excuse."

The dragon beside her laughed low and deep. "Smart. It's true, that would be something she'd do. I bet Gabriel warned you to think that way, didn't he?"

"Yes. He's less trusting than I am, thank goodness."

"There is no goodness in this palace to thank. As always, Gabriel's training has made him as annoying as a jurinfly during summer."

"I don't know what that is."

He laughed. "Of course you don't. He met you on Earth. You've never been here before have you?"

She remained silent rather than explain her previous visit.

"A jurinfly is a biting insect that is attracted to sweat. Even dragons sweat in summer. A cloud of jurinflies will pick the flesh off your bones if given the chance."

Something occurred to her and her eyes narrowed in the dark. "You said as always. Do you know Gabriel?"

"Everyone in the kingdom knows Gabriel."

"But does Gabriel know you?" Silence. She was on to something. "Why don't you tell me who you are?"

"It wouldn't help. He wouldn't believe me."

"Try me."

"The box. If you bring me the box, I can get us out of here."

She'd had just about enough of this. "If you want to get in my good graces, stop calling my husband an annoying insect and tell me more about this object you want me to steal. What's inside the box? Why do you want it so badly?"

He hesitated. She tried to look through the grate but could only see flashes of pale skin. Not enough to build a description for Gabriel.

"Inside the box is a stone," he said. "A jewel. Specifically, a garnet. The stone holds my magic. It was taken from me before I was imprisoned here."

Raven furrowed her brow. A dragon's magic when they were in their human form was housed in a gemstone ring made from the same jewel as their heart. As far as she was aware, there was no way to remove the ring without killing the dragon. This man had said he was a dragon, a dragon whose power was taken from him. Who was he? How had Eleanor taken his ring? Why was he here?

"How long have you been in this dungeon?" she asked.

"A few weeks." His voice cracked. "At least I think so. The only way I know to gauge the time is by marking off when they bring food and water."

Raven lowered her voice. "Where were you before that?"

This time he hesitated even longer. "An island off the coast of Everfield."

"Everfield. That's the fairy kingdom?"

"Yes."

"Where Aborella is originally from?"

"Yes, although the people there would be loath to claim her as their own. They consider her an abomination."

She chuckled. "I believe I'd enjoy meeting the people of Everfield."

He sighed heavily. "You'd love it there. The food is like nothing you've ever tasted. Fairies have a complete connection to nature. They can collect the pollen from a flower as easily as any bee, and they cook with it. When you bite into a crizzle roll, it tastes like spring come to life in your mouth. The people themselves glow in the dark, and when they sing..."

He trailed off, and Raven could have sworn she heard a sob on the other side of the grate. "Everfield is home for you," she said softly.

"Yes. I was born here, but Everfield is home, and if I had it to do again, I would have never come back here. This place was always a prison. I was stupid to think I could make a difference."

"I'm sorry. I hope... I hope somehow you find your way back there."

His voice was all grit the next time he spoke. "Find the box and I will."

# CHAPTER THIRTY

Nathaniel dressed in his finest suit. There was no label. The oreads had made it for him out of a fabric they'd woven themselves. It was as light as linen but draped like the finest wool, perfectly tailored to his athletic physique. The suit was important, not because he wanted to impress anyone but because it had pockets, hiding places, and built-in enchantments that came in useful in a pinch.

He loaded those pockets with his pipe, his tarot cards, and a selection of Warwick's specialized tobaccos. He also brought his shadow mail candle. He didn't bother with weapons; he was no good with them anyway.

He joined Alexander, who seemed comfortable in a white T-shirt, leather jacket, and jeans, and Rowan, who was dressed in a red sundress and a pair of Louboutins.

"Really, Rowan?" Nathaniel shook his head at her stilettos. "We're going to Paragon to recover our brothers, not a garden party."

She shrugged. "If you can wear a suit, I can wear this dress."

"Can you even run quietly in those?" He furrowed his

brow.

She rolled her neck. "As well as in a pair of Nikes." Rowan ran her pinky nail along the edge of her perfectly applied lipstick. "I'm a dragon female, Nate. I have all sorts of secret talents."

"I can attest to that," Nick said. "I have personally witnessed her run up a marble staircase in high heels without making a sound. It's uncanny."

"It's a gift." She beamed at her mate and directing a flirty wink in his direction.

Together they were an unlikely set, Nathaniel thought. Alexander looked pale and wired. Rowan looked like a contestant in the Miss New York pageant. And Nathaniel might have been attending a play or the opera. But they were three dragons. That kind of magic could not be underestimated.

"So, who opens the portal?" Rowan asked nervously.

"I do," Nathaniel said. "I can target the palace grounds, inside the wards."

Rowan did a double take. "I know you said something about that before, but how? The wards are specifically designed to be impervious to magical invasion."

Nathaniel grinned. "I know. I helped design those wards. You might say I have a key to the back door."

Alexander shook his head. "You don't think she's changed the locks since we've been gone?"

He shrugged. "I'm not sure Mother ever understood the spell to begin with, but I suppose it's possible. There's only one way to find out."

Rowan regarded him with mounting respect. "Why do I feel like there's a lot Alexander and I don't know about you, Nathaniel? Didn't we grow up in the same palace? When were you helping Mom with wards?"

"We may have had the same parents, but we didn't have the same childhood," Nathaniel said. "Tonight I'm going to show you a part of the palace you likely never knew existed. It's time."

The three turned to their respective mates to say their goodbyes. Nathaniel took Clarissa in his arms as Rowan allowed Nick to sweep her off her feet as if she were human, and Alexander and Maiara embraced.

"Keep your head attached to your shoulders," Clarissa said.

He raised an eyebrow. "If Grindylow couldn't take it off, I think my chances are better than average."

"Are you going to have the world's worst family reunion?" she asked. "Make up for three centuries of missed Mother's Days with a ricin-flavored ice cream cake?"

"I prefer mustard-gas-emitting lilies. What do you take me for, Clarissa? I have some standards after all."

"Some." She rose on her tiptoes to whisper in his ear in her most sultry voice. "Thankfully, for my sake, not too many." She gave him a kiss that belonged in a bordello, and he was of half a mind to delay their quest and haul her to bed for another few hours, but she pulled back before he could get carried away.

"Seriously, this is safe, right?" she asked softly.

He scoffed. "We are going to sneak into the Obsidian Palace, free my brothers and the witch, and if all goes well, few others will even see us."

"If all goes well..." Her face softened, all the teasing and levity melting away. "Please come back to me."

He reached into his interior pocket and showed her the silver taper. "Stay close to your shadow mail candle. I'll send a message if I'm delayed."

She nodded. "Will it work?"

He winked. "Theoretically, yes, but time flows differently between our worlds. Try not to worry if you don't hear from me for a few days."

"Days! Nathaniel, what happened to in and out?"

"Think of it like two rivers running parallel to each other. The water in each flows at a different pace. When I open the portal, I will be effectively jumping from one river into another. At the moment of my crossing, there is a temporal connection between the two streams. We could theoretically call it X or just the starting point. But as I stay in Paragon, hours and days will pass at a different rate than your river here. X + P in Paragon, X + E on Earth. There is no exact equation to predict when I will step back into this time flow, although I will attempt to make it soon."

"I'll keep the candle with me always," she promised.

He backed away from her and turned to his siblings. "Ready?"

They parted reluctantly from their mates and gathered at the edge of the Persian rug in the parlor. He lit his pipe and held out his elbows for Rowan and Alexander to link to.

"Here goes the old college try. Let's hope Mummy hasn't reset the password."

Blowing a smoke ring, he waited for the magic to form a dial, a pentagram with ancient runic symbols in each of its quadrants. His amethyst ring glowed brighter, and he drew the symbol for Paragon in the air. Reality ripped in two like a sheet of paper, its edges curling as if someone held a lighter to it.

Nathaniel inserted his fingers into the dial and twisted and turned like he was cracking a safe. The magic glowed brighter, then dissipated. Everything went dark, then split open to reveal a Paragonian sunset. Together they took one giant step forward.

# CHAPTER THIRTY-ONE

*Paragon*

Raven woke sore and thirsty on the stone floor of her cell. Her tongue felt like a dry slab of leather in her mouth, but there was no water to be had. The guards had not refilled the trough between her cell and the stranger's that afternoon. The stranger had allowed her the last hot, sulfur-smelling cup, suggesting she needed it more as a human. That might have been true, but she suspected it was also a ploy to earn her trust. He'd gone quiet after that, and she wondered if he regretted his choice.

Two guards arrived at the door of her cell.

"Come with us now!" one yelled to her.

"I can't," she rasped. Her muscles were cramping, likely from dehydration. No way could she walk on her own.

The guards entered her cell and hauled her to her feet, then ushered her up the stairs and back to Gabriel's room. When Gabriel saw her, he rushed to gather her into his arms. A moment later she was in his lap and cool water poured into her mouth. She sipped it. Turned her head to cough, then greedily drank the glass dry.

"What did they do to you?"

"The dungeon is hot. Too hot for a human without magic."

He sat her in a comfortable chair and poured her another glass of water.

"There isn't enough water for both of us, me and the dragon I told you about."

"By the Mountain, I will kill her," he murmured. "Did she even feed you?"

"No." Raven tried not to cry. She wasn't sure she could produce tears anyway.

Gabriel removed a cloth from his jacket and unfolded it. There was a pastry inside. Without a second thought, she snatched it from his hands and took a bite. The warm, savory flavors, similar to beef, garlic, and thyme, filled her mouth. She ate quickly, desperate to sate her hunger.

"I didn't take any chances. I snuck this from the buffet."

Buffet. A flicker of anger and jealousy sparked within her. While she was suffering in the dungeon, he was flirting with princesses from the five kingdoms at banquet after banquet. She ate what remained of the pastry, shaking her head.

"Raven, I wouldn't play along with Eleanor if I didn't know she would kill you if I didn't."

He reached for her hand, but she pulled it away, covering her face as she choked back tears. Her skin felt crusty where her sweat had dried.

"I'm tired," she said.

"Do you want to go to bed?" he asked softly.

"I need a bath. I'm covered in sweat." She ran her hand over her hair, which was now matted and caked.

Gabriel shook his head. "I won't let her take you again."

"How will you stop her, Gabriel? She has an army. She's separated you and Tobias to weaken you. She'll snap my neck at the first sign you aren't compliant."

"I'll refuse unless she betters your conditions."

"Don't kid yourself. Eleanor is a master of lies and deception. The minute she's appeased you, I will get more and worse. And if you push her too far, she will kill you, Gabriel, the same as Marius. And she'll find a way to twist it in her favor. You broke the law when you mated a witch. She's within her rights to call for your head. She'll pretend she didn't know."

"I hate this."

"I do too."

He swept her out of the chair and carried her into the bath, started the water running.

While he was helping her get undressed, she made up her mind. "We have to find the box so I can bring it to the prisoner in the dungeon."

"Raven, we talked about this. We can't trust him."

"He told me there's a stone in it. I think it's his ring."

Gabriel poured bubbles into the water and stirred them in with his hand. "Impossible. Our rings cannot be removed."

"He all but confirmed it. I think your mother figured out how to magically amputate it. He has no magic now. He says if I bring him the ring, he can bust us both out of the dungeon."

Gabriel shook his head. "Now I know he's a fraud. The dungeon is near the center of the mountain. There's no way out but the way you went in. And you know as well as I do that the cells are impervious to dragon magic. We were in one with you the day we were brought here, remember?"

"I don't think he's a fraud. He knows about you. He said he was born here, and you know, Gabriel, I got the sense he meant *here*, like in the palace."

Gabriel's face fell. "Then why won't he tell you his name?"

"I don't know."

She slipped into the cool water and washed herself quickly while he retrieved a fresh set of clothes for her. When he returned to her side, his expression was cold, somewhere between rage and calculated resolve. "You can't do anything about this stranger's ring, Raven. You need to rest."

"But—"

"Trust me." He lowered his chin and fixed her with a fiery stare. "I will find a way to make things better for you."

She did trust him, but she wasn't sure this was something he could fix. Could anyone? And as for the ring, even if she'd wanted to find the box, her body wasn't strong enough to leave this room. Gabriel was right that there was nothing she could do.

He helped her out of the bath and into bed, but he didn't crawl in beside her right away. From beneath the blankets, she watched him walk the periphery of the room, his emerald ring glowing as he muttered something and drew symbols in the air. He was warding their room, the same way dragons, for all of their existence, warded their treasure. She was his treasure and would always be.

She'd tasted Eleanor's power and Aborella's. She knew the ward wouldn't hold once mommy dearest decided to take it down. The empress would drain the magic from the room or threaten her life or Tobias's until her beloved removed it. But he was doing what he could. Gabriel knew this world. He knew his mother. And Raven trusted him.

She closed her eyes and allowed herself to sleep.

# CHAPTER THIRTY-TWO

Nathaniel appeared at the side entrance of the Obsidian Palace with his brother and sister flanking him. This wasn't the beautiful front garden where the royals of Paragon entertained their Highborn guests. It was a servants' entrance—wild, overgrown, and infested with vermin that feasted on the rubbish waiting for disposal. Humidity hit him squarely in the face along with the tropical scent of overgrown vegetation that warred with the stench of refuse.

"Welcome back to Paragon," Nathaniel said. "Let's hope this visit is short. I can already tell you it won't be sweet."

"By the Mountain, you've done it," Rowan whispered. "We're inside the ward."

Alexander released his arm, his gaze passing over the door and then tracing up the side of the mountain. "I fucking hate this place."

Rowan rested her hands on her hips. "I'm not much of a fan either. What's the plan, Nathaniel?"

Nathaniel tested the door and found it unlocked. Good.

He'd thought as much. At this time of day in Paragon, the day shift would be finishing their rounds and transitioning their duties. He'd hoped they wouldn't have locked up yet. He reached into his pocket and pulled out his pipe, tamping down Warwick's tobacco and giving it a light. He worked the smoke over his tongue, gathering magic.

"Really, brother, is this the time for a smoke?" Alexander asked.

Nathaniel glanced at his brother and nodded, then released three tiny smoke hummingbirds from his mouth. He cracked the door to the servants' entrance and allowed the birds inside.

"First we must find out where Gabriel, Tobias, and Raven are. Thus the birds," Nathaniel said. "Then we divide and conquer." He waited, listening at the door.

Alexander narrowed his eyes at his brother. "It's frightening what you can do with that pipe, and this is coming from someone who witnessed Raven bring his mate back from the dead."

"You should see what I can do with a stone circle." Nathaniel concentrated on his smoke. A tiny green puff rose from his pipe, and he opened the door. The three smoke birds fluttered in front of him, then flew directly back into his mouth. He inhaled them, digesting what information they contained, then coughed violently.

Rowan patted him on the back. "What is it? What did they see?"

"Tobias is in his room. He appears well. Gabriel's room is warded. They could not confirm he's inside it, but the magic does seem to have been performed from the inside. Likely his ward, not Mother's. There's a prisoner in the dungeon, but the birds could not identify who it is. The enchantments down there likely interfered with my magic."

"I can get Tobias," Rowan said. "His old room was across from mine. I know a servants' passage that was rarely used when I was a kid. I used it to sneak out."

Alexander frowned. "I can try Gabriel's room. If he did lay the ward, he'll let me in."

Nathaniel agreed. "I'll investigate the dungeon. The wards there are complex and there will be guards. If Mother is holding one of them there, I'll have the best chance of getting them out."

"It's a plan," Rowan said.

"It's very important we meet back here. You can't open a portal without me on this side of the wards. If you run into trouble..."

Rowan brushed her hair back from her face. "We get it. Don't get into trouble or we may be fighting our way out the front door."

Nathaniel tipped his head in agreement, then blew a puff of gray smoke over both of them. Members of the Obsidian Guard were trained to detect invisible assailants, a necessity when most of the population of Paragon could become invisible. "That will mask your scent for the next several hours. Make them count."

Both Alexander and Rowan blinked out of sight. The door opened and he felt a disturbance in the air as they disappeared inside. Following suit, Nathaniel made himself invisible and slipped into the hall. Sounds of pots and pans clanging in the kitchen met his ears and then the gossiping voices of the kitchen staff.

"Sir Tobias is fantastically handsome. I'd never seen him up close before. He was gone before I started working here. I finally understand his reputation," a woman's voice said.

"Mountain yes, but Gabriel is far more desirable. He's

the heir after all. The dragon who catches his eye could be queen," another woman quipped.

Nathaniel glanced into the kitchen as he passed, frowning. It sounded like his brothers had been welcomed back into the fold. And odder still, the servants seemed not to respect Gabriel's mated relationship. That was rare for dragons.

"Don't you believe it," a heavyset woman washing dishes growled out. "The empress will never step down. Mated or not, Gabriel will be playing second fiddle to his mother for centuries. Mark my words. You couldn't pry the power from that woman's hands if it were tied to a mountain horse."

A chill of apprehension ran along Nathaniel's shoulders, and he hurried toward the dungeon. The servant women didn't even seem to know about Raven. That was ominous. He'd never met the witch, didn't know her well enough to inherently care for her well-being, but Clarissa's power was reliant on Raven surviving. Avery's happiness too. They were three sisters, and although he didn't yet understand the nature of their connection, he knew his mate would never have what she wanted most without it.

He reached the stairs that led down into the dungeon. Two guards stood at attention on either side of the door. He drew a puff from his pipe and blew a cloud of purple smoke in their faces.

"Do you smell that?" one guard asked the other.

Before either could react, their eyes rolled to the back of their heads and they flopped to the floor as if their bodies had gone boneless. He stepped over them and entered the stairwell to the dungeon.

As he descended, he took another puff, this time blowing blue smoke rings, one after another. The magic drifted out in front of him, passing undisturbed around the bend of the staircase, and he descended slowly behind them. It wasn't until he reached the third level that the smoke slid into an invisible barrier before circling back toward him. A current of air brushed his cheek, and he took another puff of tobacco and blew. The outline of a man appeared in the smoke.

"Who's there?" the invisible guard asked before slumping onto the landing, unconscious.

"Thank you, Warwick, old pal. I knew I liked you for a reason." Nathaniel used his foot to shove the man aside, then reached down and retrieved the set of keys from the man's belt, slowly and carefully slipping them into his own pocket to avoid making any noise.

He strode through the door into the dungeon behind another blue ring of smoke. Apparently palace security considered it almost impossible for someone to get this far, because there were no more guards here, just torches illuminating a row of cells behind iron bars.

He strode down the aisle, peering into each of the cells. Empty. Empty. Empty. He paused in front of the fourth cell. The smell of human was strong, but the dark room was empty. She wasn't here anymore.

*Fuck.*

A growl rumbled from the next cell over. The stench of filthy dragon met his nose, an animal scent, unwashed and feral. Nathaniel eased over and peered into the shadowy interior. A man paced in the shadows, pale skin, chestnut hair. Nathaniel moved closer to get a better look, but the dragon was agitated, mumbling to himself, and Nathaniel couldn't see his face.

"Got to bring the box. She's got to bring the box. Tell Gabriel to bring the box," he mumbled.

"How do you know Gabriel?" Nathaniel asked.

The dragon swung his head around and raced toward the bars, his eyes sweeping the hall. He was filthy and his hair hung in his face, but Nathaniel recognized him immediately. He dropped his invisibility.

"Sylas?" He hadn't seen his younger brother in centuries. Not since they'd parted ways in northern Italy back in 1698. But he would never forget the face of his kindhearted sibling.

"Nathaniel? Praise the Mountain it's you."

Nathaniel fished the keys from his pocket and began trying each one. The lock rattled with his efforts.

"Why are you in here?" Nathaniel asked.

Sylas opened his mouth and closed it again. "You mean you didn't come for me?"

Nathaniel furrowed his brow. "I didn't even know you were here until this very minute."

"Then why *are* you here?"

He didn't have time for this. "This is very important, Sylas. Have you seen a girl, Gabriel's mate?"

"Yes. They bring her to the cell beside this one during the day. Poor human bakes in here for twelve or more hours before they take her back upstairs. I was afraid she'd die today. It's not meant for her kind down here."

"It's not meant for any kind." Nathaniel frowned.

"So that's who you came for, the girl?"

Nathaniel looked both ways. "Perhaps, but now I'm here for you."

Finally the latch clicked and he opened the cell door. His brother stepped into full light. He was thin. Pale. Wild-eyed. And dirty.

Nathaniel growled. "How long have you been here?"

"Three weeks, I think. Maybe longer."

Nathaniel bristled. "Did they feed you at all?"

"Every second or third day," Sylas said flatly.

Nathaniel felt sick. If Eleanor could do this to her own son, she could do it to anyone. "Make yourself invisible. I'll help you get out."

The agony that passed through his brother's expression shook Nathaniel. When Sylas finally spoke, his voice was raw with emotion. "I can't. She took my ring."

Nathaniel looked down at his brother's bare hand and had to swallow down the urge to vomit. "How? She'd have to... she'd have to remove its connection to your heart."

He nodded slowly and his face turned into a mask of suffering. "It hurts, Nathaniel, when she does it. It's dark magic. Blood magic." He rubbed his chest. "It feels like she stripped my soul right out of me. I watched her put it in a box and store it on a shelf in her goddamned library. For weeks I've sat in that cell without it, feeling empty, feeling like I'd never be whole again. I have to get it back."

"You asked Raven to bring it to you. That's what you meant by wanting her to bring you the box."

"Yes."

Nathaniel opened the cell that whiffed of human. "What's the girl like?"

"Kind. Honest. Nothing like Mother."

Nathaniel spotted something on the floor in the corner and swept it up. *Interesting.* He slid it into his pocket. "So why were you arrested in the first place?"

"Rebellion," Sylas said. "We call ourselves the Defenders of the Goddess. We've been gathering forces from all five kingdoms. More and more citizens see that what Eleanor is doing is wrong. Someone had to do something, so I stepped up."

Nathaniel did a double take. "But how did you end up back here? I left you in Italy."

"I returned," Sylas said, his brows rising. "A long time ago. Something didn't seem right to me about Marius's death."

Nathaniel waited for more of an explanation, but none came.

"How is it that Gabriel fell in love with a human anyway?" Sylas asked as Nathaniel came out of the cell.

"Didn't. She's a witch," Nathaniel said bluntly. "Eleanor stole her power the same as she stole yours."

Sylas grunted. "A witch? It's a wonder Mother hasn't killed her already. But then Raven did tell me Eleanor needed something to hold over our brother's head."

Nathaniel thought about that along with the conversation he'd overheard among the kitchen staff. It all made more sense now. He tucked his pipe between his teeth and held out his hand to his brother. "Come, let's find your ring. I'm going to need your help."

Sylas grabbed on and Nathaniel turned them both invisible. He led his brother out of the dungeon, over the collapsed guard, and into the palace proper.

## CHAPTER THIRTY-THREE

Raven felt like she'd barely fallen to sleep when she heard a familiar voice come from the direction of the door. At first she thought she might be dreaming, but a loud whisper came again from that direction.

"Gabriel? Are you in there?"

She stirred and shook Gabriel by the shoulder. He grumbled out something that sounded like "not yet."

"Gabriel, there's someone at the door. It sounds like... Alexander."

When he didn't move, Raven scrambled out of bed and opened the door. She could see Alexander through the wavy magic of Gabriel's ward although she knew he would not be able to see her from the outside. He looked nervous and glanced furtively down the hall.

"Raven? Gabriel?" he whispered. "If you're there, let me in."

Finally awake, Gabriel leaped to his feet, his wings flexing. He held a hand in front of Raven's chest. "Wait. It could be a trick. Dragons can make themselves appear any way they choose. That could be Eleanor."

Alexander couldn't see through the ward, but apparently he could hear through it. His expression turned annoyed.

"By the Mountain, Gabriel, I watched Raven bring Maiara back from the dead with a bowl and some stones. Don't leave me out here. I had to snap this idiot's neck to get this far, and I'd prefer not to have to incapacitate anyone else." He reached beyond the door, just out of sight, and lifted the head of a guard into view, then set it back down.

"Is he dead?" Raven stage-whispered.

Gabriel shook his head. "He is a dragon. Alexander broke his neck, but in order to kill him he'd have to completely sever the head. He'll heal, but he'll take a long nap before he wakes."

"It's Alexander. Let him in!" Raven said.

Gabriel's emerald ring glowed to life. He drew a few symbols in the air. Alexander passed through the ward, and Raven closed the door behind him. Clearly Gabriel no longer questioned Alexander's identity because he embraced him before Raven could even say hello. She was so tired she felt nauseated, but she was also incredibly excited to see a kind face.

"What are you doing here? How did you get in?" Gabriel asked.

"We have to go. We're busting you out of here," Alexander said.

Gabriel's eyes widened. "How? There's a legion of Obsidian Guards protecting the boundaries of the palace."

"Nathaniel," Alexander said.

"You found him? Truly?"

"Yes, we did. In London. He understands Mother's magic. It turns out he helped her develop it."

"What?" Gabriel's eyes narrowed.

"He has a magical key that got us through the side of the ward. All we have to do is get you out the servants' entrance behind the kitchens and Nathaniel can get us all home." He pointed a hand toward the door.

Wild-eyed, Gabriel took Raven by the arm.

"Wait!" She turned toward Alexander. If she didn't ask now, she'd be afraid to ask when her voice might give them away. "How is the baby?"

"Li'l Puff is fine," Alexander said.

"Li'l Puff?" Raven shook her head.

Alexander blushed and rubbed the back of his neck. "Your, uh, sister named it. We couldn't call it 'the egg' forever."

Her mouth gaped as Gabriel ushered her through the door and turned them both invisible. A trail of bodies dressed in red and black lined the hall, and Raven raised her eyebrows. She hadn't known Alexander had it in him. But then, he'd fought the Wendigo and won and he'd trained in the same pits as Gabriel. Since they were heirs to the kingdom, their father, Killian, had made certain they were prepared to lead the armies of Paragon. They'd all been trained as soldiers long ago.

But Alexander, having spent so long grieving his lost mate, Maiara, had always seemed more fragile to her than the others. Perhaps that fragility had been connected to his grief. Certainly, based on what she was seeing now, he hadn't lost his edge.

They were almost to the end of the hall when a tall and handsomely dark, uniformed soldier appeared in their path, a familiar-looking orb in his hand and a silver rod Raven knew was a weapon at his hip. The orb was a Paragonian grenade, and Raven was all too familiar with what it could do to a person. It was the Paragonian equivalent of nerve gas. It would cause her muscles to seize to the point she couldn't breathe. Without her magic, she wasn't sure she would survive it.

"I know you're there." He glanced at the bodies of the soldiers in the hall and lifted the orb. "Touch me and we all go down."

Gabriel released her hand and lunged. The soldier dodged, holding the grenade above his head. Gabriel's hands wrapped around his neck.

The man's nostrils flared. "Careful, *Gabriel*. Will your mate survive it now that she's a fragile human?" he rasped. His gaze fixed on Raven, who was no longer invisible now that she wasn't touching Gabriel.

Gabriel dropped his invisibility and Alexander followed suit. "Ransom, let us go," Gabriel said. "By order of the prince of Paragon."

"Who do you think you're fooling?" Ransom grinned condescendingly and shook his head. The dimple in his chin reminded Raven of some darkly evil Ken doll. "It's been a long time since you held any power in this court."

"Fuck you, Ransom," Alexander said, eyeing the man's uniform. "Captain of the Guard? They replaced Scoria with you? Mountain, Mother is scraping the bottom of the barrel."

Ransom's gaze raked over Alexander. "You should talk. You look like you've spent the past three hundred years in the underworld."

"Don't try to butter me up," Alexander said. "Compliments don't make you less of a douchebag."

"How exactly did you get past the guards at the gate?" Ransom asked him pointedly.

"Never mind that now. Ransom, you must let us go,"

Gabriel said. "Can't you see what Eleanor is doing? How long do you think she can get away with this?"

Ransom snorted. "Forever. We will get away with this forever."

"We? You can't possibly think..." Raven stopped herself. Of course he did. This was how Eleanor worked. She made the vulnerable believe she was partnering with them. She'd probably told this young dragon she wanted him as her consort, possibly even slept with him. He'd do anything for her. Until it suited her to have him out of the way.

Gabriel spread his wings and lowered himself into a fighting stance. "Alexander, get Raven out of here."

Alexander shook his head and whispered, "Be patient." Of course! Alexander wasn't here alone. All they had to do was distract Ransom until help arrived.

"Yes, my son, patience is a virtue." Eleanor turned the corner and entered the hall behind Ransom, Aborella by her side. "I am surprised to see you here, Alexander. Aborella, please show my sons back to Gabriel's room and Raven back to the dungeon."

Aborella's fingers crackled with dark lightning, and Gabriel nudged Raven behind him. "You're not taking her anywhere!"

Eleanor opened her mouth to speak, then balked, her head whipping around to stare down the narrow hall to their left. She frowned. "Ransom, Aborella, take these fools back to Gabriel's room and lock them inside until I return. It appears we have another visitor."

"Shall I call more men in to help, Your Highness?"

"No," Eleanor said. "I'll take care of this one myself."

Nathaniel strode into the palace library and inhaled deeply. There was no one here. He released Sylas's hand.

"This wasn't where she did it. It was here, but it wasn't." Sylas rubbed his forehead, his eyes wide.

"Of course not." Nathaniel waved a hand around the room. "This is all for show." He pointed at the large grimoire under glass. "Do you think my mother would keep her grimoire in an unwarded room, even if that room was inside a fortress? No. She's not that stupid. This library is a distraction, and the memory you have in your head of where she hid your ring is a false one."

He dug his nails into the side of his head. "The girl..."

"Even if she'd tried to find it, she would have failed. Mother keeps her magic the same as she keeps her treasure, well hidden and guarded by the only person she ever actually trusted—herself." *And me*, Nathaniel finished in his head. He knew it was true, and it still hurt to admit it.

He weaved through the shelves and stopped before a tapestry on the southernmost wall. It was a needlepoint of Hera in her garden of golden apples. He remembered it from his youth, ran his fingers across its stitching. The wall behind it was hard, solid.

"How do we get inside?"

"I have a trick for that." Nathaniel tamped out his pipe and dumped the tobacco, then repacked it with a different blend. "While I'm doing this, tell me about what brought you back to Paragon."

Sylas leaned his back against the wall beside the tapestry and frowned. "You won't believe it."

"Try me."

"All of you were going north once we reached Italy. I

decided to go in the opposite direction, back the way we'd come."

Nathaniel continued carefully layering magical tobacco but gave Sylas a sideways glance.

"I thought it would be safer. Mother had said to stay apart, but you, Xavier, and Colin headed in the same direction. It didn't make sense to me. So I returned to Greece. Spoke more to the oreads. They told me about an island, one that humans couldn't reach. It was called Aeaea."

Nathaniel paused. "The home of the mythological goddess Circe?"

Sylas snorted. "She is no myth, Nathaniel, and her island exists south of Rome in the Tyrrhenian Sea. The goddess still resides there. I've met her myself."

"Sounds like the perfect hiding place. How did you end up here?" Nathaniel asked as he lit the tobacco.

"I fell in love with a fairy named Dianthe. She invited me back to her homeland of Everfield."

"Everfield? As in the kingdom of Everfield?"

He inclined his head. "Yes. Aeaea straddles worlds, Nathaniel. We took a ship to Everfield, where I met Dianthe's family and learned what Mother and Brynhoff never wanted us to know. They've been tyrants for centuries, bleeding the other kingdoms dry, rewarding the corrupt leaders that keep the people in rags, and returning just enough to them to make it seem like the kingdom of Paragon is keeping them afloat when, in actuality, they are hoarding riches at the expense of the other four territories. They've been doing it since before we were born. Corruption among the Highborn keeps anything from changing. Eleanor has them in her gilded cage. They feast on the suffering of their people."

Nathaniel didn't have time to fully digest what Sylas

was saying. He needed to focus on the task in front of him. He brought the pipe to his lips and blew a puff of smoke against the tapestry. The smoke formed a pentagram, similar to the one he'd used to break through the wards around the palace, but this magic was even stronger. The runes marking each of the sections were specifically designed to analyze the magic behind the tapestry and find its weaknesses. He had known the recipe for the wards around the palace. This magic he did not know, so he had to deconstruct the components himself.

He reached out and turned the symbol, reading the runes like they were numbers on a dial, instructions to unlock his mother's ward. The smoke had read her magic beautifully, and when he mastered the break, the tapestry fluttered.

"After you," he said, brushing the tapestry aside.

Sylas looked between him and the open mouth of the treasure room beyond and tentatively strode inside. With a snap of his fingers, Nathaniel lit the candelabra that circled the room. The pile of treasure at the far end rivaled any he'd ever seen, at least five times the size of his own. An entire family of dragons could sleep inside its riches.

"She certainly hasn't denied herself any good thing, has she?" Sylas said gruffly.

"No." Nathaniel moved his focus to the front of the room where shelves of magical texts, dried herbs, and crystals lined the walls. He remembered doing magic in this setup, although back then these things were in a parlor in a separate area of the house. As he'd suspected, Mother had become more protective of her magic over the centuries.

He glanced down to where an arcane circle marked the stone floor. "This was where she performed the spell to strip you of your magic," Nathaniel said. "Do you remember where she put the box with your ring?"

Sylas closed his eyes. "I can see a black box closing, my ring inside, and then she's putting it up on a shelf, behind a book called *The Saddle of Arythmetes*. I feel small, like I'm a child."

"Hmmm." Nathaniel cursed.

Clearly that was a planted memory, meant to humiliate him. It wasn't enough to take his power, she had to make him feel helpless. Nathaniel pondered the best way to find his brother's ring. If he swapped out his tobacco, he could produce another hummingbird, but this room was so steeped in his mother's magic he was afraid the smoky beast would not be able to sense the ring.

Instead, he tried to think like his mother. She'd want it somewhere safe. This was her son's immortality, and given that Sylas was leading a rebellion against her, she'd prefer to keep him alive with something to hold over him. He scanned the shelves.

His eyes caught on a dragon skull. A baby by the size and shape. The skull rested on the uppermost shelf, its dark, empty eyes glaring toward the circle with hollow antipathy. Whose skull had it been? Which dragon child had been murdered to bring her the power of its blood or bones? His stomach turned as he spotted a rolling ladder and pulled it over, then climbed to look into the eye socket of the murdered baby.

Just as he'd suspected. She was a sicker bitch than he'd thought, hiding her son's heart and magic in the skeleton of her victim. He reached in and pulled out the black box.

"That's it. That's the one!" Sylas reached for it, but Nathaniel shook his head.

"See these symbols?" He pointed to the arcane marks all

over the polished ebony. "This is magically bound shut. The spell must be broken, not forced. If you try to force it, it will destroy what's inside."

Sylas folded his arms and bent in two as if his stomach hurt. He moaned softly.

"Easy, brother. If I can break Mother's treasure ward, I can break this one. Give me a moment." He gave Warwick's tobacco a couple of sure puffs, set the box down on the workbench beyond the arcane circle, and blew out the symbol again. For a moment the smoke rearranged itself, finding the right symbols, then it formed another dial. Nathaniel gripped it at its center and set to work on creating the key.

A pulse of energy rolled through him, almost knocking him off his feet. He kept going. Almost there. Almost there.

"Did you feel that?" Sylas said nervously. "Nathaniel?"

The lock clicked. He opened the box, and inside was his brother's garnet. He tore it from the satin mount and tossed it to his brother, who slid it on his finger and moaned as light shimmered across his skin.

"Praise the Mountain!" Sylas's voice trembled with relief. His wings extended, and Nathaniel watched him draw a deep, quivering breath, his pale skin taking on a slight golden glow.

"Prepare yourself. Mother knows we are here, and she's on her way."

"How?" Sylas's gaze roved wildly toward the library.

Nathaniel got to work changing out the tobacco in his pipe once more. He was about to need the heavy artillery. "That pulse you felt was the alarm she set on the box I just opened. It was undetectable. I tripped it."

"So she's coming here now? Shouldn't we run?" Sylas asked frantically.

Nathaniel held the freshly lit pipe between his teeth. He withdrew the shadow mail candle from his pocket and lit it up, then removed what he'd found in the dungeon earlier and laid it on the table beside the candle. A lock of Raven's hair. If Aborella had taken a lock of Clarissa's hair before unbinding the sisters, then it was likely hair that could rebind them. Clarissa would have her own and Avery's, but this, this could change everything. Quickly he licked his finger and scrolled a message to Clarissa, then watched as the shadows twisted around the hair and carried it and his message to the one he loved. He prayed to the Mountain that she could figure out how to use it.

"Sylas, the moment we walked into this treasure room, I knew we were not getting out of this palace without facing our mother. Even if she hadn't had a tripwire somewhere, eventually the guards would wake up and find you missing and we'd be in deep water anyway." Nathaniel watched his message fade and extinguished the candle, returning it to the inside of his pocket.

"What should we do?"

Nathaniel brushed the sleeves of his suit and straightened his vest. "We face her." He watched all the color drain from Sylas's face. "Or you could hide in the library and let me handle this."

Sylas didn't even hesitate. He blinked out of sight and was gone. Nathaniel couldn't blame his brother. The dragon looked like he hadn't had a square meal in weeks, and clearly he had experienced the dark side of his mother's magic. It wasn't surprising that he didn't want to sign up for that again.

Nathaniel closed the empty black box; then he waited as the sound of footsteps in the library drew near.

## CHAPTER THIRTY-FOUR

Clarissa felt like a woman whose husband had gone off to war. She stared at the book that was in her hands, but it might as well have been upside down for how many words she'd read. Beside her, Avery chewed the side of her nail while she blinked absently at the egg toasting happily in the fire. On the other side of the room, Maiara was whittling a piece of wood that Tempest had procured for her. It was turning into a carving of a horse that she said was for Li'l Puff when he or she joined the world. Nick had gone for a run on the grounds to burn off some steam.

But it was the tall redhead who paced the room that made Clarissa truly nervous.

Sabrina had arrived just after Nathaniel and the others had left. She'd gone to the London flat and then used her resources to track them back to the crossroads outside Mistwood. Then she'd caused such a fuss that Tempest had noticed her, realized who she was, and let her in.

Sabrina was Tobias's mate and she was a vampire. Clarissa had never met a more intimidating woman in all her years, and that included many pop stars and divas. The vampire's green eyes seemed to burn into her whenever she looked in her direction, and she hadn't sat down once since she'd arrived.

"How long have they been gone?" she asked, pausing her pacing by the fire and crossing her arms.

"About twenty-four hours," Clarissa said. "But our time does not line up to their time in Paragon. For them, I have no idea how long it's been."

Sabrina started pacing again. "Tobias told me something of the sort. Perhaps we should try to help. I can bring a team of vampires."

"There's no way to open a portal without one of their rings," Clarissa said.

Sabrina planted her hands on her hips. "One of them should have stayed behind in case there was trouble. Now we can't help if something goes wrong."

"Nathaniel is extremely powerful. I'm sure he'll succeed." Clarissa closed the book. It was futile to try to read with her stomach in knots like this.

"Tobias is extremely powerful," Sabrina murmured to no one in particular.

Out of the corner of her eye, Clarissa saw the shadow mail candle blaze to life. She'd kept it beside her constantly since the moment Nathaniel had left, but it had never ignited.

She raised one hand in excitement. "It's a message from Nathaniel."

Clarissa grabbed a pen and flipped to the last page of the book she was holding. All the women gathered around. The flame flickered, the shadows dancing and coiling. She copied the letters one by one.

"Use Warwick's blood," she read aloud. The candle

flickered out. There on the nightstand was a strand of black hair.

"Is that...?" Avery stared, looking slightly sick. "Why would Nathaniel send back a strand of Raven's hair? You don't think she's dead, do you?"

"If she was, he wouldn't be suggesting I have Warwick rebind us together." She reached for her phone and dialed the old man's number. It rang and rang again.

"Where do I find this Warwick?" Sabrina said. "I will bring you his blood."

Clarissa looked up at her and whispered, "Chill. You are super scary right now."

The vampire crossed her arms and backed toward the fire. "Sorry. I miss my mate."

Warwick's greeting finally came in her ear. "If you're calling me yourself, it must be an emergency."

"It is. Nathaniel sent me a message from Paragon. I need your help."

# CHAPTER THIRTY-FIVE

Nathaniel wasn't sure what to expect. After all, he hadn't seen his mother in three hundred years. Dragons didn't age the way humans did. However, immortal as they might be, over the course of time, things changed. From popular fashion to hairstyles and culture, older dragons had trouble keeping up. Often one could tell the age of a dragon simply by their appearance. His three-piece suit was an example. It certainly wasn't representative of modern London, but it was what he was comfortable in.

What would his mother be comfortable in? What illusion would she bring forth?

The tapestry shifted and he found out. Eleanor, Empress of Paragon, stood at the opening to the chamber, dressed in a strappy onyx dress with a satin sheen. She entered the room, her shoulders squared, her chin high, and peered down her nose at him. All the softness he'd remembered from his childhood had been stripped away and replaced with a gaunt and angular visage marked by thin lips and flat, soulless eyes.

He sighed, his heart turning to lead in his chest. "Hello, Mother."

"Nathaniel? You're the last person I expected to see. Why are you here?" Her voice was as flat as her eyes, betraying no emotion. Did she think there was a chance that his motives were benign?

He ran a hand down the front of his vest. "I could say the same. You see, when I helped you develop the spell to send the nine of us to Earth, I thought we were doing it to save us all from a planned attack by Brynhoff. But then Marius was killed anyway, and you didn't make it through the portal with the rest of us. I've labored under the assumption all these years that you died in the coup."

Her lips twitched, showing a little teeth. "Brynhoff is dead. I was able to subdue him, take control of the kingdom, and have him executed."

"Hmmm." Nathaniel took a step toward her. "And afterward? Why didn't you come for us?"

She shrugged, her perfectly shaped eyebrows rising toward her expertly coiffed hair. "I couldn't find you, spread out as you were. It seems you followed my advice too well. You were impossible to track down."

Part of Nathaniel wanted to believe her, the boy within who'd spent years joyfully mastering magic by her side, but he knew it was a lie. Rowan and Alexander had told him she'd ruled with Brynhoff and her appearance here, now, proved as much. Alexander had spoken of one of Aborella's trackers being worn by a monster in the late 1600s. And then there was Scoria who'd hunted Gabriel, Tobias, and Raven, ordered to return them to her dead or alive. They'd had to kill him to survive. His mother was not the woman of his memories. She was a monster.

"I've missed you, son," she said, approaching cautiously. "You were the only one who ever truly understood me."

"Likewise," he said flatly. "You've changed your magic room. I remember more plants and less skulls." He glanced at the skull of the dragon child on the top shelf.

"We underestimated the power of blood magic," she said, running her finger along a shelf laden with sorted bones.

"Blood magic is very powerful indeed. Our blood powered many spells when we were together."

She shot him a sideways glance. "Not just our blood. The blood of others. The blood of children is the strongest." She sighed and shook her head. "I am so strong now, Nathaniel. Stronger than the Goddess of the Mountain."

He gasped. "Blasphemy."

"It's true." She turned to him, her dark eyes hollow and soulless. "There are greater gods and goddesses, and once I obtain their book of spells, I will be the most powerful of all."

Nathaniel inched toward the door. "Is that your goal, to be more powerful than the gods?"

She whirled on him and laughed. Her eyes flashed. "Isn't it yours? Who wouldn't want the power of a god?"

He stared back at her in confusion.

"Do you remember the first time we ever did magic together?"

"Of course I do. We transformed a dove into a narwit."

"I'd never seen you happier. Nathaniel, you were never designed for the pits like the rest of them. You weren't a warrior destined to brandish a sword or flex his muscles. No, you were my boy. You were a creator, an engineer of the arcane. From the very beginning, you could see the magic in everything, take it apart and put it back together. What is that but playing God?"

He scoffed and shook his head. "You have it all wrong. Yes, magic involves rearranging the power around us, but not to play God. Its purpose is to bring balance. The power requires balance or it will corrupt. It will kill. And the rot will eat you from the inside out. You know that. You taught me about balance."

"I was wrong. Balance is unnecessary." She spread her hands. "Here I am, Empress of Paragon, breaking all the old laws. Nothing has happened to me." She paused, a feral smile stretching across her thin lips. "No, that's not true. Something has happened. I am now more powerful than ever."

He frowned. "So that's why you stopped looking for us. You have no intention of relinquishing the throne to Gabriel or Tobias. You intend to rule forever."

"For the good of Paragon!" she proclaimed. "I am the only ruler who can keep this kingdom safe. I'm the only one who can keep this world safe. I will unite the kingdoms and be their single, benevolent goddess. Who else could rule in my place? I am the only dragon with magic."

Nathaniel raised his pipe to his lips and blew a smoke ring toward her. It turned into a pentagram and widened, forming a shield between them. Her lips parted on a sneer.

"Not the only one," he murmured. He backed toward the door.

"Stay, Nathaniel. We can rule together. I can show you a new kind of magic." She raised her ring and shattered his shield as if it were nothing.

"No. Using the blood of children? You're an abomination!" he yelled.

"Traitor!"

Yellow lightning zapped from her fingers. Nathaniel sidestepped it but the blast left him shaken. That was new. He blew another shield.

"Traitor? I'm not the one forcibly holding onto a crown that isn't mine. You've been deceived by dark magic, Mother. Your mind is poisoned by it. Can't you see what it's done to you? To us? Don't you remember what we used to have?"

The electricity crackled around her ring once again, this time coiling into a whip. "I do remember. You were a part of all this once."

"Then pocket your magic and let's talk."

She bared her teeth, and for a moment he thought he saw memory flare in her eyes, but it was only a flash, a glimmer, and then they turned hard and cold once more. "Never. You're the most dangerous of my children, Nathaniel, and your blood will make me more powerful than I could imagine."

He held up a hand. "Mother, think about what you're doing!"

Her eyes narrowed and her next words came through her teeth. "I know exactly what I'm doing."

She swung the electric magic above her head and snapped it out, shattering his shield. How was she doing that without symbol or spell? He blinked out of sight, but she kept coming, the air around him crackling with her power. He blocked her magic and puffed confusion charms at her as fast as he could, but she seemed immune to his smoke. She was too strong. Too fast.

He could breathe fire or shift into his dragon form, but neither would be any use against her. Eleanor was as fire-proof as he was, and older dragons were stronger in their beastly form.

Breath short, he could only produce one last puff with his pipe before it sputtered and burned out. Eleanor's magic whip cracked. The lightning wrapped around his body, sending a sizzle of pain through his skin. Dragons couldn't burn, but this magic had teeth. He flopped to the stone, muscles trembling uncontrollably.

She pried the pipe from his grip and looked at it more closely. "Ingenious to use your breath this way. If only you had learned to use your blood."

She adjusted the ring on her finger, and he could see her hand was bleeding under the band. A rune glowed between her thumb and forefinger and then faded. That's how she did it. Eleanor was walking blood magic. She'd likely taken a page from Aborella's book and tattooed herself with magical symbols, then affixed a blade to the inside of the ring to instantly add blood to the mix when she needed it.

She wasn't just powerful. She was terrifying. He'd underestimated her descent into madness. The places she'd taken her magic had corrupted her to her marrow. Darkness and death were now her lovers.

Two guards hustled to her side at the snap of her fingers.

"Lock him up with the others, then search the grounds. Sylas is free. I can smell him all over this room."

"Yes, Your Highness."

One of the guards lifted his boot and brought it down upon Nathaniel's head, and everything went black.

# CHAPTER THIRTY-SIX

*Mistwood Manor*

"Tell me again exactly what the oracle said." Warwick wrinkled his pointed nose and stared at the hair she'd given him.

"I asked how to get my power back, and Grindylow said, 'Rebind thee to thy sisters.' That's it."

"And you believe this hair belongs to the third sister. You two, I assume, are the other two?" He glanced between Avery and Clarissa.

"Yes!" Clarissa tossed up her hands in agitation. This was taking too long. It had taken Warwick thirty minutes to get here and then she'd had to explain everything. Now they were in Nathaniel's study and he was staring at the hair like he hadn't a clue what to do with it. "Nathaniel said to use your blood."

"My blood?" Warwick placed a stubby-fingered hand on his chest. "Why on earth would we do that? My blood holds no power."

Clarissa held her head. "Nathaniel knows what he's talking about, Warwick. There is a reason he wanted me to bring this to you. I have reason to believe it was a piece of my hair that was used to unbind us, so this hair must be able to be used to bind us, right?"

Warwick stroked his round chin, his bushy gray brows low over his eyes. "In theory. I would think if we braided the three strands, performed a binding spell, and added an activation agent, we could redo whatever was undone between you. But what agent? Why, if Nathaniel was here, I'd suggest his blood, but..." Warwick's squat face twisted in concentration. He began to laugh a deep belly laugh.

"What is so funny?" Clarissa asked in frustration.

"He doesn't mean *my* blood. He means his blood in my possession. I keep a vial of Nathaniel's blood to use to prepare his tobacco and certain other spells. Sometimes I have to test things." He circled his hand. "You understand."

"Yes, yes," Clarissa said hastily. "Do you have any of the blood left?"

"Oh, of course I do. In fact, I have it with me." He patted his pocket. "I always keep it with me. There is no safe place to store dragon blood."

Avery spread her hands excitedly. "So can we do the spell? If we reignite this bond and give Clarissa and my sister back their power, maybe Raven can come home."

Warwick nodded. "Worth a try! I can call in the coven tonight."

"No. No!" Clarissa said. "We have to do this now."

"We can't. We need more power to raise the circle, even with Nathaniel's blood. You currently have none."

"What does raise the circle mean?" Avery asked.

Clarissa cleared her throat. "There has to be enough

mystical energy to activate a magic spell. The blood has it, but that's our catalyst. Warwick has it, but he's only one person. Normally, three or more are required to raise a circle."

"What about me?" Sabrina said. Clarissa had forgotten she was there, pacing at the back of the room.

"You are?" Warwick inquired.

"Sabrina the vampire." She dropped her fangs, and Warwick's eyes grew large.

"Perhaps. Vampires are magical creatures. That's two. Is there a third?"

Nick waved two fingers in the air in a kind of casual salute. "I've swallowed a dragon's tooth. I'm human, but I'm tied to Rowan."

"Hmm. Might be enough," Warwick mumbled.

Maiara lifted her chin. "I was raised from the dead."

Warwick blinked at her. "I have no idea if we can draw on that power, but your participation is welcome."

"We could use the egg," Clarissa said. "It's very powerful. Avery could hold it."

Avery tucked her hair behind her ears. "I don't know. Could this hurt it? I can't put Li'l Puff in any danger."

"Oh no, of course not," Warwick said. "I wouldn't lead a circle that would put a child at risk. It's completely harmless."

Avery nodded. "Okay then. Yes. I know my little niece or nephew has power. Enough to knock a grown dragon on his ass."

"Then if you please." He held out his hand.

Avery pulled a long black hair from her head and draped it over Warwick's hand. Clarissa followed, laying her platinum hair with its dark roots next to Avery's.

Clarissa stood. "I'll show you to Nathaniel's ritual room."

Warwick scowled as if he couldn't believe what he was hearing. "He gave you access to it?"

She raised an eyebrow. "Yes indeed, he did."

# CHAPTER THIRTY-SEVEN

*Paragon*

Nathaniel came awake surrounded by his siblings. His head throbbed. A wave of apprehension barreled into him and he reached into his pocket. *Fuck*! His pipe was gone.

"Are you okay?" Rowan asked. "You had quite a bloody gash in your head, but it's already healing."

He ran his fingers through his hair, flakes of dried blood sticking to them. "Fine. As fine as a dragon who just discovered that he and his siblings have all been captured by their megalomaniac mother can be."

"Tobias is here too. And the others," Rowan said. "Aborella and that tool Ransom caught us all."

Alexander's hand appeared before him and helped him into a seated position. They were in Gabriel's old room. The place had changed remarkably little in the past three hundred plus years.

"Aborella rounded us up just before we reached the door and threw us in here with the rest of the family,"

Rowan said. "Fucking fairy. My fingers are still twitching from the zap she gave me."

Nathaniel rubbed his aching head and regarded the room. His eyes locked on Gabriel and Tobias. "Hello, brothers."

They hurried forward and helped him to his feet, embracing him in a greeting worthy of centuries of absence.

"Alexander told us what you did for us," Gabriel said. "Thank you for coming."

"Wait to thank me until we find a way out of this," Nathaniel said.

Tobias pinched the bridge of his nose. "*If* we find our way out of this. I'm fairly sure Eleanor wouldn't have locked us in here together if we had any chance of walking out of this room alive."

The two dragons moved aside when a woman who looked alarmingly like Clarissa and Avery sidled up to Gabriel. "Aren't you going to introduce me?"

"You must be Raven," Nathaniel said. "By the Mountain, you do look like them." He took her hand in his.

"Them who?" she asked.

"Your sisters. Avery and Clarissa."

Raven shook her head. "I don't know anyone named Clarissa."

He shot her a knowing smile. "You will."

Raven's eyes locked with his. "The day Aborella took my power, she braided my hair with one of Avery's and another, blond..."

"That was Clarissa's." Nathaniel nodded. "Bleached platinum. She's a musician. It suits her."

"The third sister." Raven glanced toward Gabriel, her blue eyes sparking with realization. "That's how Aborella did it. She unbound us from our ancestry. She separated me from my source of magic."

Gabriel growled. Now that Nathaniel had a chance to peruse the room, he noticed Sylas was not among them. With any luck, he'd escaped. Or perhaps that was why Aborella and his mother weren't here. They were likely searching for him.

Rowan's heels clicked on the floor. "I hate to interrupt the family reunion, but can we get the hell out of here? Nathaniel, can you do the smoky lock-and-key thing and break us from this room?"

He shook his head. "She took my pipe. I do have a bit of tobacco left if one of you has another at his disposal."

One by one, they shook their heads.

"She hasn't changed a thing in the room," Nathaniel said.

"Some of my clothes are still in the drawers," Gabriel grumbled.

"No chance you hid a smoke in here when you were a boy?"

"Sadly, no. Not a habit I was fond of." The dragon scowled.

Alexander turned from the window and laughed. "It's not exactly the same. The pattern on the bedspread is different. It used to have more blue. And she's replaced the tapestries. They used to celebrate the Goddess of the Mountain; now there's some other figure in them."

"Leave it to an artist to notice the differences," Nathaniel said.

Nathaniel shuffled to the closest tapestry. "Rowan, you recognize her, right? It's not just me."

Shrewd amber eyes focused on the wall hanging. "It's Hera."

"Same thing in the library," Nathaniel said.

"You were in the library?" Tobias asked. "What were you doing in the library?"

"I was accessing Mother's treasure room and retrieving Sylas's ring." Nathaniel brushed invisible lint from his sleeves as everyone turned inquiring eyes on him. He didn't keep them in suspense. He explained about the dungeon, about Sylas being the head of the rebellion, about their mother stripping Sylas's magic, the skull of the baby dragon, and her intentions to rule all five kingdoms.

When he was done, they all looked a little sick. But then, he felt sick too. His mother, a woman he'd once loved and respected as the inspiration behind his magical ability, had chosen a path of narcissism and murder. Even as he raged against her, a part of him was dying, curling in on itself. He had to reframe his entire childhood, and he didn't like what remained.

"It was Sylas in the cell next to me!" Raven said to Gabriel, whose pupils burned with internal fire. "The reason Eleanor needed Gabriel and Tobias to endorse her reign was because she'd caught Sylas and learned there was a coordinated rebellion to overthrow her."

"Yes." Nathaniel nodded.

"Sylas tried to warn me. He tried to tell me she would use me to make Gabriel do what she wanted and then kill me when it suited her. I should have believed him and helped him find his ring."

"You couldn't have," Nathaniel said. "She had it locked down in her treasure room. I used magic to disassemble her wards and return the ring to Sylas's finger."

Raven padded across the room. "So he's out there somewhere?"

"They're likely looking for him," Nathaniel said.

Tobias darted a glance at Gabriel. "How convenient for Mother to have us all in one place. Who wants to place bets that when they find him, we are all going to be invited to a party that ends with our hearts on a platter just like Brynhoff's?"

Gabriel growled. "She'll say we tried to help Sylas escape. She'll come up with some other lie, say we were traitors all along."

Raven's hand went to her mouth, and Gabriel took her into his arms. It was clear to Nathaniel that Raven was a strong woman, just like his Clarissa, but by the looks of her gaunt cheeks and pale skin, she hadn't been treated well during her time here. He supposed she was exhausted and worn down.

He closed his eyes and prayed to the goddess that Clarissa had understood his message and what to do with the hair. Eleanor had taken his pipe. Had she taken the candle? He patted the secret pockets of his suit. The candle was there, but so was something even more powerful. His fingers dug for the square lump over his breast, and he pulled out his tarot cards from his inner pocket. This was why he loved this suit. She'd never even thought to look there.

As he shuffled the cards, one flipped out of the deck as if it couldn't wait to give him its message. He watched it tumble to the floor and land face up. A dark, spontaneous laugh bubbled from Nathaniel's chest.

Alexander squinted at the card. "Wheel of Fortune. What does that mean?"

"It means I'm going to need everyone to buck up and put your thinking caps on. That includes you, Raven. What would you do if you had your power back?"

"Tear the walls down," she said through her teeth.

"Blow through this palace like a dark wind just to slap your mother across the face so hard my child and her aunt a world away could hear it."

"I suggest you and everyone else in this room think of something more practical to get us the hell out of here, because this card means we are about to experience a reversal of fortune, and if everything goes as I expect, Raven will be at the center of it."

# CHAPTER THIRTY-EIGHT

*Mistwood Manor*

No matter how hard she tried to forget about her last time in Nathaniel's ritual room, Clarissa could still smell traces of her own vomit. It was all in her head of course. The oreads had made sure the room was cleaned to impeccable standards, and the dried herbs hanging from the ceiling ensured the only smell in the room was herbal and warm.

Sabrina kept rubbing her nose, probably sensitive to the strong scents. Eventually, she stopped breathing all together. Clarissa had no idea vampires could do that.

Beside her, Avery cradled the egg, which was strapped in a sling around her body. "Can we do this quickly? Li'l Puff can't get cold."

"Yes, please. Let's get this over with," Sabrina added. "There is an herb in here that burns my lungs when I breathe."

"This is for healing," Maiara said, breaking off a small dried piece of something that hung from the ceiling and bringing it to her nose. She waved it in front of Sabrina. "The stink is from the medicine. It is the way the Great Spirit tells us it is good to use."

Sabrina held her nose. "Maybe for humans. Not for vampires."

Across the room, Nick tapped on a jar that held what looked like an embalmed eel. The entire wall was filled with specimens preserved in liquids that ran from clear to yellow to green. Clarissa didn't like to look too closely at those jars.

"Nathaniel's into some crazy shit, even for a dragon," Nick said.

"He told me once he was the only dragon besides his mother who had learned to perform magic like a witch," Clarissa told him.

"Yeah, well, it's creepy, but I hope it keeps my Rowan safe." Nick's yearning for his mate made Clarissa equally anxious to get hers back. This had to work!

Warwick raised his hands. "If everyone would take their places on the circle please, we can begin."

The wizard stationed himself on the northernmost point of the circle at the tip of the pentagram. Clarissa stepped onto the southernmost arc, between the two legs of the star. Sabrina stepped on the arc to her left, Maiara spaced out evenly beside her. Nick took the space beside Warwick.

Avery hesitated, holding the egg in its carrier against her chest.

Clarissa held out her hand to her and smiled. "Come. You can be the witch of the west. Well, the southwest anyway." She pointed to the space across from Sabrina.

"Wasn't that the most wicked one in the Land of Oz?" Avery asked, smiling sweetly. It was hard to imagine Avery being anything but sweet, although it was clear to Clarissa she had an inner strength.

With a laugh, Clarissa took her hand. "There's nothing wrong with being wicked, especially considering present circumstances."

Everyone in their place, they quieted as Warwick began to braid the three hairs. His mouth moved in a barely audible chant. She couldn't make out what he was saying but thought it might be Latin.

"Please join hands," Warwick commanded.

Once everyone did, he released the braided hair, tossing it into the center of the circle. At first the braid floated toward the floor, but as soon as Warwick took Nick's and Maiara's hands, it stopped and rose to hover between them.

Clarissa felt the circle rise.

Beside her, Avery's eyes widened. "I feel it," Avery said. "It's like my feet have left the ground. I feel... weightless."

"Concentrate," Warwick barked. "Picture the hairs being bound to one another in your head." He began to chant again.

The magic in the room built to a glorious tension, the air flowing thick into Clarissa's lungs. She stared at the hairs, willing them to fuse.

A wind picked up in the circle, whipping Clarissa's hair against her face. There were no windows in this room, but the formerly thick and stale air became crisp. Sabrina took a real breath.

"Holy fuck!" All the color drained from Nick's face.

"The Great Spirit is upon us." Maiara's gaze lifted toward the ceiling.

Warwick's irises glowed silver gray as power pulsed through the circle.

Avery gasped. "Oh my God." The egg in her arms pulsed peacock blue.

Even Clarissa, who had participated in many circles in her time, had to admit this was weird. The power flowing was more in line with what she would feel from an entire coven of expert witches and wizards, not this motley crew of magical novices.

Her throat opened. She had the sudden urge to sing. "Now, Warwick! I can feel it!"

"Nick, Maiara, hands on my shoulders please!" Warwick commanded.

They obeyed, their hands sliding up his arms. He produced a vial of Nathaniel's blood from the inner pocket of his jacket. Dabbing a drop on his thumb, he reached out, his cheeks flapping in the circle's gusting magic, and pressed the blood to the braid. Almost instantly, the three strands fused into one and disintegrated into dust that circled in the cyclone that had become the room.

The magic didn't let up. As Warwick slid the vial back into his jacket and returned his hands to grip Nick's and Maiara's, a howl rose. Gradually, Clarissa became aware it was her voice! All of theirs! They were all yelling into the wind as it lifted them. She couldn't hold on. Her feet floated another inch from the floor.

Lightning branched from the center of the circle, zapping into her and the others. She lost her grip on Sabrina and Avery, crashed to the floor, and rolled onto her back. She lay perfectly still, shock waves coursing through her body in a way that wasn't unpleasant but was scary as hell.

Avery sat up first and checked the egg. "You okay, Li'l Puff?"

The egg's heartbeat seemed to pulse softly in response.

Sabrina got to her feet and held her hand out to help Clarissa up. "How do we know if it worked?"

"Only one way to find out." Clarissa opened her mouth and sang. There were no words to her song, just a single note that began low and rose in pitch like a soaring bird. Light gathered between them—a ball of light that hatched into an electric-violet butterfly. Her creation cruised around the circle, raining sparkles like stardust.

"Holy shit," Sabrina said.

"I guess it worked," Nick mumbled.

Warwick brushed his palms against each other and straightened his tie. "Of course it worked. Who do you think you're dealing with?" He pointed one meaty finger at Clarissa. "Tell Nathaniel he owes me." He strode from the room like he was a foot taller than his actual stature.

Avery hugged the egg and stared at Clarissa, wide-eyed and anxious. "What happens now?"

She thought for a moment, but there was only one answer. "Now we wait."

# CHAPTER THIRTY-NINE

## *Paragon*

Raven couldn't stop shaking. Wrapped inside a blanket, she huddled on the edge of the bed, Gabriel's arm around her shoulders. It was only a matter of time before Eleanor came for them, and she was terrified. Between the empress, Aborella, Ransom, and the rest of the Obsidian Guard on high alert, it seemed impossible that they'd escape. But they had to. They had to find a way, for each other, for their child, and for Paragon.

Gabriel was ridiculously still by her side. All of them knew what they had to do, but waiting was torture. Not knowing when or how Eleanor would strike was a nightmare.

Finally, the door flung open and Eleanor appeared, Aborella behind her and Ransom by her side. The captain of the Guard shoved a man into the room, filthy and naked from the waist up. His pants were barely more than rags. Raven immediately knew it was Sylas, although she'd never seen his unobstructed face. He resembled Alexander in build and face shape, although his hair was somewhere between Tobias's blond and the dark brown and black of his other brothers, and his eyes were the same shade of gray as Nathaniel's. The resemblance was undeniable.

"Well, well, well. It seems we have a full-blown family reunion happening here. What a nice surprise," Eleanor said.

Aborella, whose skin still hadn't regained its normal deep purple hue, glared at her. Raven quietly triumphed in the fairy's lengthy recovery. She would never suggest Aborella was weak, but she was weakened, and that would have to do.

Sylas's gaze sought hers out. "Raven, I presume."

"Yes. It's nice to meet you without the iron grid between us." She glanced down at his finger where the garnet rested. "And with your birthright returned to you."

"Oh, shut up," Eleanor said, her yellow ring shining against her black dress. The colors reminded Raven of a hornet; she had no interest in feeling her sting. "Whatever power Sylas has, it is useless to you. Do you understand? You are mine."

Ransom snickered from where he'd stationed himself near the door.

"Now, should I ask if Xavier or Colin are here as well?"

No one said a word. Unless Sylas had been in touch, Raven was sure no one in the room had any idea where the last two brothers were right now. The family hadn't kept in contact over the years. Saying so now didn't seem advantageous though. Sometimes it was better just to keep one's mouth shut.

Eleanor joined her hands in front of her hips. "Let me explain how this is going to work. Each of you will swear allegiance to me and allow me to remove your rings."

"Fuck you," Alexander murmured.

"Or," she continued, ignoring him, "when the suns rise in a matter of hours, I will invite the Highborn families to a trial where you will be found guilty of treason and executed." She gestured toward the balcony and the night sky beyond.

"You'd murder your own children?" Raven loaded her words with all the disgust she felt for Eleanor.

Eleanor's mouth widened into a wicked grin. "You may have mated my son, but you could never be a queen. You are the reason I *have* to do this. You are a danger to the kingdom. You are the witch the prophecy said would bring Paragon to its knees. Yes, I will do what has to be done to preserve our way of life. That's what an empress does. We have to make the hard choices to keep our people safe."

From the corner of the room, Nathaniel started to laugh. "Odd. I live in a country with a queen, and the royals haven't offed anyone's head in a century. Are you sure it's a requirement?"

Eleanor whirled to face him. It took her half a second to notice the symbol, drawn with an oil pastel that Alexander had squirreled away in the inner pocket of his leather jacket. Apparently he always had a drawing utensil of some sort with him. This one had the added advantage of being black, which meant the symbol was barely visible against the obsidian floor.

Raven had helped Alexander draw the runes around Nathaniel. It was a more powerful method than having the dragon draw them himself, allowing the circle to be bigger, the symbols more intricate and perfectly proportioned. The pentagram was pure genius, a testament to Nathaniel's magical aptitude, and intimidating in its intricacy and its potential.

Time seemed to slow as Nathaniel slashed his arm and blood doused the symbol he was standing in. Rowan, Alexander, and Tobias dove behind him as Eleanor tried in vain to defend herself. But they'd caught her off guard. She wasn't fast enough.

Nathaniel produced a pulse of power like nothing Raven had ever experienced. Eleanor, Aborella, and Ransom were blown away, their bodies crashing into the far wall. To Raven, it felt as if a hurricane had gusted from Nathaniel's circle, and although the power wasn't directed at her, all her ebony hair blew forward and she lifted off the bed onto her feet. She tossed the blanket aside. Gabriel's wings spread protectively beside her.

Nathaniel uttered a spell, and the circle pulsed again. His pipe tore from Eleanor's pocket, tumbled through the air, and landed in his hand. The empress scrambled to her hands and knees, drawing breath as if it hurt.

"Ransom!" Eleanor barked.

Ransom fumbled for the Paragonian grenade on his belt, still stunned by the blow. Rowan's wings punched out and she leapt over Nathaniel's head, tore the tapestry off the wall and tossed it over Ransom. As it turned out, Rowan, even in her high heels, was the fastest of the siblings. She wrapped Ransom and the grenade into a tight roll and dragged his body to a spot beside Nathaniel so quickly Raven had trouble following her movements. She stood with her stiletto on his throat, her wings out.

"Sorry, Mother, this one is indisposed." Rowan flexed her wings, her fists landing on her hips.

The empress shook off the remains of Nathaniel's attack and lashed out, her talons extended. Tobias was there, his sword blocking her attack with the clang of metal on claw. The element of surprise definitely worked in their favor.

Eleanor hesitated for a split second, focusing on the blade. "Where did you get that?"

"Never mind, Eleanor, I'll handle this." The air crackled with energy. Aborella had recovered from the blast and was raising her hands. Two storms of black lightning formed in her palms. She focused all her energy on Nathaniel. His mouth twitched and Raven held her breath, praying she wouldn't notice the smile. Would she take the bait?

Eleanor's eyes widened and Raven saw with a certain satisfaction the moment she put two and two together. Someone had to have summoned the sword in her son's hand. The empress's mouth formed the word no, but it was too late.

Aborella unleashed all her power toward Nathaniel.

"*Cogitatio!*" Raven leaped in front of Nathaniel and crossing her arms. Up until that moment, it had been all she could do to hide the fact her power had returned. The blanket had helped, as did Gabriel's arm around her and then the distraction of Nathaniel's magic. Now she joyfully let it all out. Just as it had in Sedona, the mirror spell wrapped around her and reflected Aborella's lightning. Only, unlike in Sedona, the fairy was in a confined, reflective space.

Raven spread her hands, broadening the shield to protect Gabriel, Tobias, Rowan, Alexander, Nathaniel, and Sylas as dark lightning reflected off her magic and ricocheted against the polished obsidian walls. This was no ordinary magic. Dragons were impervious to electricity, heat, or fire. But, as Nathanial had suspected, Aborella had used her deep knowledge of their anatomy to design her spell especially to target their kind. Now the fairy sorceress's most powerful weapon against dragons plowed into

Eleanor and herself, magnified by Raven's spell. Their bodies sizzled and smoked, collapsing in the assault.

The resulting magical storm was violent and hot. Raven howled with the effort of keeping her shield up. But as intense as it was, it also felt like coming home. It was like going for a long run for the first time after being cooped up all winter. Raven thought about her time in the dungeon, how Eleanor had murdered Marius, and how she'd planned to marry Gabriel off to the highest bidder despite their mating and rage bubbled up inside her. It bolstered her power. She poured every ounce of her wrath into the spell.

Her knees buckled and Gabriel gripped her shoulders, holding her up.

"A little longer, Raven. Almost there. You can do it!" His breath warmed her ear. She could do it. She would do it. To save her family.

Finally the storm fizzled. Eleanor and Aborella lay motionless on the floor. Raven dropped the shield and collapsed into Gabriel's arms.

# CHAPTER FORTY

As soon as Raven dropped the shield, Nathaniel was ready. He'd packed his pipe again and blew a ring of smoke at the door. The ring formed into a pentagram and then revolved, symbols flashing in its sectors. Finally the spell found the combination to the ward around the room. He stepped over his mother's twitching body and dialed the combination as fast as his fingers could move.

"Kill her," Gabriel yelled at Tobias. From her place in his arms, Raven could feel his rage. He was vibrating with it. "Use the sword. Behead them both. Let's finish this now."

Tobias raised the sword. But when he brought it down toward his mother's neck, it bounced harmlessly off a hard shell of air surrounding her and Aborella, who had thrown an arm and leg protectively over the empress. Raven's gaze snapped to the fairy. Her skin was charred and mostly white, but a symbol on her leg was spinning. Wild eyes locked on hers and she bared her teeth. That silver gaze was as cold as ice and as determined as a bulldog's. Aborella would die for Eleanor. Why? Raven would likely never know. But it was all there in the way she sheltered her with the remains of her magic.

"It's down," Nathaniel said.

"Wait!" Gabriel commanded. "Raven, can you break through Aborella's defenses?"

Tobias raised the sword again over Eleanor's neck.

Raven wanted to. She would have loved to watch Eleanor's head roll, followed by Aborella's. But she'd used everything she had on the reflective shield. She couldn't even walk yet. "I've got nothing left."

"Nathaniel?" Gabriel asked.

"Only enough tobacco to get us back home."

Raven wondered if that was true. She saw tenderness in the way Nathaniel looked at Eleanor. At one time, Tobias had struggled to believe his mother was evil, but his mind had been changed when she'd sent Scoria to try to kill them. Nathaniel knew what his mother was. He'd been there as she threatened to kill them all. And although he'd been a large part of the plan to fry her, there was only sadness in his expression now. If Raven had any skill at all at reading people, and usually she did, she would guess that Nathaniel did not want to watch his mother die.

Gabriel's gaze darted around the room like a caged animal. "We cannot let her live. She must pay!"

Sylas grabbed his shoulder and shook it. "We will have our day, brother, but if we don't leave before she wakes up, we will never make it out of this palace."

"He's right," Raven said. "We have to leave before she's strong enough to call for help or we'll have the whole of the Obsidian Guard to contend with."

Gabriel cursed but thrust through the door with Raven still in his arms. Rowan, Tobias, Sylas, and Alexander rushed after him. Once everyone was through, Nathaniel's ring glowed to life. Raven realized he was sealing the room with his own ward.

"It won't hold them for long," Nathaniel said. "We need to make it outside the castle. I can't move this many people from inside."

Sylas motioned. "This way."

But when they reached the end of the hall, the sound of running feet pulled them up short.

"The guards! They're coming!" Rowan said.

They all turned on a dime and rushed in the opposite direction, toward the front of the palace, but slowed when they came to a forked hallway. Raven squirmed in Gabriel's arms and he put her down.

"Which way?" Nathaniel whispered.

A flash of gold to her left claimed Raven's attention. She could have sworn she saw a woman with two golden eyes, a shimmering dress, and long, flowing black hair. *Circe.* But the moment she thought it, she was gone.

"This way," Raven said, chasing after where the image had been.

"Wait, are you sure?" Tobias whispered, but she was already halfway down the hall.

The others followed after her. At the end of that hallway, there was a flash of gold to her right and then another around the bend, until she could have sworn she saw the goddess melt through a door in the side of the mountain.

Raven rushed to the door and found it unlocked. Beyond it, stairs led down into darkness. She held it open as the others rushed into the stairwell and descended. Gabriel helped her close and lock it behind them.

"What is this place?" Nathaniel asked from several stairs below.

They jogged down, one flight, then two.

"I don't know," Raven answered.

Gabriel darted an uneasy glance in her direction. "How did you know to come here? How do you know it's safe?"

She opened her mouth to try to explain but couldn't find the words. Had she really seen the goddess? Or was it just a hunch?

Rowan came to her rescue as she reached the final level. "I know this place. Raven, you're a genius!"

"I am?"

"How do *you* know this place, Rowan? I've never seen this part of the palace before." Tobias raised an eyebrow at his sister.

Rowan lit a torch on the wall and cast light across the chamber. "That's because you shouldn't be here. No male should be. This is the sanctuary to the goddess. It's where dragon females come to lay their eggs."

Raven's gaze roved over the rough-hewn walls of the stony chamber. The temperature and red glow from deep within the cavern beyond were even hotter than the dungeon.

"It's too hot for you," Gabriel said to her. "We need to get you out of here."

"I've got this." As exhausted as she'd been moments ago, she suddenly felt a surge of energy. She whispered an incantation, and it began to snow above her head. Instantly, she felt cooler. "Is that the goddess?" Raven asked, pointing to the far wall, closer to the heat.

Rowan and the others turned to see where she was looking. A mural constructed of gemstones rose from the floor to the ceiling of the cave. It depicted a woman with obsidian hair and red armor that flowed over her torso like lava. She was muscular, larger than life, and reminded Raven of

Wonder Woman. This goddess was formidable. She was a warrior.

Rowan answered. "Yes it is. The Goddess of the Mountain."

"Does she have a name?" Raven asked.

"It is told only to females," Rowan said. "Technically, I'm the only one who should be down here, and I'm supposed to bring an offering. Her name is Aitna. Mother of dragons."

"I thought Circe was the mother of dragons?" Raven had tried to learn Paragonian history but was still putting all the stories together.

"Circe gave us the ability to transform into our *soma* forms, this form," Rowan patted her chest. "Aitna came before Circe. She's older, from a family of titans. It is said she wove the first dragon from the fabric of the universe."

Raven stepped closer to the mural and its altar. There were craters in front of it, each just large enough to hold a dragon egg. "Is this where dragon mothers incubate their young?"

"We call it the cradle. Yes," Rowan said.

"This is where our child would develop if we were here," Raven said softly. Her gaze drifted up the mural to meet Aitna's red-hot gaze.

Pounding steps came from the back of the cave and Sylas burst into the chamber from an opening in the stone. "There's a passageway. Looks like an old lava tube. It's tight, but it's a way out of the palace."

"Wait." Raven glanced at Rowan. "We have to leave the goddess an offering to thank her for our safe passage."

"It's a sweet thought, Raven, but please hurry," Gabriel said, glancing up the stairs. No doubt the guards were on full alert by now.

Raven glanced down at her hand, at the emerald ring Gabriel had given her when he'd asked her to marry him.

"Raven?" Gabriel asked.

"You can make me another. It's the most valuable thing I have. Anything I conjure won't be a sacrifice. This is the best offering I can give her." She looked at him with pleading eyes.

He nodded. "Very well."

Raven tossed the ring onto the altar.

Outwardly moved, Rowan hastily removed her shoes and set them next to the ring. Immediately she began to sob.

"Why are you crying?" Raven asked her.

"Those were Louboutins." Rowan wiped under her eyes and strode toward Sylas and the lava tube. "They were works of art... and really comfortable."

Gabriel tugged at her hand. "Come, little witch."

They followed the others into the tube. Eventually they emerged in the front garden, just as the suns rose over the horizon.

"Link arms—this isn't going to be easy," Nathaniel said.

Alarms blared in the distance.

Raven looped one arm through Gabriel's and then her other through Nathaniel's. Tobias, Rowan, and Alexander linked on his other side.

"Where's Sylas?"

They all searched, but he was gone.

Nathaniel frowned. "He was never going with us. He has a rebellion to lead."

"Get us out of here, Nathaniel," Gabriel said.

Nathaniel blew a puff from his pipe and unlocked the ward surrounding the palace, then with a sweep of his ring sliced open a portal between worlds. All six of them toppled, panting and drained, onto a Persian carpet in what appeared to be a manor parlor.

Dragging six people through a portal between worlds had only required Nathaniel to move a few steps, but it felt like he'd carried a house on his back as he did so. It had required all his strength and all his magic. He landed limp, exhausted, and sore in a cozy room with a blazing fire.

A scream of delight pierced the space and then a woman with bright red hair swept Tobias off the floor beside him as if the dragon weighed nothing and kissed him like the only oxygen left in the world was in his lungs.

"I take it that's Sabrina," Nathaniel murmured, trying to sit up and failing. He gave up and lay flat on his back again. No one answered him.

Out of the corner of his eye, he watched Rowan collide with Nick, the human spinning her around in front of the bookshelves. Gabriel and Raven rushed to hug Avery and coo over the egg, which pulsed happily in the fire. Maiara and Alexander approached each other slowly, touched foreheads, and closed their eyes as if their spirits were connecting first before their bodies followed suit and they embraced each other.

Nathaniel watched the happy reunion and longed for his own. But when he inhaled deeply, trying to place her in the room, he couldn't smell Clarissa. She wasn't here. He swallowed hard. He needed her right now.

"It is good to see you, my dragon," Tempest said, his pale face appearing over him.

"Where is she?" he whispered to the oread.

291

"At the O2. Preparing for the concert this evening. Her voice was restored."

His heart sank. He'd wanted her to go, wanted her to sing, but her absence was crushing. Cold, hard doubt seeped into his soul. What if she hadn't truly loved him? What if everything that had occurred had been a ploy to get him to do what she wanted? She had what she was after now. He'd restored her voice. Would she leave him as she had before? His heart felt hollow and his body ached just thinking about it. What if she left for good again? Would she even come home after the show? Or just leave without another word? He closed his eyes and longed for the feel of her fingers in his hair.

"I need the treasure room," he whispered.

Laurel appeared by Tempest's side, and the oreads helped him to his feet. That caught the attention of his siblings, who promptly circled him. He refused their offers of help and hobbled toward the parlor door.

"She wanted to stay," Avery called, cutting through the murmurs around him. Everyone quieted and turned their attention on her. "Clarissa would have been here if we'd known when you'd be back. It absolutely tore her apart to leave. But she told me you made her promise. We waited for you. She's hardly slept since you've been away. It's been days since we did the spell. She would have stayed had she known. No matter what."

He closed his eyes and allowed her words to sink in. Avery wasn't a liar. Her face was genuine and sure. He believed her. Her words were a balm to the ache in his heart. "Thank you."

Avery smiled softly. "It's the least I can do. Thank you for bringing my family back."

Her family. He supposed she was talking about Raven

and Gabriel, but the way she said it, he almost felt like she meant all of them. Avery Tanglewood was a unique woman indeed. A fitting sister to his Clarissa.

He nodded his adieu, and with the last of his energy hobbled to his room and took refuge in his treasure.

# CHAPTER FORTY-ONE

Aborella could still hear the voices of Eleanor's filthy, indignant children as she curled on her side on the cold obsidian, her limbs wrapped protectively around Eleanor. She brought her hand to her face, and her skin was so pale it was nearly white. The runes carved into her flesh had dulled, even the ones she used for restoring herself. When she swallowed, her throat ached. Truly she was in need of healing, but she'd saved the empress. She'd done her duty.

Eleanor's eyes opened and her lips pulled back from her teeth. The growl that came from deep within her seemed to reverberate in the room as the empress scrambled to her feet. "Get. Off. Me."

Aborella looked up at her, unable to rise herself. She was too weak.

"Find them! I want their hearts mounted to my throne! I want to water the gardens with their blood!"

"I... I don't have magic yet," Aborella admitted, showing the empress her depleted skin.

"Guards! Guards!" Eleanor yelled, ignoring Aborella entirely.

Pounding feet approached and then a dozen men in red and black entered the room. They unwrapped Ransom from his tapestry cocoon. The captain woke, shaking his head.

"Find them. Find them!" Eleanor commanded, spit flying from her lips. "Search the castle. They can't have gone far." She cursed as the men rushed from the room, her blazing stare focusing on Aborella. "That's not true, is it? They can go anywhere. My son wields the same magic I do, and now he has a witch by his side whose power is unparalleled."

"How?" Aborella shook her head. "How did she get her power back?"

The empress spread her hands. She was already healed from the attack, and yellow lightning zapped between the tips of her fingers. "You tell me! Someone must have rebound the three sisters."

Aborella had to do something. As a seer, she should have known this would happen. Only, she'd never fully recovered from the damage Alexander and Raven had inflicted on her in Sedona. She needed rest, but Eleanor kept pushing her to do more. There was always a reason the empress demanded her at her side. She'd barely slept and hadn't had enough time in the forest to rejuvenate herself since she'd returned.

Still, if she didn't do something about this situation, Eleanor would have her head as well as the others. She got to her feet. She had no magic to fuel her second sight, but she could still see. She would search for them herself.

"I can fix this," she said.

Eleanor bared her teeth. "You'd better, or there will be consequences. Do you know who Raven is? She is the one from the prophecy, Aborella. She is the one who can bring this kingdom down."

"I told you we should have killed her before—"

"Find. Them." The empress whirled and charged from the room.

Aborella pulled herself together and searched. At times she thought she could smell them, but then she'd lose the trail. After an hour of searching every room in the palace, she was at a loss. Where could they have gone? Then again, with the power the empress claimed they had, they truly might have escaped. The suns were rising and the Obsidian Guard, who'd spread out and searched within the palace and over the grounds, had similarly come up short.

Exhausted and only half-alive, she made her way to the gardens and into the forest beyond, passing effortlessly through the wards thanks to the rune Eleanor had burned into her skin. She leaned against one of the trees and closed her eyes. Waves of energy flowed into her, and for the first time in hours, she took a long, deep breath.

The leaves above her turned yellow, then brown, then fell from the branches to the ground around her. Her skin darkened. When the energy stopped, she moved to the next tree. She had just placed her hands on the third tree when Ransom's rich baritone reached her ears. He was calling her name.

She hastened back to the palace and found him in the garden.

"They're gone. We've searched every inch of the grounds and the palace."

Aborella cursed. "Have you told Eleanor?"

"Not yet. I thought you could... do what you do." Ransom focused his large brown eyes on her. The man was pretty but truly dumb, and his eyes held less intelligence than a mountain horse.

*Think. Think. Think.* She had to assume the spell to unbind the three sisters would no longer work, even if she'd had more hair from the three of them. Nathaniel would never allow lightning to strike twice. He'd make sure protections were in place. Protections. Security. Exposure. She thought back to all she had learned on Earth and had an idea.

"Go to Eleanor and tell her what you've told me. I will handle this."

Ransom scoffed, incredulous. "How? You know she'll want specifics."

Aborella took a deep breath and let it out slowly. "The three sisters can't be bound if one of them is dead." Today it was kill or be killed. "Tell Eleanor I am going to end this once and for all."

CLARISSA STOOD BACKSTAGE AT THE O2 ARENA, thinking of Nathaniel. What if he returned while she was doing the show? Then again, there had been no word in days. What if he wasn't coming back at all? Her stomach clenched at the thought. Would she feel it if something happened to him?

Surely some kind of madness would come over her if half her heart was torn from her body? She was only here because he had made her promise she'd do the show, voice or no voice. He'd said he'd come with her on tour. He was ultimately supportive of her career.

But as she stood backstage, waiting to perform the song that he'd inspired, she had a hard time remembering why this was so important to her. Her career felt empty and cold tonight. A false love.

Tom came up behind her and rested his hands on her shoulders. "You've got this, babe. Do your thing. Prove to all these people you've still got it."

A harsh laugh broke from her throat. "Is that what this is? My opportunity to prove I'm worthy? The millions of records I've sold haven't done that?"

"You know how it goes. You're only as good as your last performance."

She sighed and turned to face him. Tom had been handsome when they'd started working together. He'd been a Rob Lowe look-alike with a square jaw, blue eyes, and a dark coif. But now, all she saw was the Botox, the thinning hair he tried to hide with a thick layer of product, the contacts he wore to make his eyes more blue. He wasn't much older than her, but this life, the loneliness, the constant travel, it aged you.

He was her Dr. Frankenstein, and soon her prescription would include a surgeon's knife or a syringe. She knew it. Even with her magic, she would never be enough for him or for the audience.

A deep sense of peace came over her. In that second, she knew exactly what she wanted. For millions of people, what she was about to do was a dream. They'd do anything to be right where she was. And she realized, down to her bones, that she was no longer one of them.

She nodded at Tom. "Then let's make sure this one brings down the house."

She turned around and he slapped her on the ass. She would have said something, but the beat dropped and it was time. She strode out onto a stage of leaping dancers and joined in, stomping and swaying with the music. Her magic sparked to life, twinkling between their bodies and syncing their moves until they were one organism, pulsing to the musical heartbeat.

She opened her mouth and began to sing:
*Your night, it crawls to meet*
*the darkness inside me.*
*Don't you know that your energy*
*is the thing making me me?*

The train she was wearing detached and rose behind her as if carried by a breeze, folding itself into an origami beast, a dark, twinkling dragon with huge wings that flapped above her and the dancers. As always, the crowd went crazy. That's how she noticed her. The redheaded woman who'd stolen her hair, who'd taken her power. She was there. The only body motionless in the front row. Aborella.

*I was once a dying thing.*
*You helped me find my wings.*
*Though you were my everything,*
*I broke away and felt the sting.*
*Free from you, free from us.*
*Free to rule the skies above.*

She had no choice but to keep singing, although her stomach tightened. What was she doing here? Aborella wouldn't dare attack in public, would she? She was too far away, and if she tried to get any closer, her security team would take the woman down.

*Bring on the night.*
*I will be its queen.*
*Bring on the night.*

*I will rule the wind.*
*Bring on the night.*
*I welcome it. I'm ready. I'm ready.*

She spread her arms and climbed the pyramid of stairs that rose out of the floor until she stood on a platform, the origami dragon hovering over and behind her.

*But it's cold without your fire.*
*It's cold without your fire.*
*If I could take the blame*
*and lure back your flame*
*I'd hold you once again*
*and things would never be the same.*
*Your flames, they lick my skin.*
*Let it burn.*
*Your love, it changes me.*
*Let it burn.*
*Lure back your flame.*
*Let it burn.*
*I'm burning at your stake.*

The crowd gasped and stared over her head. She followed their pointing fingers. The origami dragon was gone, replaced with a real one. Nathaniel's amethyst heart glowed through the chest of his black and purple scales. His horned head reached over her, his wings spreading. She missed her cue, but he filled in the break in the music with a stream of fire that blazed over the heads of the crowd.

The arena exploded with cheers. She'd never heard them this loud or this wild. She looked between Nathaniel and Aborella. *Just try it, bitch.* She sang on.

*Your light, it crawls to meet*
*the darkness inside me.*
*Don't you know that your energy*

301

*is the thing making me me?*
*Bring on your light.*
*I will be your queen.*
*Bring on your light.*
*I will rule your world.*
*Bring on your light.*
*I welcome it. I'm ready. I'm ready.*
*Let it burn. Let it burn. Let it buuuurn.*

Aborella seethed at Nathaniel and then at Clarissa, her evil mind seeming to come to some nefarious conclusion as the music waged on. She raised her hands and black sorcery crackled like lightning.

Her security was on it. They moved for her first, then feeling the danger, ushered the crowd back, giving Aborella room. The audience went along, clearly thinking it was all part of the show. Aborella didn't even seem to notice.

She unleashed her power straight at Clarissa. It never reached her. Nathaniel's scales flashed in front of her, shielding her from the attack.

But Clarissa wasn't about to allow Nathaniel to take the brunt of the blow. She sang out her next note and held it, her magic forming a protective barrier around his scales.

Black lightning crackled and hissed. Her lungs began to burn and she could feel her face redden, but she poured her entire self into the music. All the love she felt for Nathaniel loaded her voice. She would not fail.

Aborella's magic sputtered and died. Clarissa stopped singing. Nathaniel uncoiled and faced the fairy, his amethyst heart glowing as bright as a spotlight. Clarissa had a clear view of Aborella's look of terror as Nathaniel's massive taloned paw slammed down on her body, flattening her into the concrete just as the music came to its conclusion.

She met the gaze of her mate. His dragon's beautiful amethyst eye winked at her, before he disappeared into thin air, leaving nothing but a smear of blood on the floor of the arena and a crowd whose screams and applause rattled the walls.

## CHAPTER FORTY-TWO

Nathaniel plunked down beside Gabriel in the last row of section 412 and watched his mate continue her performance as if a fully grown dragon hadn't crushed a fairy right in front of her not five minutes ago. The crowd had closed the gap where he'd been, some even fighting over what remained of Aborella's clothing even though it was stained with her purple blood. Everyone here thought it was part of the show.

"Are you sure she's dead?" Gabriel asked. If he hadn't been a dragon, he'd never have heard his brother's whisper over the music. Good thing. The fans packed around them didn't even turn their heads.

"No. Aborella's magic is dark and she's an immortal. I drained her completely and destroyed her physical body on this world, but what I washed from my hands and what remained on the concrete was not all of her. All I know for sure is that she is vanquished. For now." Nathaniel gripped the armrests of his seat. He'd never trust the bitch was dead, not unless her body was actively decomposing in front of him.

"I thought not." Gabriel frowned.

"You know you'll have to go back, right?" Nathaniel looked at Gabriel with conviction. "The throne is rightfully yours, and Mother will destroy the five kingdoms if left to her own devices."

"I know. I think Raven knows too. I always thought the law about dragons and witches was a warning. Now I realize it's a promise." Gabriel's brow furrowed, the warrior Nathaniel knew he was coming to the surface. "I'll need your help. You're the only one who understands Mother's magic. Without you, she'll smite us from this world and the next."

"You have my word," Nathaniel said. "I promised Clarissa I would go on tour with her, but she'll understand periodic absences."

Gabriel nodded slowly. "You do understand that your mate is the third sister."

Nathaniel's skin prickled. "In theory. I understand my mate is bound with Raven and her sister Avery in some way. Aborella came for her tonight to kill her, not because she wanted Clarissa dead but to take away Raven's power."

"You don't remember then, the tale of the Three Sisters, from school?"

Nathaniel's eyes widened and he turned from watching the performance to focus fully on Gabriel. "Ancient history, Gabriel. These are not the same three sisters."

The hard truth that sparked in Gabriel's eyes was totally and completely chilling. "No. They are their descendants and the ones the prophecy foretold. Together, they are more powerful than anything in this universe. Even Raven does not understand the full extent of it. She does not know the prophecy or the history as I do."

"Then how do you know it's real?" Nathaniel asked. "There are many stories and many prophecies."

Gabriel threaded his hands over his waist. "My mate had a vision of the goddess when she delivered our child. She was dead, Nathaniel. Her heart stopped beating. When she came back to me, she told me she'd met Circe. And the prophecy she shared with me was too close to the one we learned to be a coincidence."

Nathaniel swallowed. "The whelp... Your child is the result of mating between a dragon and a witch. You are the heir. Your child is the prophesied destroyer of the kingdom of Paragon."

"Yes." Gabriel stared at Nathaniel's mate onstage as if he hadn't even heard it. It took a full minute for Nathaniel to put it all together.

"Your child is the only hope for Paragon," Nathaniel whispered. "We always thought the destroyer was a bad thing. The mating was forbidden because we feared the result. But now, it means... this means..."

Gabriel glared at him, his jaw tight. "My family will sit on that throne and bring peace to the five kingdoms, and not because we desire to conquer but because we desire to liberate. We will save Paragon from the empress. We are the ones the goddess foretold."

Nathaniel's hand instinctively sought out the pipe in his pocket, anxiety flipping his stomach. "And Clarissa is part of it."

Gabriel leaned back beside him as they both took in the crowd, the lights, his mate's magical voice. "Yes."

## CHAPTER FORTY-THREE

It was late by the time Clarissa had wrapped up her act, met with fans, and signed autographs. She'd stripped off her costume, hairpiece, and makeup. Then there was the hard conversation with Tom. Words were said, words that could never be taken back. But that's what happened when you violated someone's expectations. She'd figured as much.

Tom had staked his career on her ongoing success, and she'd told him she wasn't interested in being a pop star anymore. All things considered, she thought he handled it well.

Security walked her out to her car, where she anticipated Emory would be waiting. Instead, she found Nathaniel leaning up against the Mercedes and staring at the stars. When he saw her, his mouth spread into a wide smile.

She took off at a run and leaped into his arms, wrapping her legs around his hips. He did not disappoint. Catching her, his big arms enveloped her in protective warmth and his face buried in her neck.

"Oh God," she said. "My God, Nathaniel, I thought you'd never get back. And Aborella, she would have k-killed me if not for you."

"Shhh. Shhh." He kissed her cheek. "We got her. I have you now. You're safe."

He opened the car door for her and she slid in. Once he was in place beside her, she tucked into his side again as Emory took off for Mistwood. "I missed you so much. Tell me everything."

He gave her the condensed version. "I had no idea that Aborella would strike tonight. I simply came to see you perform and acted when I saw her in the crowd. Truthfully, I thought it would take her longer to recover from what we did to her in Paragon."

"I'm lucky you did. Even with my voice and magic in place, I'm not sure I could have stopped her from hurting me or one of my dancers by myself."

He placed a kiss on her temple.

"Why do you think she came after me? Why not Raven?" It was a question that had weighed on her all night.

Nathaniel thought about how to tell her the truth. "In my world, there is a legend, part history, part folklore, about three sister witches. In the early fourth century, long before I was born, the kingdom of Paragon was attacked by the kingdom of Darnuith—in our world, the kingdom of the witches. The witch queen of Darnuith, who attacked Paragon—which was under the rule of my uncle King Brynhoff at the time—was one of three sisters. She'd risen to power quickly, and her magic was unparalleled. The uprising was thwarted, and Brynhoff credited the Goddess of the Mountain with his victory.

"He claimed the goddess had decreed that for the

greater peace, there must be an alliance of kingdoms. The Highborn Court was formed with Paragon as its head, thus giving the kingdom of Paragon power over all five territories. Although each kingdom is independent on paper, Paragon, as the protector of all, has ultimate power over all. Since then, there has been a tenuous peace. But there is a marked difference between the way Paragonians talk about the five kingdoms and the way others do. We say that the realm of Paragon is divided into five kingdoms, led by the kingdom of Paragon."

"And what do the others say?"

"Before the uprising by Darnuith, the realm was called Ouros and Paragon one kingdom among five. Many outside of Paragon still call our world Ouros. But while ancient maps are labeled Ouros, all maps since the Witch War label our world as Paragon with the Kingdom of Paragon delineated as the capitol."

"I can't imagine the other four kingdoms appreciate that. No wonder there's political unrest. But how does that translate into Aborella trying to kill me?"

"There is a prophecy among the Darnuith that one day the descendants of the three sisters will return and that the progeny of a witch and a dragon will destroy the kingdom of Paragon. Aborella tried to kill you tonight to get at Raven because Gabriel and Raven's child is believed to be the destroyer, the one foretold, the weapon the three sisters would use to conquer the kingdom of Paragon. You were the most vulnerable, so she targeted you. I can only assume she'd learned you'd be at the O2 the last time she was here, the night she took your hair."

A dull humming had started in her ears, and Clarissa shook her head as if to clear it. "Are you saying that my existence... my connection to you and to Raven and Avery... that you believe it was prophesized in your world. Like... like... in your mythology?"

He nodded. "We think, perhaps, yes. I didn't believe it at first, not until Gabriel brought it to mind. But there's no doubt Raven and Gabriel's child is the one foretold. It all fits."

*Ooookay.* She leaned back against the seat and swore. What was she supposed to do with that? "It's a lot to process."

"Right, well, you don't have to worry about anything." Nathaniel brushed a hand over the sleeve of his suit. "I'll be there, every night at every concert, from now on. I'll protect you. No one from Paragon or anywhere else is ever going to hurt you again, and Gabriel and Raven can go about their lives and decide what to do about Paragon. We don't need to be involved."

She swallowed. "Aside from the idea that I should or could simply set aside what you've told me about Paragon to pursue my career, there's something you should know." She turned to look him in the eye. "I told Tom tonight that I'm retiring. There're a few more appearances I'm contractually obligated to complete, but then I'm ending it."

He placed his hands on her shoulders, his brow furrowing. "Why? Clarissa, I promise you, nothing that has happened requires you to sacrifice this. You love to sing. You live to sing. I know my world is terrifying right now, but I swear to you I protect what's mine—"

She shook her head and laughed. "I know. I know I *could* do it. Tonight was our best performance ever. We're trending everywhere. Everyone is talking about the show. Tom said it was a concert for the history books."

"Then what's the problem?"

"I'm not willing to pay the price of fame anymore."

"Clarissa..." Nathaniel looked contrite, like he regretted what he'd said to her over breakfast about her chosen profession.

"No... no. Nathaniel, you were right about that. All these years, I've been terribly lonely. Surrounded by fans but always alone. I thought it was enough. But spending every holiday with the people you work with because you have no real friends or family isn't living. It's a prison."

"You'd have me. I'd be there for you, always."

"Yes. I know. But I don't want it anymore. I love to sing. I'll always sing. I want to become an indie artist. Release music on my own terms. Perform in small venues, intimate ones for me and a few dozen fans. No more arenas. No more crowds of thousands. No more Tom." She placed a hand over his heart. "I want to have a home, maybe a family. Let's face it, I have more money than I could ever spend. I don't need to work and I just... I just..."

"What sort of family?" Nathaniel asked. Dark clouds moved in behind his irises, and his expression became gravely serious.

She drew back. Had she made a terrible mistake? Her words rambled out all at once. "I... I thought because we were mated that your family would become my family. I mean Nick, Maiara, Sabrina, Avery, and I seemed to bond while you were gone. I felt connected for the first time." She sighed. "Oh hell, I was wrong. They don't like me, do they? I'm so bad at reading people."

Her hands went to her head, but Nathaniel caught her wrists. "No, you're not. My family is your family and always will be. Any of my siblings would do anything for you."

"Then why do you look so grave?"

"Children between dragons and witches are rare," he

said. "Forbidden, as I mentioned. Gabriel and Raven's child was conceived with the help of a magic spell. She died giving birth, and although they were able to revive her, it was touch and go for a time. Children won't happen naturally between us, and the magic to make them happen would be dangerous."

"Oh." She blinked at him. She'd known he couldn't impregnate her. They'd covered that much before when they'd become lovers. She'd just never fully understood why.

"We should have talked about this... before." He tucked her hair behind her ear.

She sent him a soft smile and tugged at the cuff of her sleeve. "It wouldn't have made a bit of difference, Nate. You are mine, and our claiming each other was long past overdue as far as I'm concerned. But truly, when I said family, I didn't necessarily mean children, although someday I wouldn't mind providing a home for a child who needs parents— an orphan like me. Right now, I just mean you, your siblings, Tempest and Laurel if they ever warm up to me. A home... Love... Warmth. I'm tired of feeling like my every breath is pulled into my lungs for someone else."

Nathaniel ran his fingers along the inside of her thigh from her knee to the hem of her dress. "Then so it shall be. If you truly want to make a change, we can build you a studio at Mistwood."

"Life is too short for anything else."

Nathaniel turned serious. "There's something else I need to tell you."

Her stomach tensed. Was her mortality a problem for him? "Yes?"

"There is a way I can make you immortal like me, and I hope you'll accept it."

It felt like all the blood had drained from her face. Her skin went cold. She thought she'd understood what it meant to be mated to a dragon, but never did she assume it came with immortality. "Are you serious?"

"Yes. If I feed you my tooth, you will live as long as I do."

"Your tooth."

He nodded once. "It is how it always has been and always will be for dragons. Do you think you could be bonded with me for all eternity? The tooth will keep you young and impart you with health and strength."

"Are you sure?" she asked. He squinted at her. "I mean, have you ever done this before?"

"With Emory."

She mulled it over for a few long moments.

"Does the length of the commitment scare you?" A muscle in his jaw twitched. She realized his bond to her was already eternal. He would love her for the rest of his life, not hers.

At once she knew her answer. "No. It doesn't scare me."

"Then yes?" His eyes met hers and flashed amethyst.

"Yes."

He reached into his mouth, and with a tug she thought must have hurt, extracted something white and too long to have fit in his jaw. He closed his fist around it. A surge of magic rippled across her skin. When he opened his hand again, there was a purple pill the size of a Tic Tac in his palm. "Take this and it is done."

"That's it? Just swallow it down?"

He nodded. She took the pill and placed it on her tongue, then swallowed it without hesitation. Immediately she felt warmth bloom from her stomach and branch through her limbs like lightning. She closed her eyes as

315

energy charged through her blood and her connection with Nathaniel became a palpable thing, a taut, invisible string between them.

Her eyelids flipped open and he was there, focused on her, his masculine presence almost overwhelming. She wanted him. Wanted him in her.

Every cell in her body came alive at the feel of his fingertips lightly caressing the sensitive flesh along the inside of her thigh. She desperately wanted to yell at Emory to drive faster. She remembered the feel of Nathaniel rising behind her onstage, felt the sheer power that seemed to surround him. All that magic, all that feral, tightly coiled strength, was right here in her arms. She needed him. She needed to feel him inside her, to know he was hers on every level.

By the time they pulled into the drive at Mistwood, she was a raw, hungry nerve. They slipped into the manor through the back door and went directly to his room, where he wasted no time trying to strip her out of her dress, his mating trill rumbling in his chest. She dodged.

"So impatient. I don't recall giving you permission to touch me," she said through a smile. There was nothing she wanted more than to feel Nathaniel move inside her, but patience was a virtue, and a game would make the prize all the sweeter.

His hands dropped to his sides and his lips twitched. "I can't touch you?"

"Not until I say. What good is having a dragon to ride if he can't take direction?"

His eyes narrowed. "You'd like to be in control, Ms. Black?"

She grinned. "Oh, I *am* in control. Hold absolutely still."

She raised herself onto her tiptoes and grabbed the lapels of his suit jacket, pushing it off his shoulders. It fell to the floor in a heap. To his credit, he did hold absolutely still. And didn't that make her feel powerful? All that brutal potential, that lean, hidden power, was completely at her command. She swaggered around him, her eyes raking his body, then slid her hands over his ribs from behind.

Arms wrapped around him, she unbuttoned his shirt, tugging the tails from his pants and sliding it off his shoulders from behind. She scraped her nails along his ribs, enjoying the hard peaks and valleys of his chest and abs. Her fingers dipped inside his waistband.

"Clarissa," he whispered, and her name on his lips sent a wave of heat through her. He said it with reverence.

"Hmm." She took a step back and then swept her fingers up his spine and into the hair at the back of his head. His muscles twitched and flexed under the soft graze of her nails. She pressed her hand between the two crescent-shaped marks on his shoulder blades. "Show them to me."

Obediently, he unfurled his wings. They were glorious, sparkling and purple tinged. She allowed herself a moment to take in their magnificence. She ran her hands along the place where they sprouted from his body, petted the flesh along the webbing.

He moaned, his breath coming faster. She stroked along the bony edge and then scraped her nails along the underside. A shiver traveled over his skin, and she grinned in triumph. She was just getting started.

"For the love of the Mountain, Clarissa, I'm going to ruin my pants."

"We can't have that." She reached around his waist, unfastened the buckle of his belt, then circled to the front of him to pull the strip of leather off in one quick snap. She folded the leather in half and placed it in his hand.

"What do you want me to do with this?" he asked lasciviously.

She backed up a few steps. "Hold it in both hands, behind your back."

He obeyed, the motion causing the muscles of his arms to bunch and strain. Her blood pounded in her veins. She was going to enjoy this. She unbuttoned his pants and slid them and his briefs down around his ankles. He stepped out and toed off his socks. She tossed them over the chair against the wall.

He was hard and erect. Magnificent. Her eyelids felt heavy. Deep inside, her body opened and wet heat bloomed between her legs.

"Well, Ms. Black, what do you plan to do with me?" His irises had turned bright, burning violet, the way they always did when he was doing magic. Behind him, his wings tensed. Desire flowed off him in waves.

"This." She dropped to her knees and wrapped her mouth around him.

Nathaniel felt the leather in his fists stretch as Clarissa drew his erection into her mouth. He was going to need a new belt. Her tongue slid slick and wet along the underside of his shaft. By the Mountain, he'd never felt pleasure like this. The act itself was delicious, but the way she reveled in controlling the pace, in absolutely owning him, ignited the thrill.

She opened her throat and drew him in deep. His mating trill boomed loud enough to rattle the walls.

"You'll make me come," he whispered.

She slid her mouth faster, wrapping her hand along the base of his shaft. His release rushed through him and his wings spread as the belt finally snapped and dropped from his grip. He laced his fingers in her hair as she licked the last bits of his release off him.

"Mmm, so you *can* take direction," she said in a tone that was nothing short of indecent.

"You are an exceptional taskmaster."

His hands found the hem of her dress and pulled it over her head. He made short work of her bra and her lace thong. Her breasts mounded warm and heavy in his hands, her nipples budding hard between his fingers. His mouth found hers and tasted the salty remains of his passion on her lips.

Nathaniel had lived a long time, but there was only one thing he knew for sure: she was his other, his true and permanent partner.

His fingers trailed over her abdomen, then lower to the junction of her thighs.

She sighed against his lips. "I love you, Nathaniel."

He drew her against his chest as he hastened the work of his fingers. "Love isn't a strong enough word for what I feel for you. You are my heart, my greatest treasure, the fire in my blood."

She arched her back and pressed her breasts into his chest as an orgasm rocked through her. He lowered her onto the bed through the aftershocks and thrust into her just as her body softened beneath his.

"And the student becomes the teacher," she whispered, tilting her head back.

He kissed the underside of her jaw, moving inside her, magic building between them once more. "I think there's plenty left between us to learn."

Together they found their release, their hearts and bodies entwined, but the bond between them ran far deeper. All his life he'd practiced magic, both the dark and the light, but he'd never experienced power like this. Or love like this. And that was the strongest magic of all.

# CHAPTER FORTY-FOUR

A very should have been happy for her sister. She watched Raven cradle her child in her arms with Gabriel behind her and thought that, despite the oddity of it, they seemed like the perfect little family. Still, all she felt was jealousy. Not of her sister's happiness though. No. She was happy about that. She wouldn't want anything less for Raven.

No. It was Li'l Puff. Up until Raven had returned, Avery had a purpose. She was the only one who could handle the egg. Now no one needed her. What would happen next? Would she go home to New Orleans, go back to waiting tables and try to forget that dragons, witches, and vampires were real? That her sister was one? Would she ever know the feeling of raising a circle again?

"We have to name him or her, Gabriel," Raven said. "We can't keep calling it Li'l Puff. It sounds like a rapper." She looked over her shoulder at him. "What about Michael?"

"It could be a girl," Gabriel said hopefully. "Why not Phoebe?"

"Then what if it's a boy?" Raven giggled.

"Charlie," Avery said softly toward the fire.

"What?" Raven and Gabriel both looked at her.

She spread her hands and shrugged. "Charlie. Charles if it's a boy. Charlotte if it's a girl. Charlie for short. Works now. Works for both genders."

Raven glanced between her and Gabriel. "Charlie." She tried out the name, and the egg pulsed brighter in response. The silhouette inside pressed a hand close to hers. "I think he or she approves."

Gabriel grinned. "Charlie it is." He pressed a kiss to the side of Raven's head.

Avery stood and headed for the door. "My work here is done. Just in time too. I'm exhausted. I'd better go to bed."

"Night," Raven said. "Talk more over breakfast? There's so much—"

She held up a hand and nodded. "Yes. In the morning." She slipped out of the room and into the hall.

Nathaniel woke to the soft rhythm of Clarissa's breathing and extracted himself from her side. His stomach was growling. Between the magic he'd expelled coming back from Paragon and what it had taken to vanquish Aborella, not to mention the hours of lovemaking with Clarissa, he'd built up an appetite. He could mentally call for Laurel or Tempest to fix him something, but he wasn't sure what he wanted, and a thorough dig in the refrigerator was what was called for in this situation.

He donned pajama pants and a gray T-shirt and jogged barefoot down to the kitchen. His wings unfurled in alarm when a face appeared in the dim glow of the appliances.

The person's hands shot up. He'd scared her as much as she'd surprised him.

"By the Mountain, Avery! What are you doing up at this hour?" He flipped on the light.

"Couldn't sleep." She looked down into her teacup. "I thought some chamomile would settle my nerves. You?"

"Starving. I was about to make myself a sandwich. Care to join me?"

She nodded. "Please."

He crossed to the fridge, pulled out some leftover curried chicken salad, and found some bread in the pantry. Some lettuce and he was on the road to proper sandwiches. He nabbed two plates and started assembling.

Avery watched him from the table. "I'd offer to help, but you seem to have things under control."

He nodded. "Relax. I've got it." Her face fell again when she thought he wasn't looking. "Something on your mind?"

"I'm wondering if I should go home now. Charlie is back in Raven's arms."

"Charlie?"

"Li'l Puff. Raven and Gabriel settled on a real name."

"Ah. Yes. Charlie. Could either be a girl or a boy. Brilliant."

"Thank you. It was my idea." Her eyes drifted down to her cup again.

"You don't want to stick around and be there when the little omelet hatches?"

She chuckled. He brought the sandwiches to the table and set one in front of her.

"I really don't have an excuse to stay. I've already been away from home a long time. My mother can hardly keep up with things at the Three Sisters on her own."

Nathaniel stopped. "Wait... That's the name of your mum's pub? The Three Sisters?"

She snorted. "Yeah. Weird coincidence, huh?"

"Very." He took a bite and chewed. He didn't believe in coincidences.

"The day Warwick raised the circle and we re-bound Raven, Clarissa, and me together, I felt it. Magic. I floated off the floor... three inches. How do you go from flying to mopping up vomit from the last patron who didn't know when to quit? Or having your ass pinched and getting flogged with beads the next Mardi Gras? I'm just so over it, Nathaniel."

"So don't go back." He bit into his sandwich and chewed.

Avery laughed. "I... I have to go back. I don't have the money to stay."

"Clarissa told me she thinks of you as family. I do too. I need help at Relics and Runes if you want to work. If you don't, we have plenty of room and resources here to keep you quite comfortable until you figure out what your power is."

She snorted. "I don't have any power."

He lowered his sandwich. "Of course you do. I thought we settled this, that afternoon when you showed us all you were the only one who could hold the egg?"

"Yes. We figured out that Charlie tolerated me for some reason. So what?"

He shook his head. "I think it's something more."

She took a bite and spoke around her sandwich. "Like what?"

He raised a finger. "Wait here." He flashed up to his study, grabbed his pipe and his cards, and returned to the table.

"I will never stop being freaked out by how fast you all are."

He shrugged. "All part of being a dragon." He shuffled the cards in his hand. "Let's consult the tarot about your future, shall we?"

She gave him a skeptical look and took another bite. "This sandwich is sinfully delicious. What is that... sweetness?"

"Mango chutney and cinnamon. It's Laurel's specialty."

"Mmmmm." She glanced at the cards. "I come from New Orleans. As a rule, I don't believe in tarot or other forms of divination. There's a psychic on every corner, and most couldn't tell you when their next meal is coming."

"Well, not everyone finds what they're looking for in the cards, but tarot can be a way of tapping into your deepest intuition. The cards, after all, are just cardboard. The magic, if there is any, comes from you."

She set the stub of her sandwich down and licked her fingers. "All right. What do I have to lose? Deal a spread or whatever it is you do." She waved at the table.

He stopped shuffling and laid three cards in front of her. "Past, present, future."

"What do I do, turn them over?"

"Unless you want me to do it for you. I think it's better if you do it."

She nodded and wiped her hands on the napkin next to her plate. "Here goes nothing." She flipped the first card. "The Hanged Man."

"Reversed," he said. "The position of the card to you makes a difference."

"Okay. So what does it mean?"

"It means imprisonment. Forced sacrifice. Martyrdom."

She scoffed. "In my past?"

"Yes."

Her face turned from disbelief to wonder. "Maybe I underestimated tarot cards."

"You see some truth in it?"

"You may have heard that Raven had brain cancer. She had the front seat in our family for most of my life, which was fine with me. She needed my parents' attention more than I did. But it wasn't exactly what I would have chosen for myself. I wouldn't say I was a martyr. I just did what I had to do. I mean, she was dying."

"But she's not dying anymore."

"No." She scowled. "And now I find that all that energy I poured into loving her has nowhere to go."

"Which brings us to the present." He gestured toward the center card.

She flipped it and gasped. A skeletal figure on a horse. She placed a hand on her chest. "Death?"

Nathaniel shook his head. "The death card does not mean physical death. It means change, rebirth, transformation. You, Avery, are the caterpillar in the cocoon."

"Cocoon, huh? No wonder my life feels so suffocating."

"Change could mean opportunity."

"Or tragedy."

He nodded toward the third card. "Why not check what the cards see in your future?"

She shrugged and rubbed her palms together. "No whammies. This butterfly would like to spread her wings."

"Whammies?"

"Old American game show. It means I only want good luck." She bobbed her dark eyebrows and reached for the third card. "Let's see what the future has in store." She flipped the card.

Nathaniel stared at the exposed face of the moon and rubbed his chin. Difficult. Very difficult.

"What? What does the moon mean?"

"This one has many different meanings. You can see how it depicts a crab crawling out of the primordial sea? That represents evolution in action, which makes sense given the card before it, Death. You are becoming, Avery. That is for certain. But what you are becoming is shrouded. This card almost always denotes some dark mystery."

Avery covered her face with her hands. "Excellent. So my future is a shadowy uncertainty. Thanks for clearing that up. The cards were a great idea." She gave him two very sarcastic thumbs-ups.

"There is one more-pleasant meaning associated with this card."

"What's that?"

"It usually portends romance."

"Now I know these cards are liars. There is no one in my life that leaves the slightest whiff of roses in their wake. No one." She rolled her eyes.

He leaned back in his chair and took her in. As a mated dragon, he wasn't attracted to Avery, but in a strictly objective way, he could say with some certainty she was an attractive person. And her kindness and courage were undeniable after what she'd been through. Plus he was sure there was more to her. Although he didn't understand its nature, it was clear that magic lived just under the surface of her person. It just needed the right circumstances to wake it.

He folded his arms and studied her. "You're a grown woman, Avery. You can make your own decisions. I've invited you to stay. I've shown you what the cards say. Now you have to decide. Just realize, if you go home..." He pointed to the Hanged Man. "You'll be an almost-butterfly trying to crawl out of its cocoon a caterpillar again. You've already been changed. You can't be the same as before. Not without cutting off your wings."

Her jaw dropped open. He cleared the plates and left her to her thoughts.

# CHAPTER FORTY-FIVE

*Three days later...*

Nathaniel would never grow tired of sharing the company of his siblings or their mates, and the bond between them was perhaps stronger now than ever before. From the head of the table, he watched them over his wineglass, absorbing their endearing idiosyncrasies.

Across from him at the foot of the table, Gabriel was singularly focused on his mate Raven, who sat beside him.

"What about this one?" Raven said, showing him a picture on her phone of a crib made of some dark, polished wood.

Gabriel smirked. "Where is the top?"

"Top!" Raven squealed.

"It's a crib, not a cage," Avery interjected, laughing.

Gabriel shrugged. "Human babies don't fly. Dragon babies do. You need a top. And, while we are discussing dragon realities, I would suggest you avoid wood in place of something that won't burn."

Avery and Raven looked at each other in openmouthed

horror. Without another word, they both reached for their wine and drained their glasses empty.

On Gabriel's other side, Sabrina and Tobias enjoyed the lamb that Tempest had prepared.

"Nathaniel, my compliments to your oread," Sabrina said, her green eyes shifting in his direction. "This is the best I've ever had."

He was sure a large part of her enjoyment hinged on the fact that Tempest had left her portion extremely rare. In fact, he believed he'd done little more than warm the bloody chops that populated her plate. The rest of the dishes, including Tobias's, were far more cooked.

"I'll let him know," Nathaniel said.

Tobias raised his fork. "We eat well in Chicago, but I have to say there's something about this animal. Every bite I take is more complex than the last. It's like I can smell the grass it fed on."

"Because it was raised here, at Mistwood," Nathaniel explained. "There's magic in the groundwater."

Sabrina had gone to great lengths to stay as long as she had, calling her father in to help run the Chicago vampire coven in her absence. As Tobias chatted easily with her over his dinner, Nathaniel had to smile to see his traditionally stoic and fiercely academic brother fill with light in her presence. Tobias rarely took his eyes off Sabrina when she was in the room.

Beside Avery, Maiara was playing with Alexander's phone. He'd recently taught her how to take selfies, and she was experimenting with the functionality.

"You've got to look at the little hole," Alexander said. "That's the camera."

She showed him a picture of the side of her head.

"No. No. See?" He helped her take one. He was

smiling in the finished photo, but her eyes were narrowed like she didn't quite trust the phone. Why she needed a selfie, Nathaniel would never understand. Alexander sketched her at least once a day. He never seemed to tire of it.

Nathaniel's attention drifted to the other side of the table when Rowan tossed her fork down and yelled at Nick. "How can you think Taylor Swift is unrelatable?"

Nick spread his hands and shrugged. "Look what you made me do? It's totally the perspective of a narcissist."

"You are nuts. You're crazy." Rowan got in his face. "She's making a point about how celebrities are unfairly characterized by the media and that jokers like that guy who sued her try to weaponize their reputations against them for profit."

"Huh. Really?"

Rowan rolled her eyes toward the ceiling. "Yes! Do you take this stuff literally? You've got to read into it. Listen to the words."

Nick waved a hand in the air. "I miss when she used to sing sweet country songs."

"I've met her, you know," Clarissa interjected.

Rowan and Nick both froze like she'd manifested in front of them although she'd been sitting there the entire time.

"Really?" Rowan asked.

Clarissa nodded. "At an industry party in Nashville. She is one of the kindest people I've ever met. And talented. Not a lick of magic. Does it all on her own."

Nick's mouth popped open. "Huh. Ain't that somethin'?"

Rowan flashed him a smug grin and raised her glass to Clarissa.

Nathaniel leaned over to whisper in her ear. "So is this what you had in mind when you said you wanted family?"

She winked one bright blue eye. "Exactly what I had in mind. I was wondering about something though."

"Hmm?"

"When you told me about what happened in Paragon, you mentioned Sylas and how he was leading a band of rebels. A long time ago, you told me you were one of nine. Your oldest brother, Marius, was murdered. Gabriel, Tobias, Rowan, and Alexander are here. Assuming Sylas returned to wherever he was staying in the kingdom of Everfield, where are your last two siblings?"

"I'm not sure about Colin." Nathaniel swirled his wine.

"And then there was one." Clarissa rubbed his thigh expectantly.

"Xavier," Nathaniel said. "As it so happens, I do know where he is. The hard part is reaching him."

She squeezed his thigh. "I know that look. You have an idea."

His gaze settled on Avery. "Yes, I do. A hunch really, based on the guidance of the cards. It won't be easy, but I believe the Treasure of Paragon will be together again soon, and when that happens, Mother better make her peace with the goddess, because we are coming for her. And when we do, she will pay for her lies and deception. There will be no mercy."

# EPILOGUE

Eleanor tapped her fingers against the arm of her throne, waiting for Aborella to return. Her jaw hurt from grinding her teeth, and heat throbbed at her temple. She should have killed the witch while she had the chance. How could she have known Nathaniel would come?

She cursed. He could be a real problem. Aborella should have seen him coming. When the fairy returned, Eleanor would make her pay for her incompetence.

A sound like a pop echoed in the room and a smear of purple landed on the floor in front of her with a splat. What was left of Aborella gaped up at her like a fish. Half her skull was smashed, leaving one eye to rove wildly in its socket. Her legs were completely missing, along with one arm. Her skin was pure white, like freshly fallen snow.

Eleanor's lips drew back from her teeth. "You do not have my permission to die, seer!"

With Brynhoff dead, she needed the fairy. Without her, she'd have to get her hands dirty dealing with the uprising in the lesser kingdoms. She despised the thought. It might put her in danger, and it was imperative she be the one on the throne.

Aborella grunted. "Kill... me...," the fairy whispered.

Eleanor responded with a wicked laugh. "Oh no. That would be much too easy. You have failed me, Aborella, and you need the opportunity to make things right."

Opening her mouth, the empress reached inside and tugged a molar from her jaw. There was a sharp pain, the taste of blood, and then the tooth in all its long, razor-sharp glory dangled from her fingers. Aborella stared at it in horror.

"You know, I've never done this before for anyone," she said to Aborella, whose breath rattled in her lungs and came in uneven gasps. "You should feel special."

The tooth shrank to the size of a small stone. The empress tipped it into Aborella's mouth and watched it worm down her throat. The fairy gagged, her pale torso, stained with purple blood, convulsing with her effort. Eventually the tooth disappeared.

"Ransom!" the empress called.

The captain of the Obsidian Guard appeared at the side door, his disgust evident when he saw Aborella's state. "Yes, Your Highness. What can I do for you?"

"Carry her and follow me." The empress stood from her throne.

"Of course. Allow me to get a covering to wrap the remains." He motioned in the general direction of Aborella's bloody body.

"She's not dead and her blood won't hurt you unless you drink it. Pick her up. Now. We don't have much time."

Ransom took a step toward the body and then another. His lips twisted as he lowered himself to her and wedged his hands under the fairy. Purple blood soaked into his red sleeves, but he managed to lift her from the pool of her own filth.

Once he had the fairy in his arms, Eleanor led the way out the side door of the palace and deep into the jungle to the place where a large moss-covered tree grew from rich volcanic soil. With a wave of her ring, a shovel appeared in her hand.

"Bury her here," Eleanor commanded.

Ransom set Aborella down, the fairy's mouth still gaping soundlessly, and took the shovel in his bloody hands. Soon the hole took shape and he lowered the fairy into it.

"N-no. Please no," Aborella begged from the grave.

Eleanor rolled her eyes. "You won't die. I've given you my tooth after all. You'll simply..." She waved her hand dismissively. "...be out of the way until your body regenerates itself. I've put you right on top of the roots of this tree. A few months in this grave and you'll likely be good as new."

"No." Terror filled Aborella's eye, and the fairy begged in ragged gasps for mercy.

Eleanor placed a hand on Ransom's shoulder. "Bury her. Then make sure all the blood is cleaned up. Destroy this uniform. Get another from storage. Do you understand? I do not want to see a single trace of her."

"Yes, Your Highness." Ransom dug the tip of the shovel into the loose dirt and emptied it on top of Aborella. Then another and another. Her one remaining arm flailed with her protests.

Eleanor strode back to the palace, the sound of Aborella's strained screams growing faint behind her.

THANK YOU FOR READING THE DRAGON OF CECIL COURT. If you enjoyed Nathaniel and Clarissa's story, please leave a review.

For the first time in her life, Avery is putting herself first and striving to define herself separate from the needs of her family. When Nathaniel informs her that she is the only one capable of reaching their brother Xavier inside a protective magical ward in the Scottish Highlands, she agrees to go on a quest to retrieve the dragon sibling. Only she isn't prepared for what the journey will require of her or for what Xavier will awaken in her.

Read HIGHLAND DRAGON, available now wherever you buy books.

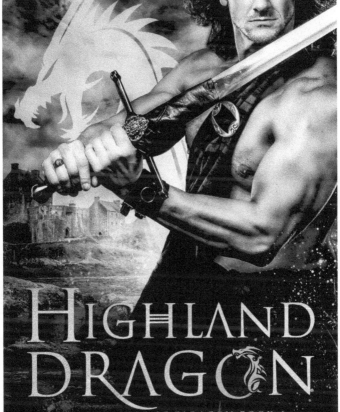

# HIGHLAND DRAGON

## THE TREASURE OF PARAGON BOOK 6

*USA TODAY* BESTSELLING AUTHOR

# GENEVIEVE JACK

# PROLOGUE

*Paragon*

I n a dark, lonely, and unmarked grave beyond the boundaries of the Obsidian Palace, Aborella waited like a seed planted in the dirt. She'd lost track of how long she'd been trapped beneath the earth. Unconsciousness had relieved her suffering periodically, but without a source of light, she had no idea how many days had passed since the empress had sentenced her to this fate. All she had left was the hope that Eleanor would change her mind and come to collect her.

Her chest ached thinking about the woman she once considered a friend. The betrayal Aborella had experienced at her hands caused her more pain than the crushing weight of being buried alive. The fairy sorceress had drained herself to the point of death trying to protect the Empress, but things had gone horribly wrong. Aborella was fatally wounded in battle, and although the empress had saved her life by feeding her a dragon's tooth, she'd taken out her anger and frustration on Aborella, abandoning her to fester in a shallow grave. Eleanor, it seemed, did not tolerate failure, even from her.

Her spirits lifted when the sound of a female voice grew near, until she realized it was a soothing timbre, not Eleanor's shrill, nasal tone.

"Sylas? Sylas!" the voice called in a loud whisper.

Aborella became more alert in her earthy tomb. Whoever this was must be in league with Sylas, Eleanor's eighthborn son and rumored leader of the rebellion.

"Oh Goddess of the Mountain! Sylas?" The female voice was closer now, just above Aborella. The sound of digging, not by shovel but by hand, met her ears. The owner of the voice must have noticed the grave and thought she was Sylas. Aborella waited, hoping, praying to the goddess the woman would succeed in reaching her. If she could enjoy a single breath of fresh air and see the stars above her, it would be the sweetest mercy.

Already the weight over her was lighter. And then dirt brushed her cheek and was lifted away. Aborella stared up at a dark shadow within a deep red hood. Gloved hands, filthy with dirt, hovered over her face, two full moons acting as dual spotlights behind the woman's head.

"Thank the goddess," the woman murmured as she determined Aborella wasn't the dragon in question. "Sylas, I'm going to kill you."

She reached toward the pile of dirt beside the grave, and Aborella's heart raced. Was she going to bury her again?

Aborella couldn't let that happen. She had to show this hooded creature she was alive. Using all the energy she had, she tried to raise her hand but only managed to twitch a finger, which the stranger didn't see as it was still buried. The woman scooped another mound of dirt. Aborella opened her mouth to scream and instead drew in a full, cleansing breath of night air.

"By the Mountain!" The stranger tossed the dirt aside. A short, high-pitched gasp came from inside the hood. "How are you alive?"

Aborella tried to answer, but all that came out was a gurgle. When had she lost her ability to speak? She knew that half her face was smashed, courtesy of Nathaniel, who had also taken three of her limbs, but when she'd first escaped to the palace, she had spoken to Eleanor. And she had just proved she was able to breathe. Which meant perhaps her lack of voice was due to fear or the fact she'd had no food or water for however long she'd been buried. Without making a sound, she forced her lips to mouth, *help me*.

Quickly, the hooded figure unburied the rest of her. It was a blessing Aborella couldn't see the stranger's expression inside the deep hood. Her injuries were extensive—one leg completely gone, the other severed above the knee, one arm torn off unevenly, facial disfigurement—and it would only depress her to see the stranger's disgust manifest at the sight. She needn't have worried; the hood hid any reaction as the woman hooked her hands under Aborella's armpits, braced her heels in the dirt, and dragged her from the grave.

"Oh, my dear goddess. You're a fairy!"

The woman must have seen her wings. Aborella held absolutely still, which wasn't difficult considering how weak she'd become. She was suddenly relieved her voice hadn't worked. If the stranger was looking for Sylas, she was undoubtedly a rebel and would kill Aborella where she lay if she recognized her. Fortunately, her regularly dark purple skin was bright white now, a symptom of her drained magic, and her face must be unrecognizable thanks to her injuries.

With any luck, the hooded one would assume she was some wayward fairy set upon by thieves and would leave her to die.

"Is it you?" A low, deep voice came from a thicket of trees to the left.

"Sylas?" The stranger turned, and Sylas stepped into view, dropping his invisibility as if it were a blanket wrapped around his being. "Stars and lightning! Thank the goddess!"

He rushed forward and swept her into his arms, kissing the face under the hood. "I'm sorry it took me so long. I had to wait for that young fuckup at the gate to fall asleep."

"I felt the tug on our bond and followed it here, but Hades if I knew exactly what it meant! How did you escape?"

"It's too long of a story to tell you here. I've been hiding in the gardens for days. We need to go." He took her hand and began to lead her away.

Aborella swallowed, fresh agony washing over her as a slight breeze irritated her wounds. She forced herself to remain silent. If Sylas recognized her, he'd cut off her head and feed her to the forest animals.

She was partially hidden behind the skirt of the stranger's cape, but as the woman turned, the light of the moon drenched her pale skin.

Sylas pulled up short, his gaze locking on Aborella. "What in Hades is that, Dianthe?"

Dianthe. That was the stranger's name. A fairy name. Interesting.

"I thought she was you!" Dianthe pointed a gloved hand toward the grave. "I thought that wicked mother of yours had tortured and buried you here as some sort of warning to us. Instead, I found her."

"Who is she?"

"Definitely a fairy. Probably raped and tortured by Obsidian Guard scum and left here to die. They didn't even make sure she was dead before they buried her. It's... sick!"

Sylas was shaking his head. "We have to leave her. There's nothing we can do."

"Why?" The hood turned toward him, the gloved hands squeezing into fists. "I can heal her, Sylas. You know I can. If she's survived this long, I can bring her through this. Fairies have unbelievable regenerative properties. If we can get her back to Everfield—"

"And how exactly do you suppose we do that?" He rubbed his eyes, his words tinged with exhaustion. "I'm lucky to be alive, woman! We're risking everything by lingering here."

Dianthe placed her gloved hands on her hips. Now Aborella wished she could speak. If she could make a sound, she'd protest going to Everfield. She'd been born there and was universally hated by its people. Even if the three of them could successfully avoid detection by the Obsidian Guard and make it to Everfield in one piece, the people there would surely execute her the second anyone recognized her.

"Fine," Sylas whispered, pacing nervously. "But this is on you. She's your responsibility."

"When have I ever shirked my responsibility to you or anyone else?" Dianthe's soft voice held a note of anger for the first time that night.

"Give me your cloak. It will make her easier to carry."

Dianthe removed the red hood and began unfastening the buttons. Aborella had never seen a fairy like her. Her skin was the color of roasted cinnamon and shone like silk in the moonlight. Most fairies were born the color of flower petals—the darker the color, the more powerful the fairy. Dianthe's deeply pigmented skin was highly unusual, and when she glanced in Aborella's direction, another difference revealed itself. Most fairies had green eyes. Dianthe's were the color of warm honey. She was beautiful but markedly strange, different from any fairy Aborella remembered from home.

The lights went out as Sylas tossed the cloak over Aborella's body and face, wrapped her up, and scooped her into his arms. Nothing more was said. Aborella had neither strength nor voice to change her fate. She closed her eyes and gave herself over to it.

## CHAPTER ONE

Aworld away from Paragon, in a place between places, Xavier, son of Eleanor and heir to the kingdom of Paragon, also woke to perpetual darkness. The scent of stale air, moldy stone, and the metallic tang of new blood assaulted his senses. Moans of pain echoed against unyielding stone walls. Someone was being tortured. Someone was always being tortured here.

His chest grew heavy with despair as the understanding of his predicament invaded his consciousness again. To be sure, there was nothing new about his reality. Rather, Xavier's renewed anguish was caused by the intense and realistic dream he'd had moments before. He'd been flying in the sun, the sweet smell of a tribiscal vineyard filling his lungs, his wings carrying him on a soft, warm breeze. He'd dreamed of freedom, of Paragon, of flying. He'd dreamed of the mountain.

It felt like an eternity since he'd spread his wings. He almost wished he hadn't experienced the dream. The ultimate despair of his predicament only cut deeper in comparison.

Another scream reached his ears from somewhere deep inside the dungeon, and Xavier came fully into his reality. The wail of agony echoed against the stone and then pinched off as if whatever wretched soul had uttered it had run out of breath. He stretched a talon to the stone and etched a line next to the others. Hundreds of others. If he'd calculated correctly, he'd been trapped in this cage for nearly two years.

Footsteps approached—a guard with his nightly meal. The sandy-haired young man was dressed in clan colors but was oddly a stranger.

"Ye must be new," Xavier said. "I donna recognize yer face."

Without speaking or making eye contact, the guard slid the tray he was carrying along the stone floor, through the slot in the door, and into the cage. Venison, bread, greens, and water. It was a decent enough meal, although Xavier would kill for a whisky.

"Ye might be new, but it seems ye ken the rules well enough. Why does that arse ye slave after bother feeding me if he plans to leave me to rot in this hole?"

The guard didn't answer him, but then he was already halfway down the hall before Xavier asked the question. None of them ever lingered. Feed the dragon and then leave quickly, Lachlan must have told them. Wouldn't want to risk Xavier breaking the mind control Lachlan kept them all under and perhaps convincing one of them to let him go.

Anyway, Xavier knew exactly why Lachlan continued to feed him. He had to. The very existence of the *builgean* depended on Xavier's magic. If he died, their world would collapse. If he became weak, the crops might wilt and the animals would stop producing young. His magic was keeping the clan alive. His clan.